Praise for
Eternal Hunger

"Dark, delicious, and sinfully good, *Eternal Hunger* is a stunning start to what promises to be an addictive new series. I can't wait for more from Laura Wright!"

—Nalini Singh, *New York Times* bestselling author of *Bonds of Justice*

"Dark, sexy vampires with an urban bite make *Eternal Hunger* a must read."

—Jessica Andersen, author of *Demonkeepers*

"Action, passion, and dark suspense launch a riveting new series. Laura Wright knows how to lure you in and hold you captive until the last page."

—Larissa Ione, *New York Times* bestselling author of *Ecstasy Unveiled*

ETERNAL HUNGER

MARK OF THE VAMPIRE

LAURA WRIGHT

SIGNET ECLIPSE
Published by New American Library, a division of
Penguin Group (USA) Inc., 375 Hudson Street,
New York, New York 10014, USA
Penguin Group (Canada), 90 Eglinton Avenue East, Suite 700, Toronto,
Ontario M4P 2Y3, Canada (a division of Pearson Penguin Canada Inc.)
Penguin Books Ltd., 80 Strand, London WC2R 0RL, England
Penguin Ireland, 25 St. Stephen's Green, Dublin 2,
Ireland (a division of Penguin Books Ltd.)
Penguin Group (Australia), 250 Camberwell Road, Camberwell, Victoria 3124,
Australia (a division of Pearson Australia Group Pty. Ltd.)
Penguin Books India Pvt. Ltd., 11 Community Centre, Panchsheel Park,
New Delhi - 110 017, India
Penguin Group (NZ), 67 Apollo Drive, Rosedale, North Shore 0632,
New Zealand (a division of Pearson New Zealand Ltd.)
Penguin Books (South Africa) (Pty.) Ltd., 24 Sturdee Avenue,
Rosebank, Johannesburg 2196, South Africa

Penguin Books Ltd., Registered Offices:
80 Strand, London WC2R 0RL, England

First published by Signet Eclipse, an imprint of New American Library,
a division of Penguin Group (USA) Inc.

First Printing, October 2010
10 9 8 7 6 5 4 3 2 1

Printed in the United States of America

To the sons and daughters of the Breeding Male. May I always tell your stories with truth and passion.

Acknowledgments

An Eternal thank-you to Maria Carvainis and the entire MCA crew. You are the calm sanity behind my well-intentioned madness.

To my dream team: Danielle Perez, Claire Zion, Kara Welsh, Craig Burke, and everyone at NAL who's worked so hard on this novel. Thank you so very much!

To Kara Cesare, for truly getting "them" and for truly getting "me."

To my behind-the-scenes team: Jennifer Lyon, critique partner from heaven; Julie Ganis and Kerry de la Rionda, BFFs and ledge talker-downers; and Mindy Stern and Debra Borys, PhD, my windows into mind trauma and life on the "fourth floor." Thank you ever so!

And finally, to my life, my loves, my eternal blessings: Daniel, Isa, Lucca, and the wacky canine trio. Thank you for your patience and support.

1

SoHo
11:45 p.m.

Their breath visible in the frigid air, their shadows massive against the jagged stone walls, Nicholas and Lucian Roman moved through the tunnels beneath the quiet Manhattan neighborhood, determined to save their brother's soul, yet severely opposed on how to accomplish it.

"He's not ready," Lucian growled.

Nicholas's strides lengthened as he stalked past the tunnel guards—male vampires, Impurebloods—who kept their eyes on their boots and away from the one so beautifully pale, and the other with eyes and hair as black as his unbeating heart. "I will see for myself."

"What you will see, Brother," Lucian said, his fangs twitching, "is an animal. The hunger rules him again. This time it is nearly uncontrollable."

"No. Alexander has control. He has judgment. Look

where he keeps himself." Nicholas frowned. The six-by-nine-foot cage that dwelled far beneath the New York City streets had been built long ago to quell his eldest brother's rage, starve his body, and fuck with his mind, but in the past two days it had kept him from killing anything that crossed his path.

Lucian fell into step beside him as the tunnel widened. "He nearly butchered that human woman, Nicky."

"She is fine. She breathes."

"Only because you intervened."

Nicholas said nothing, his jaw tight as a fist.

Lucian continued. "He must stay in the cage until he feels . . . whole again. Until his craving for blood eases." His voice dropped. "If it ever eases . . ."

"You want to keep him locked up like an animal indefinitely?" Nicholas accused fiercely. "Like he was forced to do as a *balas*." The ancient word for "vampire child" exited Nicholas's mouth as a bitter hiss.

"It is as he wants it," Lucian argued. "Alexander built that cage because he was addicted to the pain of his past—now he keeps himself in it to protect his future. I'm not the bastard who fucked up his early years, but I know what needs to be done now, and so does Alexander. He understands the danger he's in—that we're all in now."

They rounded the corner and Nicholas eyeballed a second set of guards as they passed by. The Impure-bloods, the powerless sons of both human and vampire, had escaped their respective *credentis*—their vampire communities—long ago, after having had their sexual appetites bled out of them by the Order, the rulers of their breed. Now they worked for the Pureblood Roman brothers, and were treated with decency and respect.

"I believe your reaction," Nicholas said to Lucian as they reached the end of the tunnel and the door that led to their brother's prison, "your need to keep Alexander contained—is based in fear."

Lucian stepped in front of the heavy iron door, blocking Nicholas's way, his almond eyes burning with aggression. "Listen to me. If he kills, the Eternal Order will be able to track him—they'll be up our asses before we have a chance to cover them."

Nicholas sniffed. "Since when have you ever cared about the laws of the Order?"

"Hey, if you want to bring a war here—because you know that's what will happen if the Order finds us and attempts to take us back to the *credenti*—I'm game. I'd have to be dead to return to my vampire community, so they'll get a good fight from me. But we must acknowledge that if they find us, everything we've created since escaping will be over." He lifted his pale brows. "This is not fear, but reality."

Nicholas stared at his brother—the terrifying angel with the shock of white hair hanging past his ears. Granted, Lucian could be a hotheaded shit who acted too quickly and apologized never, but his point, his reasoning for keeping Alexander away from the public, had merit. And Nicholas was never one to ignore reality. As a *balas* it had kept him and his mother clothed, fed, and breathing. And more vitally, it had kept them away from the *credenti* and, later, the Eternal Order—the ten Pureblood vampires who had passed on to the middle world, yet made the laws, punished the lawbreakers, and governed every vampire *credenti* on Earth.

Nicholas nodded. "All right. He stays. But I want to see him and speak to him first."

"Are you going to give him a hug?" Lucian drawled, "Tell him everything's going to be all right? Share some feelings perhaps?"

Nicholas didn't bite back. He was nothing if not controlled. It was how he survived within his own head, within the memories that lurked there. "Enough now. Open the door, Little Brother."

With a sniff of derision, Lucian turned and punched in the alarm code. When he saw "green for go," he gripped the massive door handle and pulled. The brothers entered, quickly filling the small space with their massive frames. Nicholas looked around. First thing he saw was Alexander's ancient servant, Evans, a bald, rat-eyed Impure, who had escaped a *credenti* in Maine just ten years ago, and had been found in Central Park by Alexander.

Evans paced the floor in front of the cage, which was cut into the rock wall and had no windows, except for the three twelve-inch iron bars soldered into a steel door that took three keys, an alarm code, and a retinal scan to unlock.

"Open the door, Evans," Lucian ordered brusquely.

The old Impure stopped directly in front of Alexander's self-imposed prison. Like most males who came before the Roman brothers, he refused to make eye contact. It was the fear of their father, the Breeding Male, who and what he was—it remained strong, even in those who had escaped the *credenti.* "I'm sorry, sir. He wishes not to be disturbed."

Lucian cocked his head to one side. "I really don't give a shit."

"Easy, Lucian," Nicholas said in a calm voice, well aware that the old vampire was just protecting his master, the one who had taken him in and given him a new life. "Step aside now, Evans."

"But, sir—"

"I'm a gentleman, Evans," Nicholas continued easily, "and would drain your vein quickly and relatively painlessly, but Lucian, as you know, has little self-control."

Evans paled. "Yes, sir."

"Do it," Lucian said. "Quickly."

His hands shaking, the servant did as he was told, disarming the alarm, performing the retinal scan, and fumbling around with the key as he unlocked the door. Then, without looking at either brother, he stood back and watched as the door rolled to one side.

It was pitch-black inside the cage, freezing, and smelled of disinfectant—just as Alexander liked it. Lucian was the first to enter, but was barely five seconds inside before he let loose a string of curses.

Nicholas reached his brother's side in a millisecond. "What's the problem?" When he saw the reason for the outburst, he stalked out of the hole in the rock and went directly to Evans, his nostrils pulsing with each heavy breath. "Where is he?"

Evans's entire body trembled with fear. "I couldn't stop him. I—"

"Look at me, *Impure*!" Nicholas demanded.

Evans's gaze flickered up. He saw Lucian coming toward him too, and looked ready to pass the hell out.

"How long?" Nicholas repeated.

"An hour," Evans squeaked out.

"Shit!"

Nicholas turned when he heard Lucian. "He's on the hunt."

Lucian's fangs elongated as he glared at the servant. "You stupid little fu—"

Nicholas stopped him. "No time. We need to find him. No female in his path is safe."

The West Side
Fourth-floor psychiatric unit

"Lock her in and check her every fifteen."

Before the heavy wood door closed, Dr. Sara Donohue took another glance at her newest patient. Pearl McClean sat in the center of a twin mattress, legs crossed, chin to her chest, and due to a mild sedative, calm for the first time since she'd arrived from the ER an hour ago. The seventeen-year-old girl may have looked like an ordinary teenager daydreaming about her latest crush, but the blue paper gown she wore, and the fact that she was in a juvenile seclusion room on the fourth-floor psychiatric unit of Walter Wynn Memorial Hospital, made it clear that her troubles went far deeper than unrequited love.

Sara eyed the six-foot-three mocha-skinned security guard as he snapped the lock on the girl's door. "Hey, Randy, page me if she rips off that gown again. I'm talking right away."

He gave her a casual salute. "You got it, Doc."

Sara turned away from the door and started down the hall. "Coming, Mel?" she called over her shoulder.

"Yeah, right behind you." Melanie Abrams, the social worker who'd brought Pearl to the hospital and who worked most of the juvenile cases on the floor, ran after Sara, her ultrahigh heels making little clicking sounds on the scuffed white vinyl floor. "Not for nothing," she said, her tone slightly breathless from the pace. "But when did cutting get so freaking popular?"

Her eyes on her files, Sara ran down the med schedules for the night. "Maybe when leeches became an impractical way of detoxing emotional and physical pain. But I don't know if that's what's going on here."

"How can you say that?" Melanie asked, clearly taken aback. "She has hundreds of cuts all over her body."

"I know, but cutters normally stick to one area: arms, legs, belly. An area they can hide," Sara said, while hustling down the hallway, her long legs covering ground like a Thoroughbred out of the gate.

A young psych nurse walked by them and, as usual, his eyes went directly to the petite blonde behind Sara. She could hardly blame the guy. After all, Melanie looked more like a centerfold than a tough-ass social worker, and when she was around, most women in the hospital felt like Mary Ann next to her Ginger. Not so much Sara, though. She had zero desire to be the hot one, didn't have time to be the hot one.

"Maybe she wasn't looking to hurt herself," Melanie said, ignoring the nurse as she followed Sara. "Maybe she just wanted someone to notice her."

"Could be." Sara rounded the corner, then stopped at the double doors separating the juvenile ward from main reception and the adult long-term-care facility. She slipped her key card into the wall slot and waited impatiently to be buzzed through. Once she gained access, she took off toward reception, Melanie affixed to her side.

"You know," Sara began, "she didn't say a word when I was in there with her. She didn't answer one question, but she did flinch every time I mentioned the mother's boyfriend."

Melanie looked thoughtful. "The guy seemed kind of shady to me, but he did act concerned when we came to get her."

"Course he did. Who called 911?"

"The mom. She was at the door when we got there, led the officers and me right into the bathroom. We found Pearl crouched beside the tub. Knife was a few feet away."

Sara dropped her files on the green marble desktop. "Was she wearing anything?"

"No. Naked, out of control, covered in cuts. But . . ."

Sara glanced up, saw the confusion in Melanie's pale blue eyes, and said, "What?"

"I don't know . . . It was weird. With that many cuts, you'd expect a good amount of blood, right?"

"And what?" Sara said. "There wasn't much?"

"There wasn't any." Melanie's gaze flickered to the two nurses behind the large circular desk, and she lowered her voice. "These were fresh wounds, open—and they weren't even seeping. Take a look."

Sara opened Pearl McClean's file again and flipped through the photos of her injuries until she got to the close-up shots of the girl's wounds. As Melanie had said, the cuts looked new, unhealed; no scar had formed over the hundred or so gashes and yet there was no sign of blood. In fact, she thought, pulling the image closer, the skin looked almost shiny, like an imaginary piece of tape was affixed to it.

"So?" Melanie said. "What do you think?"

"ER doc says the weapon and cuts match up." Sara stared at the photograph of the girl's back, then shook her head. "I just don't think those marks are self-inflicted."

"So what, then? Someone did this to her? The boyfriend? The mom?"

"I don't know, but I'm not letting her leave the hospital until I find out."

Melanie eyed Sara, as if she didn't want to say something, yet knew she couldn't stop herself. "The mother raved about the relationship her boyfriend had with the girl. She said he was the perfect father—that he'd do anything for Pearl."

Sara laughed. "You didn't believe that."

"No." Mel sighed, looking momentarily deflated. "So what should I put in the report?"

"Let's go with 'deliberate self-harm' for now," Sara said, closing the girl's file. "It'll give me more time—"

Sara was cut off by the long bleating sound of one of the nurse's pagers. She turned to see Claire, a reception nurse in her late thirties who always worked graveyard and was obsessed with bright blue eye shadow and cinnamon Certs, checking the readout on her pager.

"Who is it?" Sara asked her.

"LTC, 412," she said.

Shit! "Buzz me in." Sara pushed away from the reception desk and Melanie, and raced through the door to Long-Term Care. Gray. She'd just seen him an hour ago; he'd been fine. Her heart beat louder and faster as she ran down the hall. What the hell had happened?

Her breath pulled hard from her lungs as she burst through the door to his room. Her gaze shot to the bed, which was sans patient and stripped of all linen. Then she caught sight of Gray, completely calm, sitting on a chair by the window, staring out at the building across the airshaft and its handful of rooms that were dotted with light and life. His hands were splayed on his thighs, and his dark blond hair was disheveled. Several longer bits stuck out in places like weeds in the grass.

The rational part of Sara's brain warned her to chill out and feign professionalism if she didn't want any questions coming her way later, but it was almost impossible to be cool. Without a word to the nurse who stood beside Gray, Sara went to him and knelt down beside his chair. She fought the urge to wrap her arms around his long, lean frame and protect him from whatever crisis he'd encountered in the past five minutes. Instead, she took his hands, misshapen and discolored from decades-old burns. "What happened, Gray?" she asked him gently.

Nothing. Not like she expected anything else.

"Will you look at me?" she asked him gently. "Let me see you're okay?"

Gray didn't move, just continued to stare out the window as if nothing but a light breeze had blown through his door. Sara looked up at the nurse standing beside her. "Jill?"

"I found a stockpile in his mattress," the nurse said. "Klonopin." She nodded toward the metal meal cart next to the bed.

Sara followed the nurse's gaze and saw the small hill of round, yellow pills. *Goddammit*. How was this happening behind her back? How had she not seen signs of hoarding, and of his mental state deteriorating to this point? She turned back, stared at the once-handsome young man curled into himself like a child on the plastic chair.

Stockpiling sedatives was the road to intentional overdose. Anger, fear, and untamed guilt swam like piranha in her blood. She wanted to shake him, force him to look at her, but she had to be careful how she dealt with Gray in front of staff. As psychiatrists went, she was one of the more hands-on docs, but that didn't mean she could get all weepy and emotional with a patient without attracting attention.

"When you found him," Sara asked Jill, a practiced calm in her voice, "was he taking anything from the stash?"

The nurse shook her head. "Just adding to it. He was on the floor beside the bed stuffing the pills inside. I think he used a fork to jab a hole in the mattress."

Sara stood, pulled out her stethoscope and placed the diaphragm on Gray's back, listening to his heart and lungs. When she was satisfied by what she heard, she eased the buds from her ears. "Jill," she said. "Get rid of the meds, but make sure he takes his regular dosage. And I mean watch and check, okay?"

"Of course, Dr. Donohue." Jill raised her dark brows. "Do you want him back in bed for the night?"

Sara winced. The question was a valid one in a situation like this, but the phrase "back in bed" was code for "Do you want him strapped down?" and there was nothing she wanted less in that moment. "No, he's fine where he is. But I'm going to get a new mattress in here, and in the meantime I want you to check the room for anything else, anything that might be a problem, then look in on him every ten minutes and call me if there's any change."

Jill nodded. "Sure thing, Dr. Donohue."

When the nurse left the room, Sara went to stand in front of the window, in Gray's line of vision. She hoped he'd lift his gaze to hers for just a moment so she could connect with him. But when he did, the weight of his unhappiness read so loud and obvious in his steely gray eyes that Sara could barely keep her emotions in check. Her breath trembled as she leaned toward him, and she hated herself for it. "Just give me a little more time," she whispered.

His jaw twitched; then his mouth settled into a frown, and after a moment, he turned away and shut his eyes.

Sara didn't say another word, just turned and left the room. She headed straight for her office, to the tiny bathroom that was all her own. When she got there, she shut the door and turned on the cold water. What was she supposed to do? What did he expect her to do? Let him go? Let him die? Just give him the tools to kill himself and walk away? He was fucking kidding himself if he thought she was going to do that.

Tears burned in her throat and she hauled back and smashed her fist against the bathroom door. Pain shot through her wrist, then up her forearm. It felt good for a moment—her anger was alive, and the sudden release of emotional pain felt almost druglike in its quickness. Was this the release-high some of her juvie patients got off on? she wondered before the pain suddenly jumped and intensified. Sucking air through her teeth, she stuck her throbbing hand under the faucet and let the frigid water numb her skin. She glanced at the door, made sure she hadn't left an imprint.

All she needed was more time. There would come a day, one day soon, if she could get her ass in gear, that she would get it right, and Gray would finally be released from the memories that haunted him. *And hell, you'd be released from them too, wouldn't you?*

The loud knock on her office door startled her, but pulled her back to reality. She quickly dried her hand, left the bathroom, and called, "Come in," as she walked over to her desk and dropped into the black leather chair behind it. She eyed the four half-empty takeout cups scattered around the top of her messy desk, and ached for a hot cup of coffee.

Dr. Peter Albert walked into the room with an expression of a man who was long on criticisms but short on patience.

Sara didn't wait for the middle-aged ward chief to

ball her out. One second after he sat in the chair opposite her, she shook her head and said, "Amazing. It's close to midnight, staff's changing over, and yet the Dr. Albert spy contingent rolls on."

The man smiled dryly. "I would hope so. Who knows when or if I'd have heard about it from you."

He was right, but Sara didn't say it. She didn't have to. Pete had known her for four years now, and he'd come to expect certain things. Her honesty and loyalty were his when it came to every patient but one.

She shrugged, tried to sound casual. "There's nothing to worry about here. He's fine. Nothing drastic went down."

Pete didn't buy it. "Only because a nurse caught him before it did."

"It's my fault. The sessions this week have been particularly brutal. He's been bombarded by flashbacks of the fire—"

"Get serious. That pile of Klonopin was more than a week in the making."

Sara sat up and grabbed one of the half-empty cups of coffee on her desk. "We're getting so close, Pete. I can feel it. Isn't that why you brought me on? To find the switch? Turn off traumatic memory for good?"

"Yes, that's why I hired you, *and* why the donors continue to throw money at the Neuro Psych department—it's also why I allow you to have Gray here." Tense lines formed around his mouth. "But if anyone finds out—"

"No one's going to find out," Sara assured him, taking a sip of coffee. *Ugh. Cold.* She drank it anyway.

"If Gray regains his ability to speak—"

"He wouldn't tell anyone. He wouldn't want me to lose my job."

Pete's brow lifted. "Even if you were the one preventing him from permanently checking out?"

His words stopped her cold, because in truth, the possibly was a valid one.

Pete was quiet, his gaze dropped from her eyes to her mouth and remained there a second too long before he said softly, "Listen, Sara. I've got to protect myself and this hospital."

"I understand that."

"Good, because I've decided to change Gray's current situation."

"What does that mean?" A prick of fear moved through her.

"I'm having him moved to lockdown."

"Hell no!" She slammed down her cup. "No, Pete. I won't keep him in a cell, strapped to a bed, no group therapy. He's already a prisoner."

"You're not thinking clearly. You're making choices based on emotion, not what's right for Gray. I think maybe you should consider putting him under the care of another doctor—"

Sara was adamant. "Not going to happen."

"Sara—"

"If you make that change without my say-so, you

can consider it my resignation." Sara leaned toward him, her tone deadly serious. "And all of my research—every study on PTSD, every unpublished finding I have on memory pain in military vets, every question, every curiosity, every idea I have will go with me."

Worry etched Pete's expression, and something beyond a professional loss. She knew he liked her, more than a boss should. And if she were anyone else, someone with a past that was free of tragedy and a future that offered clear possibilities, she might have given him a chance. After all, he was a decent guy, nice to look at. But she had nothing to offer anyone, not now—not yet.

Sara stood, grabbed the stack of files from her desk. "I have to go. I have patients."

Pete stood as well. "If the truth gets out, I'm going to have to deny all knowledge. It's your career that'll be destroyed."

Sara nodded. "Understood." Poor Pete, she mused. He was a good man, just not a brave one.

Sara walked out of her office and didn't stop until one of the nurses called to her from the nurse's station. "Dr. Donohue?"

"Yes?"

"Tom Trainer's calling for you again. It's his fourth call tonight. I tried to tell him you weren't available, but he insisted on holding."

Sara sighed. "He's no longer a patient here. Tell him you'd be happy to recommend a doc outside the hospital, but I won't be speaking to him now or ever."

The young woman nodded. "Okay."

Sara walked away from the nurse's station. She needed to see Gray, see if he was all right and in the room she'd left him in. The hallway was quiet, with most of the patients asleep. She grabbed his chart from the wall and entered his room. When she saw him asleep on the dormitory-style bed, a single white sheet pushed down to his knees and no restraints at his wrists, she sighed with relief.

She watched him for a few moments, the shaft of light from the hallway illuminating his pale face. Her little brother was twenty-seven in real time, but to Sara he still looked like the boy who used to chase her around the house pretending to be a hungry sister-eating dinosaur. Now he was as much a prisoner of the hospital as he was of his mind.

Sara went over to the bed and sat down beside him, laid her perfectly smooth hand over one of his fire-ravaged ones. The fire she'd caused—the fire that had not only destroyed her family, but her brother's mental and physical health, as well, the summer he'd turned eight.

The fire she'd run from and come out unscathed.

It took every ounce of self-control she had not to lie down beside him and weep against his shoulder. But she didn't deserve his care, not until he could offer it to her himself. Because the truth was, no matter how hard she worked, she'd never truly atone for her sin until she brought her brother back to life.

2

In the indigo light of predawn, Alexander Roman rounded Hudson Street and came to halt on 11th, sniffing the bitter November air like the animal he'd become. *Too many to choose from,* he thought, his fangs elongating, vibrating as hunger gnawed at his belly. He'd tried it their way, his brothers. Every hour on the hour, they'd had him feed from the stock at RB Beef Company, one of the many businesses he and his brothers owned and operated in the city. But for Alexander, the desire to find another female, human or vampire, and sink his canines into the sweet spot below her breast, drink deep and long until her heart stopped, was impossibly strong.

His father's DNA had finally shown up, two hundred years after it had been rooted in his mother's womb. Was this the kind of Pureblood male—the kind of *paven* his mother had been forced to lie with to create him? A rabid beast on a mission, pounding into her? If so, Alexander couldn't help but understand her need to despise him.

Delicate snowflakes fell around him, so white and pure until they hit the ground. The wind picked up and Alexander cocked his head to one side, the scent of blood assaulting his nostrils. *Ahhhhh* . . . It was human female, a delicacy, easy prey, something he'd rarely allowed himself to sample until the hunger had hit. Now the hunger ruled, and he was off, flying full speed down the snowy street, his fangs curling as his mouth watered.

Then suddenly, halfway down the block, something halted him like a truck jerking on its breaks. Panting, he stood immobile on the sidewalk, an odd tingling sensation building in his fingertips. He shook his hands to get rid of it, then took off running again. But seconds later, midstride, he was hit by a rod of pain that stole the very breath from his lungs.

What the fuck?

His body began to shake and heat up as the pain traveled lightning quick up his wrists, forearms, biceps, and shoulders. Instinctively, he reached out for something to steady himself. His hand clamped around a thick metal pole and he pressed his body against the hard coolness as if it were his lover.

What the hell is happening?

First hunger, now pain.

His head began to pulse like the bends of an accordion and he could feel his pupils shrink until all he could see were shadows. Panic erupted in his chest at the sudden, ugly blindness.

Get home. Get the fuck home now!

From behind him came the steady and familiar hum of the delivery truck that always passed by at this time. Alexander heard the catlike screech of brakes and a male voice call out, "Look at that asshole."

The yeasty stink of fresh bread filled the air, intermingling with the sound of shared laughter.

"I haven't been that hammered since the Mets won the play-offs," another man said. "Careful there, buddy. Don't piss yourself."

Blind as a wolf pup, his head pressed against the dirty metal, Alexander hissed, his fangs tingling with a need to strike. *If you want to remain alive and intact, keep driving.*

"Sleep it off, buddy," one of them called before hitting the accelerator.

Something that felt like oil snaked down Alexander's throat. It was thick and purposeful and heading for his lungs. Suddenly there was no air.

No air in. No air out.

The pressure was excruciating, and Alexander dropped to his knees, his hands locking on to either side of his head. This wasn't another symptom of hunger. This was something altogether different.

His ears felt stuffed with something . . . rags—rags that housed a hundred pissed-off flies. Panting to supply his aching lungs with even a whisper of breath, Alexander started crawling toward what he hoped were the brownstone's stairs. He knew that most of the brownstones on this block had garden apartments. If he could reach one, he'd have the shelter he needed. Daybreak was near and he was fifteen blocks from home and four blocks from the tunnels.

Daybreak.

Something he'd never feared in all of his two hundred years. Not until this very moment.

It should've been impossible, he thought, feeling the edge of the icy stone steps beneath his fingers. It was too soon, too early. But with every shock of pain, every instinct warning him to find shelter, he knew it was true. The change was upon him, and he had only minutes before the sun caught and seared him.

As he scrambled clumsily down the steps, a quick wind picked up, sending a tornado of forgotten winter leaves whirling around him, their sharp, crackled edges stabbing at his sensitive skin. Like the tide rushing toward the shore, his vision came back—but in a binocularlike fashion, tunneled and unfocused. He squinted, caught sight of the minishelter before him. His muscles continued to tremble with small bone-aching seizures as he got to his feet and stumbled down the rest of the stairs and into the covered entryway of the brownstone's garden apartment.

He needed to get inside. He needed full protection.

On his knees, huddled against the door, he reached up and gripped the handle, then cursed when he found it locked.

What street is this? Where are the tunnels?

Suddenly it hit, like a lightning bolt of fire, angry stabs of sunlight against his skin.

Dawn.

He glanced up. Above him, in the dome of sky, the protective shield of indigo had succumbed to the pale, dire streaks of a lavender and pink sunrise.

Alexander cried out, turned and clawed at the door. With each fiery tear into his skin, his eyes watered, his nose ran, and he tried not to vomit with the acute, lethal pain of it.

It all made sense now. The desperate hunger, the relentless pain. He was being sent through morpho before his time.

One hundred years before his time.

Mouth wide and fangs curled, he cried out into the sunrise, then collapsed in a heap against the door.

Sara walked down West 11th toward her building, pulling her wool coat closed at the neck to keep out the frigid morning air. Exhaustion licked at her mind and her muscles, making her feel like a huge wimp. Fighting for Gray had become commonplace in her daily life, but last night's episode had drained her will more than she cared to admit. She liked to think of herself as a hard-ass, someone who pushed herself and those around her until the answers revealed themselves—then on to the next mystery. But witnessing Gray's potential suicide attempt had her wondering for the first time since med school if she might come out of this a failure, if her plan to go back home to Minnesota, return a well and happy Gray to their ever-hopeful mother, was an utterly bullshit objective.

The flutters of a melancholy heart warned Sara that she was bordering on vulnerability, and she didn't do vulnerable. Clearly, she needed sleep, a solid five hours to get rid of the weak-little-kitten vibe she was carrying around. Then she could go back to work—rethink and retool.

She made her way down the brownstone steps, pulling out her ring of keys as she went. But at the bottom, she came to an abrupt halt, nearly colliding with something blocking the entryway to her garden apartment. Her heart stuttered, and sudden fear yanked her out of her exhaustion. Huddled against her doorway was a man.

She turned her key chain again and palmed the pepper spray she'd had on there since moving to New York seven years ago. There was probably nothing in it but air now, but, what the hell, he didn't know that. She flicked the nozzle to the on position with her thumb, then walked cautiously up to him. A thread of fear moved through her and she was glad it was daylight.

The man's face was turned toward her door, his large frame curled into a ball. As she crept closer, she noted that the triad of smells that normally emanated from the lost souls who found shelter at her door were absent.

She leaned down and touched his shoulder. "Hey, buddy."

Nothing.

Perfect. This was the last thing she needed today.

She tried again. "Hey, it's really cold out here. Let me point you toward a shelter. There's one a couple blocks down."

He didn't move.

Fuck. A quick fear implanted itself in her gut, one nurtured from years of living in the city and working in a profession of unpredictability. The man huddled at her door didn't fit the profile of a homeless guy, and that made him not only strange, but potentially dangerous.

She stared down at him, the cold morning wind blowing strands of her hair against her face. His clothes looked clean and expensive. Shoes, too. Maybe he was someone from her neighborhood, out partying—

HELP ME . . .

The unspoken words slammed into Sara's mind. Caught off guard, she stumbled back, but got only as far as the first step when a sudden, tortured cry erupted from the man, and his dark, closely shaved head dropped back, exposing his face for the first time.

"Oh God. Oh . . . oh, shit . . ." Heart pounding, she stared at his ruggedly male face. On either cheek, two angry red welts—symbols of some kind—had been singed into his pale skin.

"Who did this to you?" Sara uttered.

He didn't answer, just lay there, eyes closed, panting, openly suffering, back against the door. He was so huge. The width of his chest had to be twice the size of hers.

She knew it was probably a stupid move, but she was a doctor and her concern trumped her fear. She dropped to her knees beside him and cupped his face. "You need an ambulance."

The man's eyes shot open. Sara gasped, "Jesus!" Then she stared as severe, predatory merlot-colored orbs caught and held her gaze. She'd never seen anything so fierce or so beautiful in her life, and she just kept staring, transfixed as his full lips parted, then moved.

He hissed something. Then again.

She shook her head. "I don't understand."

NO AMBULANCE.

Sara's hands flew to her ears. What the hell? His voice. It was inside her head. How was this happening? Exhaustion? Was it screwing with her mind?

NO POLICE. NO AMBULANCE.

Panicked, Sara released him and shot back to the steps. When she did, shafts of sunlight broke free all around her and flooded the space. Like a snake in search of a mouse, defying all logic and reason, the light slithered about, searching for its prey. She was delusional—had to be. And yet, as she watched, white-hot rays from the sun above them clamped on to the man's wrists and forearms, searing into his flesh, branding the sensitive skin with the same strange key-like symbols that etched his face.

"Oh my God. Your skin." She shot forward again, blocking him from the light. "It's smoking—" Sara dove into her purse, grabbed her cell phone. She flicked it open.

NO! The man reached out, knocking the phone from her hand.

She gasped. "What the hell are you doing?"

IN.

Ignoring him, Sara reached for her cell phone again.

"Please," he said aloud for the first time, his tone dark and impassioned. "In."

"No!"

The man grabbed her wrist, his thick, long fingers squeezing lightly. Sara sucked in a breath as the muscles in her neck gave out and her head dropped forward. She felt instantly warm and light-headed. She didn't know how it was possible, but his fingers . . . on her skin . . . it made her feel—

"Ahhh," she uttered, electric currents shooting up her arm into her neck, her face. Her mouth started to water and she heard something in her mind again—something unintelligible. And yet she instinctually understood every word. She got to her feet, went to her door, and shoved her key in the lock.

It was incomprehensible, but she knew exactly what she had to do, and once the door was open, she bent down and curled her wrists under the man's armpits. It was like trying to move a bulldozer, and after several seconds of struggling to pull his enormous frame over the threshold, the man dug his heels into the concrete and helped her. But once inside her apartment, he let out a pained groan and collapsed on the floor, lying against the hardwood, still as a stone.

"I don't know what the hell is going on here," she said in a panicked voice, quickly drawing the curtains over the closed blinds, "but you need a doctor, like, yesterday." She ran to the couch and searched behind the cushions until she found the cordless. She was about to dial 911 when she heard something moving in her kitchen.

She stopped, looked up. "Who's there?"

There was a moment of utter silence; then a man stepped out from behind the wall that separated the two rooms. "It's me, Dr. Donohue."

Wearing a suit that was two sizes too big, the young man stared at Sara with wide brown eyes. He was tall and thin, his straight dark hair almost to his shoulders now. It had been just hours since he called the hospital looking for her, but three months since she'd last seen him, since she'd stopped treating him—three months since he'd snuck into her office and declared his love, offering her the bluebird that lay stiff and lifeless in his hands.

Sara tightened her grip on the phone as she moved to stand in front of the man on the floor in an utterly asinine attempt to protect him. "Tom . . ."

"You remember me." He smiled broadly, looking remarkably like a dimpled serpent. "I didn't think you would."

Adopting the motherly tone he'd always responded to, Sara said gently, "Tom, you need to leave now. This is very inappropriate."

His smile widened. "You said that to me once before, remember?"

"I think you should go home. We can talk later."

Tom wagged a finger at her. "No, I don't think so. I've tried to talk to you, but you won't answer my calls."

"If there's something you really need to see me about, then maybe we can schedule—"

"No!" He frowned, his eyes filling with tears. "You're lying."

Fear rose in Sara's throat, but she kept her eyes trained on him as she searched the phone's keypad with her thumb. *Where's the fricking on button?*

"I've been waiting all night for you." He moved toward her, his polished loafers making a scraping, sandpaperlike sound against the wood floor. "Where were you?"

"Working." Sara shifted her hand higher on the cordless. *To the left, then up two buttons.*

"Working with *him*, that disfigured mute you love so much," he said with an exaggerated pout. "All you care about is him. The rest of us are just your experiments."

"That's not true," Sara assured him gently. The image of Gray that shot into her mind made her all the more conscious of remaining alert and alive.

Tom noticed the man on the floor behind her, cocked his head to one side. "Who's that?" His tone instantly changed from childlike to menacing. He looked accusingly at her. "You brought someone home? Are you going to be with him? Let him touch you?"

There. Sara stabbed the call button on the phone. Knowing she had only seconds before Tom's aggressive side surfaced, she looked down and dialed. But she never completed the call. Tom descended on her, knocked the phone from her hand. Terror pulsing in her chest, Sara ran for the door, but Tom was right behind her. He reached out, grabbed her wrist, and hauled her back against him. She winced in pain, but she wasn't about to give in. The little bastard was going to get a knee to the balls if it was the last thing she did. She kicked at him, twisted in his grip, tried to bite his shoulder, get her hands free, get to his eyes with her nails.

"I like you like this," Tom hissed in her ear, clamping his hand over her mouth. "Why do I like you like this?"

Where was the phone? The front door? Was it still open?

Sara's gaze went wild, looking, searching as her breath remained jailed inside her lungs. Then she saw it—the front door. Open a crack. She had to get out, get free. She bit down on Tom's hand, then jammed her elbow into his gut.

"Bitch," Tom cursed, releasing her.

Momentarily free, Sara made another run for the door, but tripped over one of the couch legs and landed on her hands and knees.

Get up! Move!

Behind her, she heard Tom mutter the words "You little whore . . ."

She scrambled to her feet, her lungs aching for breath. But she never made it to the door. Tom caught her coattails and yanked her back. She stumbled, losing her balance as panic closed in on her. She pushed against the feeling. There was no way she was going to be taken down like this.

She scissored her legs, but just as she managed to get her feet under her, Tom grabbed her shoulders and whirled her to face him. Sara opened her mouth to scream, but before the sound cleared her throat, Tom's fist slammed into her face. Time stopped, then slowly picked up again, and then she was flying back, her head hitting the hardwood floor with a nasty thump. Blinding pain assaulted her, followed by pins and needles. *No.* She couldn't catch her breath. Her lungs ached for air, but there was none. The room narrowed. From the back of her mind, she heard a growl—slow and menacing. Was it her? No . . . didn't come from her. She struggled to stay conscious, turning her head to the side and blinking.

Again. The sound of an animal.

Her gaze lifted. *The man on the floor.* Was it him? No, he was still lifeless, eyes closed, skin pale, except for the key-shaped brands on his cheeks. Oh God, she wanted to help him, warn him, but her body felt impossibly heavy—

Suddenly, without warning, the man's eyelids popped open, his head jerked back, and within seconds, he was on his feet and heading straight for Tom. Sara struggled to stay conscious, to focus on the impossible scene playing out before her. The man was so huge, his face a mask of animal rage.

"Who the hell are you?" Tom cried out, backing up, his eyes little balls of terror as he stared at the stranger.

"Very thirsty," the man hissed.

The image of Tom's terrified face drifted down the tunnels of Sara's clogged mind. *So tired.* She just wanted sleep. Her gaze flicked upward. The man had Tom in his clutches, his feet dangling off the ground like a puppet. Tom was swinging his fists . . . hitting nothing but air . . .

Sara's head pounded with the slow beat of her heart. The last thing she saw before she blacked out was the man's teeth.

No. Not teeth. *Fangs.*

3

The puny male squirmed in Alexander's grasp. He weighed less than nothing, his jabs little more than the delicate slap of a butterfly's wings. Alexander's fangs quivered against his lips, the stinging pain from his burns fueling his ire.

"Please," the human begged, his watery brown eyes wide and scared. "Let me go."

Alexander lifted his brow. "She asked for release, didn't she, cockroach?"

"What?" he sputtered. "What? I don't—"

"The woman asked for release," Alexander roared. "And did you listen to her? Give her what she asked for?"

Trembling like a wind-up toy, Tom stared at Alexander, his bulging gaze moving from one branded cheek to the other.

Alexander grabbed the bastard's neck with both hands and growled, "Speak, human! Did you give her what she asked for?"

"No," Tom croaked.

"No. You terrified her. Wounded her." Alexander brought the man's face close to his own. "You deserve no less than that."

Tom started to cry. "Please . . . no."

Unfazed, Alexander leaned in and sniffed the air around the human. His nostrils flared angrily. "Weak blooded and pissing in your pants. You should be grateful you didn't manage to kill her, human. I would like nothing better than to end your miserable—"

Alexander's skin began to vibrate and arrows of pain shot through him, making him wince. He looked down, at the hands that encircled the human's neck, and his jaw went rigid at the sight before him. The sun-seared burns on his wrists and forearms were fading, shrinking into permanent tattoos—the markings that identified him as a morphed male, just as the ones on his face forever identified him as a progeny of the Breeding Male.

How had this happened to him? A Pureblood *paven* didn't go through morpho until his three hundredth year. He had another century, for fuck's sake! His fingers dug into the thin skin of the human's neck. Just a few days ago, he'd been a creature of the night and of the day—of a life that was his own. Then the hunger hit, followed by the sun . . .

A sound, nothing more than a sigh really, floated up to Alexander. *The woman.* She stirred. Alexander glanced down, and his temper ebbed slightly. The human woman who had heard his thoughts, who had saved his life, now writhed in slow motion on the wood floor several feet away, her heart-shaped face contorted in pain.

Alexander changed his grip on the male, one hand slipping under his arm, the other remaining around his throat. He squeezed, just enough. Killing the piece of shit, pulling the breath from his body, would surely be a proper punishment for what he'd done, but Alexander knew that such a temporary wave of satisfaction would lead to big problems, problems he and his brothers had made every attempt to avoid—that is, until the premorph hunger had claimed him.

He released the man, and with a defeated sigh, the skinny human passed out and slid to the floor, his long body hitting against the wood with a dull thud.

Alexander went to the woman and dropped to one knee beside her. She breathed comfortably, but the red bruise on her pale cheek was already starting to darken and swell. Rage rippled through him like the aftershocks of an earthquake, and his hands and fangs trembled with the desire to tear into the flesh of the human passed out behind him.

The woman stirred again, her full lips moving, her brow coiled with tension. Her color was good, but she needed rest and a doctor. Until then, Alexander would offer her what comfort he could. In addition to new powers morpho provided, individual gifts were also given to each Pureblood *paven*. Alexander already understood his as well as he understood his own name. He brushed back the woman's long, dark hair and placed two fingers on her temple, breathed calm into her blood, then watched as her body relaxed. When he believed her to be sleeping gently, he reached into the pocket of his coat for his cell phone. *Dammit.* It wasn't there. He looked around the room, his gaze quicker than it had been only hours previously. Near the threshold leading into the kitchen, he spotted the cordless. He reached in its direction and muttered a terse, "Come." The phone shook against the ground, then flew across the room and into Alexander's waiting hand. He stabbed at the numbers, then pressed the receiver to his ear.

"Alex?" Nicholas's voice was laced with panic. "Where are you?"

"I need two cars at 340 West 11th, off Hudson. Garden apartment."

"Why?" Nicholas demanded harshly.

"I have two unconscious humans and no protection."

"No protection?" A stunned silence vibrated across the line. "What have you done?"

"Protection from the sun," Alexander said angrily.

"What?"

"I've gone through morpho." The words were bitter on Alexander's tongue.

There was a pause. Then Nicholas uttered a curt "Impossible."

Yes, Alexander mused, as the brands on his hands and face twitched with residual pain. "Get the hell over here. I need to find out what's going on."

Ten minutes later, Nicholas and Lucian walked through the door. Both standing well above six feet, both broad and lethal, they surveyed the one-room apartment and its contents with the same military vigilance they'd relied upon in battle more than a century ago.

"Damn," Lucian said, his severe sand-colored gaze shifting from the man on the floor to the woman on the couch. "You did it."

"Did what?" Alexander snapped, standing sentry beside the woman, monitoring her physical condition.

Lucian tossed the black cloak he'd brought with him, a makeshift sun shield for Alexander, over one arm of the couch. "Drained them both."

"Bullshit," Alexander growled. "The woman's blood is untouched."

"And the man?" Nicholas asked, walking over to Alexander, his stride heavy with predatory grace.

"In a coma, I believe," Alexander said.

When Nicholas reached his eldest brother, his black gaze moved over Alexander's face and forearms. "Have you seen yourself?"

"No," Alexander said, his jaw tight.

"It's not pretty."

"Then not much has changed, has it?"

A quick grin touched Nicholas's lips, showing off the tips of his fangs. It was gone in an instant. "You have the markings of our father."

The circles branded into his cheeks screamed "I am descended from the Breeding Male." Alexander nodded. "Yes."

"And of your true mate," Nicholas said, eyeing the key-shaped markings within the circles. "Is this good news or bad?"

Alexander sniffed. "You mean am I relieved that I don't carry our father's gene to screw and impregnate any female that crosses my path?" He heard Lucian snort with amusement behind him. "Yes." He was glad of that, and had felt deep concern for the day he would morph and find out what future he had been given. But was this good news? Instead of a Breeding Male's empty circle, he had the mark of a true mate inside of his, and his body, without his consent, would soon be on the hunt for her.

"Going through morpho explains the extreme hunger," Nicholas said. "Is it gone now?"

"It is different," Alexander said. "I have more control, but the blood I desire isn't as random."

Nicholas's ink black brows drew together in concern. "What are you saying? You must be selective in the vein you choose? Not just any female will do?"

"The hunger remains, but it too has morphed into something I'm not exactly sure how to feed." His nostrils flared. "Blood has become the appetizer . . ."

"Not the main course," Nicholas finished for him.

Alexander said nothing.

"Sounds great. Can we finish the question-and-answer portion of this game show later?" Lucian said, impatience registering in his tone. He looked at Alexander, arching one pale brow. "Are you going to tell us what went down in here?"

A growl began to build low in Alexander's chest. "Take care not to push me today, Little Brother. I don't feel so good." He raised his chin and inhaled deeply, trying to rid himself of the unnecessary aggression surging through his blood. "Sun came up and I needed shelter." Alexander looked at the woman, felt a deep tenderness roll through him. "She provided it. Without question." His voice conveyed a hint of awe.

"What about the man?" Lucian asked.

"He was waiting for her. The little prick attacked her." Alexander stared at the bruise on the woman's face as she slept peacefully. A low snarl escaped his lips. "I should have drained him."

"Good thing you didn't," Lucian uttered tightly. "That would've been another problem we don't need."

Sensing another round of morphed male hostility in the air, Nicholas asked a practical question. "What do you want to do with the man?"

Still hovering close to the woman, Alexander eyed his brother. "You take care of him, Nicholas." He lifted one thick eyebrow. "Make sure he never comes back here. Make him forget that she even exists."

Nicholas nodded quickly. "Done. And what about her?"

"I'll take care of her," Lucian offered with a wicked grin.

"No!" Alexander snarled, his upper lip lifting, exposing his fangs. "No one touches her."

"You sure the hunger's eased, Alex?" Lucian said, his grin widening. "You're acting like an animal over a feed. Perhaps she has the vein you desire?"

Nostrils flared, Alexander stared at Lucian, ready to strike with either words or fists.

"Easy there, boys," Nicholas said dryly, stepping between the two. He eyeballed Alexander and said in a low voice, "*Duro*."

The tender word for "brother" barely registered with Alexander. Blood was rushing in his ears as he tried to keep himself under control. This was not the debilitating pangs of hunger; this was something altogether different—a barely restrained ferocity when it came to the woman who'd saved him. Jesus, how could he even think about striking his brother? The brother he'd protected and cared for, for more than a century?

Nicholas broke through his thoughts. "We need to act swiftly, Alexander. Where do you want to take her?"

"Home."

"Isn't this her apartment?"

"*Our* home," Alexander clarified. He knew the decision wasn't a wise one, but he couldn't stop himself.

Nicholas and Lucian stared at him for a good thirty seconds. Finally Lucian shook his head and muttered, "You've got to be kidding."

"She's unconscious, Alexander," Nicholas said, attempting to reason with him. "She needs a doctor."

"She remains unconscious because of me. I sedated her. Her mind is protected, unharmed, and, for the record, we have a doctor."

"She needs a doctor who treats humans," Lucian said sharply.

Alexander covered the ground between them, stood nose to nose with the white-blond vampire. "She's coming with me, Little Brother, so if you have a problem with that, you'd better get over it in the next five seconds."

Lucian stood his ground, his nostrils flaring. "We have a covenant, Brother. No humans in our home—"

"Screw the covenant," Alexander snarled. "This is different."

"How?"

"She's mine!"

"Stubborn ass." Lucian backed away, signaled for Nicholas. "You talk to him."

Nicholas had been a lion on the battlefield, but in business matters and family squabbles, he could always be counted on to remain the closest thing to unruffled and rational. "Alexander, you know what we risk if she—"

"She saved my life, Nicky!" Alexander roared, his

tone as passionate as it was fierce. "But for her, I would be the dust on your boots."

The words coated the air around them, and after several moments of silence, Nicholas nodded and said, "All right. For now, she is welcome in our home."

Alexander's gaze shifted to Lucian. "What about you?"

His jaw rigid, Lucian locked eyes with Alexander. "Do I even have a say here?" A century of fighting side by side, of helping each other escape a childhood of daily nightmares, of finding the courage to reject the race who had held them captive, had built an unshakable bond between them. At their very core, they were not only brothers—they were best friends. Finally, Lucian nodded and muttered, "Fine," but his almond eyes remained wary.

"Luca," Nicholas said, his tone serious and purposeful. "Check the sidewalk. It's early yet, but I don't want an audience when I'm hauling the human to the car."

After Lucian left, Nicholas turned to Alexander, his expression grave.

"Say it," Alexander urged, grabbing the black cloak and throwing it on.

"It cannot be for long."

"It will not."

"And above all things, you cannot bind yourself—"

"I know," Alexander said tightly as Lucian walked back into the apartment and announced that the way was clear.

"Okay. I'm out of here. See you back at the house." Nicholas lifted the bony male human into his arms and was out the door in seconds.

In the most gentle of ways, Alexander gathered the woman in his arms, feeling an odd pleasure at her supple weight.

Lucian watched him. "You look like a monk in that thing."

"Flip up the hood, will you?"

"It won't fully protect you," Lucian said.

"It'll have to do. We need to get her home."

With a wary expression, Lucian did as his brother asked, then checked the street and sidewalks once more before they all made a quick escape into the waiting BMW.

4

Tom Trainer woke up in the back of a strange car, dizzy as hell and unable to speak, his throat burning with each breath. It took him several moments to remember where he'd been and what had gone down.

But when he did, panic struck.

Whomever this car belonged to, the asshole didn't want him happy and healthy.

He lifted his head an inch, spotted wide, thick shoulders, black hair, and an unfamiliar face in the rearview mirror. The man was talking on his cell, barely above a whisper in some foreign language. He was a real looker, a model or actor probably. Whoever he was, Tom wanted nothing to do with him.

He put his head down against the cool leather seat again. What did he do? How did he get the hell out of here? As the car moved, he felt every pothole, smelled every bit of exhaust from the cars ahead of him. When they finally slowed, then stopped, Tom glanced up as quick as a gopher from its hole and saw that directly in front of them, cars were waiting at a red light.

It was now or never. His throat hurt like a motherfucker, and he hoped that when the time came he could run.

He took a deep breath, grabbed for the door handle, and pulled.

"Oh, fuck!"

The man.

Off his cell and pissed.

Go. Go.

Like a drunk, Tom stumbled out of the car. He was dizzy and felt like puking, but fear gifted him with a shot of adrenaline and he got himself together and ran.

"Come back here, you little shit!" the man roared after him.

Halfway down the sidewalk, Tom glanced back, saw that the man had pulled to the side of the road and was getting out of his car, flashing a deadly stare and a set of pearly white . . .

Oh Jesus.

Tom's mind spun back to Dr. Donohue's apartment, to the other man, the one who'd jumped up from the floor like a haunted-house freak and attacked him: impossibly large, tattoos or gang symbols carved into his skin, and the same needle-sharp pearly whites.

What are they?

Despite the pain pounding in his skull and throat, Tom whirled around and ran like hell down the sidewalk.

5

Sara awoke with a start and one hell of a headache. At first she thought she had a hangover. She squinted at the stark white ceiling, in particular a beautiful plaster medallion in the shape of a sunburst. A shot of unease moved through her as she realized she was not looking at the ceiling in her apartment.

She sat up and glimpsed only wood floors, white bed linens, and the dark cast of evening light before fireworks exploded inside her head. *Red. Gold. Bam. Pow.* She sucked air through her teeth, draped her arm over her eyes, and moaned.

Where am I?

After a moment, her head cleared and she lowered her arm, blinked against the pale light of a bedside lamp. The room was large with an incredibly high ceiling that was trimmed in stark white dentil molding. There was a white fireplace against one wall, arched windows on the other, and an alcove beyond. For a second, Sara's heart jumped into her throat and she wondered where she was—*if* she was still in New York. She turned to the windows and through the darkness saw a cut of the city skyline through the room's corner view.

Not a hospital room. She was in a bed in someone's house. How did she get here? Who brought her—

She stopped, her mind quick-dropping images that took her a moment to comprehend. Then, like a river breaking free of its rocky restraints, the memory rushed through her. As she touched her face, felt the swollen flesh beneath her fingertips, she winced. She remembered it all and her heart picked up speed. The man on her floor, the phone, Tom in her apartment, Tom's pissed-off expression and ready fist . . .

Oh God. What if Tom brought her here?

She looked around for a phone, saw none. Where was her cell?

Don't panic, Sara. Just get the hell out of here.

Whipping back the bedspread, she eased herself off the mattress. Her head felt like a stone balloon, bloated and heavy. She was missing her coat and gloves, but she spotted her shoes on the floor beside the bed. They were huddled neatly together, and she slipped them on. She had to get herself to the hospital, or to the police—somewhere safe.

She stood. Her legs felt boneless and impossible to control as she stumbled across the room to the windows. No way out. No fire escape. She turned and headed for the door. Gritting her teeth against the waves of nausea, she gripped the handle and turned the knob. When she found it unlocked, her heart jumped with the small victory and she pulled the door wide and staggered through it.

The hallway was long and wide. There was artwork on the walls, rugs on the floors, antiques and modern sculptures balancing on masculine console tables. From the small bit she could see, the place seemed lavish, museumesque. Where was she? Brownstone? Warehouse? It couldn't be Tom's place; he didn't fit here. Besides, he'd described his apartment as a "one-room shitbox."

She looked left, then right, down the impossibly long hallway. She saw it. A staircase. It had to lead to a way out. Though her head throbbed against her skull, she forced herself to walk. Just a few steps, she told herself. But soon her head was spinning and she had to grip the wall for support.

Get downstairs, outside in the air where you can breathe—

She heard something. At first she thought it was her heart knocking in her chest. But the sound was coming closer.

Someone was coming up the stairs.

Tom.

Her heart swelled in terror and she suppressed the scream that hovered in her throat. She may have been hurt and wobbling around like a drunk, but she wasn't about to let him get her. She whipped around, tried to run down the other length of hall. Her face pulsed and dizziness whirled through her again. A few feet past the room from which she'd just escaped, she lost her footing and fell against a small table, crying out in pain as the edge of the wood stabbed into her hip. Tears pricked her eyes. She heard him coming down the hall and panic flooded her senses. She wasn't going to die this way! Fuck no—unable to run or to fight, in a strange house, by some stalker ex-patient.

Clawing at the wood, she pushed herself to her hands and knees. She had to get out of here, get back to the hospital. *Gray.* He had no one to help him but her . . .

"Goddamn Nicholas. All he had to do was hold on to that human long enough to clean his mind."

Sara stilled. The voice coming from the stairs was male, but it wasn't Tom. Who—

"Nicholas said there were police in the area." Another voice. Female this time. "He did the right thing holding back."

Sara started to crawl, her left side hugging the wall. Maybe these people were working with Tom, or *for* him. Her breath was shallow and dense as she inched forward. If she could just get to a room with a fire escape . . .

"Oh, shit," the man said, his tone full of panic. "She's out of bed."

Quick, heavy footfalls echoed down the hall, and in seconds, Sara felt hands on her—large, male hands. And she was being lifted.

"No!" she uttered fiercely, struggling like a cat in the man's arms.

"Please don't fight, Dr. Donohue," he said, his tone gentle. "You'll injure yourself further."

"Let me go!"

"Sara, please."

His voice suddenly registered in her consciousness. She turned and, through her blurred vision, saw who held her.

It was him. The man outside her apartment, the one she'd helped.

Beneath long black lashes, his scarlet eyes implored her. "Sara . . ."

"You won't hurt me," she said.

He shook his head. "Never."

"I don't want to die," she said, completely spent now.

"And you won't," he said as he carried her back into the bedroom. "I will not allow it."

6

"Lie down, my dear."

The woman's voice was soft and maternally soothing. "Yes. Good. There we are."

The scene in the hallway had taken its toll on Sara and she allowed herself to be directed back against the pillow. The man was gone now. He'd deposited her in bed and disappeared, leaving her to wonder where he was and if he was coming back.

She sighed when she felt the woman's cool hand on her forehead. The gesture reminded her so much of her mother and those days she'd been allowed to stay home from school, eat Chef Boyardee, and have as many Pudding Pops as she wanted. Those normal, coveted days before the fire . . .

"Better?"

It hurt to move her head, but Sara managed to nod.

"Are you hungry? Thirsty?" the woman asked. She was somewhere in her fifties, and had eyes the color of olives and short, gray hair.

"No."

"If you change your mind, I have some fruit and juice here on the side table." The woman smiled as she placed a hand around Sara's wrist.

"What are you doing?" Sara asked weakly.

"Checking your pulse." The woman pressed two fingers into the groove along the inside of Sara's wrist.

"Who are you?"

"Leza Franz."

"A doctor?"

"Yes," the woman said, giving Sara a tight-lipped smile.

"What hospital?"

"I'm a . . . private physician."

Sara shifted uncomfortably. This was wrong. Something was wrong—she could feel it in her gut. Where was the man?

She stole a glance at the window, then the door. If she could just get up, if she could just get to a phone . . .

"You have a concussion, my dear," the doctor said gently. "But it's a mild one, and with a few days' rest, you should be up and—"

"I should be in a hospital," Sara interrupted, her tone as forceful as she could manage. "Why am I not in a hospital?"

The doctor hesitated for a moment, then looked over her shoulder. "Do you want me to . . . ?"

"No. I'll explain it to her."

Sara's pulse jumped at the sound of the man's voice.

He was here. The whole time. But how? She'd seen him leave . . . hadn't she?

She lifted her chin. Where was he? She wanted to sit up, see him, demand he tell her what was happening—but her body wouldn't respond.

"Very good, sir," said the doctor. "I'll return in an hour."

"Thank you, Leza."

The low, almost growling timbre of his voice seemed to take up residence in Sara's chest, the vibration warming her blood.

The doctor walked to the door, and, suddenly panicked, Sara called out, "Wait!"

Before the door clicked shut, Leza glanced back and smiled empathetically. "Not to worry, Dr. Donohue. You're safe here."

Safe? Who is she kidding? Pressing the heels of her palms into the mattress, Sara pushed herself into a semisitting position, then gripped the sheets when a rush of dizziness came over her.

"I can feel your fear, Sara."

Sara blinked to recover her vision. "Where are you?" she demanded.

"Right in front of you."

"No, you're not. I can't see—"

Fire roared to life in the hearth across the room. "I swear to you there is nothing to fear here."

He sat in a massive black wingback chair in the shadowed alcove directly across from the bed—a chair Sara didn't remember being there before her unsuccessful escape moments ago. He was dressed for cold weather in a thick gray sweater and black pants. He watched her intently, his arms crossed over his broad chest.

In the amber light of the fire, he looked to be somewhere in his thirties, and was far from good-looking. In fact, with the buzz cut, narrowed burgundy eyes, and those two small, black key-shaped markings carved into the hollowed flesh beneath his high cheekbones, he had a face to fear, a face that might make some recoil. But strangely, Sara felt nothing but relief under his watchful gaze. Yes, he looked relentless, ready to spring, but even so, every fear within her eased, warmed even, and the hum his voice had created within her returned.

Clearly, the knock on the head had screwed with her brain.

"Who are you?" she demanded, trying to keep her voice calm.

"Alexander Roman."

"I don't know you."

"No."

"Where am I?"

"My home. In SoHo."

The way he stared at her mouth when she talked made a muscle quiver in her thigh. "Are you going to tell me why I'm here?"

"You were attacked."

"I know that, but why am I *here* and not in a hospital?"

He leaned forward, his eyes glowing. "Unfortunately, that little bastard who attacked you got away, and I'm fairly certain he still wishes you harm." Alexander growled softly. "He will be found and dealt with, but until then I want to make sure you're safe."

The news that Tom was still walking around Manhattan and not locked up in a jail cell devastated Sara, but she didn't show it. She had another problem to contend with, an immediate problem. "I'm not safe here."

"You are," he assured her.

"No. I want to go to a hospital."

His expression was sympathetic, but there was an immovable flicker in his gaze. "I can't allow that. I'm sorry."

"You can't or you won't?"

He sighed. "I'm bound to protect you, Sara."

With those words, the vibration and the calming heat from a moment ago moved from her chest to her belly, then threatened to dip lower. She ignored it. "I don't know what you're talking about, or who you think you are—but I don't need your protection. If Tom's still out there, and he goes after me again, I'll call the police. Have them deal with it." She watched his eyes flash in the firelight at the suggestion. "Where's my phone?"

"Back in your apartment, I'd imagine."

"Then I'll use yours."

The man stood and walked to her. His size, like a cross between a linebacker and military badass, was unnerving.

He gestured to the end of the bed. "May I?"

She swallowed hard, but refused to show her unease. "Do I have a choice?"

The mattress dipped low with his weight. "Listen, Sara."

"How do you know my name? And how does the doctor know my name?"

"I know this is an unusual situation—"

"You think?" she said darkly.

"But I need you to trust me for just a little while longer."

"You've got to be kidding." She gritted her teeth and said slowly, "I want a phone, and I want it now. I have a hospital full of patients and a crime to report to the police."

His face grew serious. "I'm afraid I can't bring the police into this."

"What?" Sara sat up, struggled against the dizziness in her head. "Why the hell not?"

He paused a moment, his eyebrows lowering to meet a dangerous gaze. "I think perhaps you know why not."

"I'm not a game player, Mr. Roman."

"I cannot allow myself and my brothers to be exposed."

"Exposed," Sara repeated, surprised at the sudden

jump in her heart rate. "What are you talking about? Who the hell are . . ."

Sara's words petered out as an image flickered in her mind. It was fuzzy and there was confusion and shock attached to it, but as the seconds ticked off, the hazy memory came slowly into focus. Startled, she looked up. "You!"

The man before her suddenly opened his mouth and revealed two white, blade-sharp fangs.

Pure, white-hot terror assaulted Sara and she shook her head, drew back against the pillows as far as she could manage. "No . . ."

The man's jaw relaxed and his gaze remained even with Sara's. "It was unfortunate that you had to witness—"

"No." She kept shaking her head like an idiot. It was the bump on her head. She was delusional. "No. It's not possible." Yet there it was. He had fangs.

I AM WHAT YOU THINK I AM.

"Don't do that!" Her temples throbbing, she stared at him. "This is impossible. You don't exist . . ."

Alexander's eyes clouded over and he uttered softly, "There are many who would agree with you on that."

Cold fear rippled through Sara like a dozen icy waves—the heat and comfort of his presence completely dead to her now. Her skin bristled and her heart thundered in her chest, keeping pace with the pain that pounded in her head. This wasn't happening. Everything in her education and experience screamed at her that this couldn't be happening, yet her gut whispered otherwise.

What did she do now? Her head was throbbing so badly she felt like she might throw up. She hated how weak she felt. She dropped back against the pillow.

"You need to rest," he said, his voice as gentle as a kiss. "Have something to eat and drink."

I need to get the fuck out of here! "I need a hospital . . . I need my phone." Her words slurred and she forced her eyes to stay open.

"Your former patient is not going to give up, and until he's caught, I ask that you stay here."

"Fuck you!" she shouted, but the sound that left her throat was little more than a squeak. She wanted so badly to remain tough and resolute, but she was so tired. "I have patients. My—"

"That asshole wants to kill you, Sara. He won't stop until he does. I felt it. I felt his need for your blood."

"You . . . what?" She shook her head, refusing to listen to any more of that. "If you think you're going to keep me here against my will, a prisoner—"

"Not a prisoner, a guest."

"A guest?" she repeated. "You're insane."

"A very welcome, very honored guest." Alexander put his hand over hers, and the heat that traveled up her arm found its way into her belly, curling deliciously inside of her. She looked up at him, hating herself for wishing this feeling would never go away. "You saved my life," he continued. "And all I ask is that you allow me to do the same for you."

The confusing warmth of his touch was too much for Sara. She should be thinking about escaping, not wishing she could crawl up into his powerful arms and fall asleep.

She yanked her hand from his grasp. "I don't know who you are, what you are—the only thing I want is to know where the front door is."

Before Alexander could answer, there was a knock on the door, and an older man's heavily accented voice rang out, "I'm sorry for the interruption, sir, but Lucian and Nicholas are in the library. They ask that you meet them there as soon as possible."

"Who's that?" Sara demanded. "And who the hell are Lucian and Nicholas?"

"My brothers." Alexander stood, inclined his head. "I have to go. Please try to sleep, and if you need anything just press the call button on the bedside table."

As soon as he was out the door, Sara pushed herself into a sitting position. Instantly, she gripped her head, her brain pounding mercilessly inside her skull. She was so exhausted, nearly sick with it, but there was no way she was lying down and resting. She had to stay awake, alert—she had to find a way out of this insanity—this nightmare her mind, and the bump on her head, had created.

7

Alexander entered the mahogany-paneled, twenty-thousand-volume library with a newly acquired speed that he reviled. In the coming weeks, he would see more evidence of the powers morpho provided, along with the many shackles that accompanied it, and the thought darkened his mood.

For a century now, he and his brothers had lived unfettered among humans; the only thing separating the two species was the brothers' need for blood. But everything had changed. He could no longer walk in daylight, and though he had escaped the bonds of a Breeding Male's debauched and violent future, he would soon be hit with the irresistible need to find his true mate—the one he was destined for, the one who bore his mark.

"Drained the woman yet?" Lucian asked, descending the spiral staircase from the second level, several ancient tomes in his arms.

"Fuck you, Luca."

"How is she, Alexander?" Nicholas asked. The tall, black-eyed middle Roman brother was sitting at a long metal desk, his head partially obscured by his computer screen as he furiously typed.

"Disoriented, tough as steel." The bright light from the chandeliers burned Alexander's retinas and he dimmed all three with a quick suggestion from his mind. "She doesn't want to be here."

"Can you blame her?"

Alexander stalked across the room, dropped down on the couch. "She has nothing to fear from me."

"Not the point," Lucian said tightly.

"I just want to help her."

"Even if it's against her will?"

"If I must."

"This isn't 1875, Alexander," Nicholas said. "Females don't take kindly to males who tell them what they want or what they must do. And New York women—" He broke off, laughing. "Forget it."

"She may be tough," Alexander said, grabbing his laptop off the coffee table. "But she's also a physician and thoughtful, and she must know she has to give herself time to heal."

Nicholas glanced up. "Yes, but clearly she doesn't want to do it here."

"Well, unfortunately, she must." Alexander stabbed at the power button on his computer. It was a weak argument for keeping a human in the house and they all knew it. Sara should be with her own kind, under the care of a human physician. And yet he couldn't let her go. She had saved him. The first female in his long life to do so . . . and he owed her.

A low growl from Lucian's direction had Alexander looking up. "What?"

"You told her what we are," Lucian said.

"Yes."

"Goddammit!" Lucian dropped his books on the desk. The impact sent a cloud of dust into the air.

"She knew," Alexander told him.

"Bullshit," Lucian retorted. "You told her so you could keep her. Now her mind will be deeply imprinted."

Alexander's eyes narrowed, but he didn't move from the couch. "She saw me with that skinny human. She saw me go through morpho. She knew."

"She may have suspected something, but she could never have known—"

"Enough," Nicholas said calmly, still focused on his computer screen. "What's done is done. The woman must stay here now. But once she's well, Alexander, you're going to have to clean—"

Alexander interrupted. "I'm not going to damage her mind, Nicholas."

"You won't. Things are different now." Nicholas turned his screen so he could see his brother.

"What do you mean?"

"You're a morphed male, *Duro*. You can clean a human's mind with no fear of permanent injury."

Lucian brightened. "Good. Problem solved."

"Yes, lucky me," Alexander said dryly, his mind pushing aside one issue to deal with another. "So, speaking of my newly acquired morphed status, what have you found out?"

"Not much," Nicholas admitted. He shook his head, frustrated. "I've contacted a few of our remaining peers in the Eternal Breed who are outside the *credenti*—first with a location request for the human I let get away this afternoon, and second, for information about males morphing before their time. I kept it casual. No reason for either request to get back to our . . . families." He said the last word as though it were poison on his tongue. Even after a hundred years of separation, of freedom from their kind, the three of them still flinched whenever they were reminded of the nightmare that was their abusive adolescence.

Nicholas shook off the momentary gloom and nodded at Lucian. "What about you? Find anything in those old books?"

"I focused on the history of the breed, thinking this could be genetics." Lucian shrugged. "Our father, who he was—*what* he was—maybe we're all destined to reach maturity before our time." He snorted. "Not like dear old Dad stayed around long enough to tell us if we should expect anything out of the ordinary in this department."

It was a despised and avoided subject for the three of them, having the Breeding Male as their father, their common link. But now the questions were there. Their father had been a *paven* of purest blood whose genetic code and structure had been altered hundreds of years ago by the Eternal Order. He and two others had been given the ability to impregnate at will and decide the sex of the *balas*, in order to repopulate one sex or the other in times of dire necessity. Alexander sniffed with derision. It had been hailed as a genius move by the Eternal Breed, but had soon become a nightmare as the Breeding Males grew more like uncontrolled animals, desperate to rut and feed. The Order had been forced to cage them, and brought them out only to service the *veanas*, the Pureblood females, who were forced by their families to lie with them.

A necessity for progress, for breed survival, Alexander recalled with a sneer. And yet the stigma of being their father's sons had only made him and his brothers outcasts to their peers, watched specimens to observe and test by the Order, and reviled by their own mothers.

For Alexander, escaping his *credenti* that hot morning in August had been a truly blessed event.

Forcing his focus back on the present, Alexander continued to grill Lucian on the texts. "Have you found any evidence of genetic predisposition?"

"No past cases," Lucian admitted. "Not as it relates to morphing, anyway."

"That doesn't mean it isn't possible," Alexander said.

Leaning back in his chair, Nicholas asked, "What if

it was something in the blood you consumed over the past week? The human woman you fed from."

"Possible," Alexander said thoughtfully.

"Any injuries in the past month?" Lucian asked.

"Nothing. Could it be environmental?"

Nicholas looked skeptical. "We'd all be affected."

Evans walked in then, and the servant looked rattled, sheepish. He cleared his throat.

"What is it, Evans?" Lucian said.

"I apologize for the interruption, sir, but it's the young woman . . ."

A growl, guttural and fierce, erupted from Alexander and he shot across the room, nearly setting the floor on fire in his haste. "What is it?" he demanded, towering over the servant.

"Easy, Alex," Nicholas warned, abandoning his post at the computer and heading toward his brother.

"Christ," uttered Lucian. "Did you see that speed . . ."

Alexander's attention zeroed in on the servant. He fought to keep from shaking the answer out of the wide-eyed Impure. His fangs quivered, each word out of his mouth a terrifying warning, "What. Is. Wrong. With. Her."

"She's gone, sir," Evans said breathlessly.

"Gone?" Alexander repeated. His gut flexed with worry and disbelief. "Gone where?"

The old Impure shook his head. "I don't know. The window in the blue bedroom was open. I believe she used the fire escape."

Shit! Alexander turned and sprinted toward the door with his new hyperspeed. She was in danger. They all were.

"Where the hell do you think you're going?" Nicholas called out.

Pausing at the threshold, Alexander shot back, "After her."

"It's nearly dawn."

"I don't care!" Alexander roared.

"You'll care when that little prick finds and kills her because you've turned to dust!" Lucian barked after him.

It took supreme effort for Alexander to stay where he was and listen to reason. His head dropped forward and he uttered a pained "I need her."

"One of us will go," Lucian said begrudgingly. "After all, we can't have her running around with an uncleaned mind, now, can we?"

"I'll go," Nicholas offered. "I lost the man. I won't lose the woman."

Still shaking, Evans swallowed tightly. "Pardon me, sir."

"Not now, Evans," Nicholas said, a little less contained, his gaze trained on his morphed, and very impassioned, brother.

"But, sir, the wall . . ."

The man's words petered out as he stared slack-jawed at something behind them. All three brothers turned to see what the problem was.

"Holy shit," Lucian uttered. "They've found us."

Nostrils flared and breathing heavy, Alexander stared at the blank white wall beyond the stairs. It was moving, like easy waves on the sea, and before their eyes, a message was being carved into the plaster.

> The Eternal Order requests the presence of the first precipitately morphed male, Alexander Roman. At the third hour past midnight, in the Hollow of Shadows.
>
> As one brother must shun the light, the other two will shortly follow. Do not disregard our request.

8

Alexander stood in front of the wall, his hand moving over the inscription, his need to run after the human woman momentarily quelled.

Behind him, Lucian snarled. "Un-fucking-believable."

Alexander glanced over his shoulder. "Is it?"

Lucian's almond eyes flashed hatred. "I won't believe it. No one has the power to premorph males. Not even the Eternal Order."

"Assumption makes asses out of us all, Little Brother," Nicholas said, seated behind his computer again, typing furiously.

"Then call me the biggest ass on the planet," Lucian returned. "I don't believe it."

Nicholas glanced up, ready to say something, then shrugged and uttered a dry, "Too easy."

"Up yours, Nicky."

"Think clearly, Luca. What makes you think the Eternal Order lacks the power to premorph? If they can create an animal like the Breeding Male or remove the sex drives of Impures as though it were any normal feeding session, how hard is it to screw with morphing?"

"Not hard at all, it seems." Alexander went over to the desk and stood behind his brother. "What are you looking for, Nicky?"

"Anything on the Hollow," Nicholas said, Web pages opening and closing every two seconds. "Rumors on location, any off-the-radar vamp sites that might have some clue as to where to begin to look for the Order's headquarters."

"And?"

"Nothing."

"That's because the Order would imprison or obliterate anyone who revealed their supersecret hiding place." Lucian grinned with menace. "Pussies."

Alexander released a weighty breath and backed away from the computer. "This will be resolved. I'll leave at first dark."

"Leave for where exactly?" Lucian asked. "Unless a map shows up on the wall in the next few seconds, I'd say we're pretty much fucked."

Alexander shook his head. "The one thing I know is the Order wants me to go before them. As is their way, they will make me search like a rat in a maze first, humble me to show me just who is in control, and when that is complete, they will make themselves possible to find."

"And if they don't?" Lucian asked.

"If it becomes necessary, I'll contact the family."

Nicholas's head shot up, his normally sedate black eyes burning with sudden passion. "Family? As in *your* family?"

Alexander shrugged. "We have limited time. Theydon's uncle used to be a member of the Order. It's possible that he may know where this place is."

"You're just going to walk back into the *credenti,*" Nicholas continued, "find your mother's mate, the *paven* who once wished for your death above all things, and ask him for directions?"

Alexander went cold, his tone like ice. "If I have to."

Lucian cursed.

"You're not going," Nicholas said with a dead calm, rising from his chair.

"Try and stop me."

"Oh, you know *I* will," Lucian said, his features and massive frame tightening into pure aggressor mode. "That cage of yours is looking pretty damn perfect right about now."

Alexander lifted his shoulders, looked from one brother to the other. "Either way I'm caged," he said. "But the two of you are free, and I am going to make sure you remain that way."

"I'm not afraid of morpho," Lucian said fiercely.

Alexander stared him down. "You should be. You of all of us should be."

The heat, the anger, the need that boiled in Lucian's gaze said it all. He was the most like their father, the only albino Breeding Male. If any one of them carried the gene and would become a rutting, uncontrollable animal when he morphed, it would be Lucian.

Alexander walked back to the wall, his gaze moving over each letter, each cluster of words, the uncloaked command. "If this is not stopped, the two of you will be next, tracked by the Order for the rest of your days. The hunger—though it will ease somewhat—will become your number-one need, soon to be replaced by either the inescapable hunt for your true mate or the unstoppable desire to breed." He paused. Breathing in, breathing out. "I'm in morpho. It's done. But they will not turn the two of you."

"We took an oath," Nicholas reminded him, his tone devoid of emotion. "We left that life and everything in it. We cannot go back. For any reason."

"You're right," Alexander said, watching as letter by letter the message scrawled into his library wall evaporated. "*You* will not go back."

When the wall sat smooth before him, Alexander turned around and addressed Nicholas and Lucian in a way he hadn't since their days on the battlefield. "While I am gone, Nicholas is on Tom's trail. Lucian, you will find Sara, follow her, make sure she comes to no harm. Don't let her see you, and don't scare the shit out of her."

Both brothers stood there: Lucian's nostrils flaring with impatience, Nicholas's expression impassive, though his eyes had gone as black as a starless night.

For one moment, Alexander wondered if they were going to defy his orders. It was one thing to curse and chide, even to make brash statements of noncompliance, but the truth was in their guts, in their genetic makeup: They were the younger vampires. They could do nothing when given an order by their elder but nod and take action.

"Well?" Alexander said. "What say you?"

Lucian spoke first, his upper lip curling with bitterness. "Fine. I'll follow her, but I can't promise I won't scare the shit out of her."

Alexander's gaze shot to the dark one, the black-eyed, cool-as-ice male. "And you?"

Nicholas shook his head. *No.*

For one moment, Alexander softened. "Nicky . . . *Duro* . . ."

"Do not do this for us," Nicholas said.

"It is done." His jaw set, his mind resolute, Alexander headed for the door.

9

Euro-trance club music vibrated off the walls of the three-story town house in Brooklyn's Boerum Hill. It was what they liked—the humans—hot music and lethal sex with someone or some *thing* they never had to see again when the danger buzz wore off.

Ethan Dare walked the halls of the home his eighth wife had owned before her very fortunate passing three years ago. Internally renovated and historic, the late-1800s town house had all the original features, including a garden. But for the Impure, the only feature that mattered to him in the slightest was the eight large bedrooms he and his recruits used to fuck any and all humans as well as Pureblood and Impures who willingly crossed their path.

The scent of sex and sweat flooded Ethan's nostrils, made his head, and the stiff rod in his pants, pulse. A new and exciting development, for it had been a long time since his cock had done anything but lay limp against his leg. More than two hundred years since the night the Eternal Order had blood castrated him—him and any other Impure they could find.

But things had changed. The Supreme One, the hidden benefactor of their cause, had given his blood—granting Ethan and his recruits new life, new power.

Ethan stopped at one bedroom door, then another, observing his work in progress. His recruits, male and female Impures—those like himself with incomplete blood—were stretched out on beds, pressed back against walls, on their hands and knees rutting like dogs. His cock twitched and his forked tongue, a disfigurement gifted by a gang of Purebloods back when he was just a *balas* enslaved in his *credenti*, slipped in and out of his mouth.

The Impures, the ones who had escaped their homes and their lives of servitude and impossible desire, had given their allegiance to him, and their trust. After all, he was a savior of sorts. He had been the one to find a cure for their castrated and powerless blood.

Yes, the Impures would spread their seed and their legs for Ethan and the good of the cause because they too yearned for the extinction of the illustrious and oh so pure Eternal Breed—they too wanted to see a new Order, a new, ruling Breed of Impures like themselves.

It wasn't a quick or easy task. In the seven months of the program, only a few of the *balas* created had stuck to their hosts' wombs—Ethan's included. But if they could hang on, in two months' time the seeds of infection would bloom in the heart of vampire society and the Impure revolution would be under way.

Ethan leaned against the door frame and watched his largest male recruit pound into the excited and willing human female. Eyes closed and legs splayed, the woman moaned and hissed, gripping the male's shoulders. Ethan's groin throbbed with need, with the power of what he was creating here.

"Commander?"

The soft sound landed close to Ethan's ear and he turned away from the action to eyeball the male behind him. Alistair, a handsome Impure who had the look of an eighties surfer and a penchant for high school–age human females, inclined his head. "Forgive the disturbance, Commander."

"Is my girl locked up nice and tight?" Ethan asked.

Alistair smiled broadly, his dimples popping. "Like a fist, Commander."

"And her mother?"

"Believes her daughter is a self-destructive brat who will do anything, including cutting her flesh, to get attention. She is pleased that the girl is getting the serious mental help she needs."

Ethan nodded. "Good. Keep a close watch on her. Make sure she remains in the hospital. She carries our future within her."

"Yes, Commander."

Movement caught Ethan's focus and he waved Alistair away. His lead recruit, Mear, a thickly muscled, violet-eyed Impure was walking down the hall toward him, combat boots cracking against the wood floors. Conversely, trailing behind him was a tall, thin, impish-looking male Ethan had never seen before. He pushed away from the wall, met the pair halfway, and demanded in a curt tone, "What do we have here?"

"A new recruit, Commander," Mear said.

Ethan eyeballed the large Impure and sneered. "He's human, Mear. He can rut along with the other human male dogs here, but he will never be a recruit."

"He wishes to become *Imiti*, sir," Mear said, using the ancient word for an imitation vampire, one who can take on the characteristics of a vampire if they are consistently fed. "With my blood in his veins, he will make the change."

Ethan paused. "Your blood?"

Mear nodded.

Normally, a human could not become *Imiti* unless they drank from a Pureblood, but for Ethan and his recruits, things were different. The Supreme One had made it so. "You will feed him?" Ethan asked.

"Yes." Mear's lavender eyes glittered with anticipation.

"Why?"

"We were friends in the human's juvenile system for many years. He assisted me in my escape."

"Did he?" Ethan turned to the human, who was shaking like a dog who'd been kicked every day of his life. It was a feeling Ethan remembered well. "What is your name, human?"

"Tom Trainer," the man squeaked.

"You understand what this means, Tom Trainer?"

Looking like he was about to shit his pants, the human nodded slowly.

A smile twitched at Ethan's lips. "Our poor Mear, our best fighter, cannot bear to lay with a female. You will take care of his needs?"

Tom swallowed tightly, but again, he nodded.

"And he will work for you, Commander," Mear put in, "do whatever he's told."

"How nice," Ethan drawled, enjoying the human's fear and confusion, not to mention Mear's excitement over his new pet. "To give to the cause, without any quid pro quo."

There was a pause, then a whisper of "Sir, he does need something."

Chuckling softly, Ethan moved closer to the human, stood eye to eye with him, and asked, "What is it you want, Tom Trainer? What are you so willing to give your life for? Because, make no mistake, once you stepped into this little world of mine and offered your body to Mear, your life became mine to command."

Baby brown eyes flickered up, found Ethan's calculated glare. He whispered something unintelligible.

"Speak up, human!" Ethan demanded. "I can barely hear you."

"A woman," Tom said.

"Ah," Ethan drawled, eyebrows lifted. "You will make Mear jealous."

"Not to fuck," Tom said in an almost violent tone. "To hurt, to bleed, to kill."

"She has rejected you," Ethan said as if he gave a shit.

"Yes." Emotionally amped up now, Tom continued his tirade. "She must die. She and that fanged animal who was with her."

Ethan's gaze shot to Mear's. "What is this?"

"My friend claims that his love for the woman was interrupted by a vampire, Commander. A vampire with burning tattoos on his face."

Ethan stilled, a cold fear rolling through him. "Tattoos on his *face*? Are you certain?"

"Yes . . . Commander," Tom managed. "On both cheeks. They looked like something a branding iron would do."

Was it possible? Ethan wondered, alarmed. A descendant of the Breeding Male close by? And if so, what did it mean for Ethan's plan, his new Order?

Unwilling to show his unease over the news the human had brought with him, Ethan regarded Tom with a cold smile. "You know that there are fanged animals here?"

Tom paled. "Not like that one."

No, not like that one. Ethan's gaze bore down on Tom. "All right, human, you will drink from Mear, you will gain in strength, and your female will die at your hand. In return, you belong to me—you will fight for me." Ethan closed his eyes and pulled air into his nostrils. "Now tell me more about this singed *paven*."

10

Having run all the way from SoHo, Sara could barely catch her breath as she burst through the back door of Walter Wynn Hospital. She spied the empty stairwell and took the steps two at a time until she reached the fourth floor. Dizzy, her heart throbbing inside her chest, she collapsed on the top step and put her head between her knees.

Breathe.

Try to get some oxygen into the rational part of your brain.

Maybe she should've gone straight to the cops, or found a hotel room and slept for the five hours her body was begging for. But no, she'd searched Alexander Roman's second floor for an unlocked window and when she'd found one she'd destroyed the screen, climbed down the rickety-ass fire escape, and run to the one place she was utterly tethered to, the one place she was sure to find her sanity.

Grabbing on to the railing, she pulled herself up and

plodded over to the door, opened it wide. The psych unit was active, like a Starbucks at eight a.m. Afternoon visiting hours were in full swing, and families and loved ones were being buzzed into one ward or another, depending on the age of the patient. Just a month ago, Sara's mother had been part of that crowd, in New York on one of her biyearly visits, and just like the rest of them, she'd worn a hopeful expression on the way in, praying she'd find her son changed, healed. It was not an uncommon occurrence to leave disappointed.

Sara tried to slip past the nurse's station, heading straight for the door to the adult ward, and had her hand on the keypad when a voice called out, "What happened to you?"

Feigning nonchalance, Sara glanced back at Claire, the main reception nurse, and shrugged. "Tripped on the stairs going into my apartment. Ice was pretty slick this morning."

Claire looked concerned. "Did you get checked out by ER?"

"Yep. All good." Eager to stop the questions, Sara turned back to the keypad and stabbed in her security code. *Yep, all good. Walked into the ER and told them about the patient who attacked me and the vampire who kidnapped me and they immediately sent Cameron Phelps down for a psych eval . . .*

The door buzzed and Sara took off through it. Just like any other day, she headed straight for Gray's room.

She found him sleeping, curled up into his pillow, looking peaceful and young. The sight should have eased her, but it didn't. Every moment since the night of that fire she'd thought of nothing else but making her brother well. Every day he'd been stuck at home with their mother, voiceless and in pain, she'd been studying her ass off, waiting for the day she would graduate from med school, waiting for the moment she could come and get him, help him, fix him.

It had been four years now, four years that she'd been working with him, at this hospital, trying to take the trauma from his mind. She had performed countless drug trials, a yearlong study into levels of anxiety, depression, fear memory versus permanent memory, memory replacement, even false memory replacement, and though some of her patients had been helped, had gone home to live what she hoped would be normal lives, Gray remained unchanged. What was wrong with her that she couldn't find the answer, find a way to fix him?

Pushing away from the doorjamb, she left his room and headed for her office. She was in immediate, real trouble here—and in her world, if you were in trouble you fixed it. The scenario was simple: Patient broke into your apartment and tried to kill you. You didn't stop to think or consider the feelings of others. You called the police.

Her door was open and she flicked on the overhead lights and went over to her desk. She dropped into her chair and scrubbed a hand over her mouth, as if she were trying to stop herself from talking out loud.

Pick up the phone.

She stared at it.

What the fuck are you thinking, Sara? You're no idiot. Do it. You owe the . . . vampire nothing, no loyalty.

But was that the truth? He'd saved her life. Whatever he was, whatever he claimed to be, he'd kept her alive so she could keep her brother alive, and wasn't that worth something? Some token sense of loyalty?

You know what they call that, honey? Stockholm syndrome. Yep, you studied it in school, have patients who suffer from it.

Clamping her teeth together until her jaw ached, she pressed the intercom button, then stabbed in the numbers for Precinct 23. But before she even finished dialing, the call failed.

Without missing a beat, she tried again. But the second time, though the call went through, the ringing distorted into a strange moaning sound and wasn't picked up on the other end. *What the hell?* She pressed the call button again, got a dial tone, and punched in the numbers. This time she heard the irritating trill of a fax machine. Frustrated, she slammed the phone down, glared at the thing, and fantasized about yanking the cord from the wall and chucking the whole thing at the door. But that would be a reactionary move, not a productive one, and today of all days she needed to pretend to be flexible and sane.

She took a deep breath, grabbed the piece of paper with the number on it, then headed out of her office and straight for the adult-care nurse's station. Without a word to the crew, Sara picked up one of the desk phones and tried again. Thankfully, this time the call connected, and she sighed as the ringing continued on perfectly normal. But as it did, she started to feel a slight panic take over her nervous system. When the cops actually answered, she'd have to report the crime, not to mention explain *his* involvement in it. Or did she? Maybe she could just leave him out of it—make it all about Tom and the attack.

But Sara never had to make that choice. No one picked up, not even a machine. It just rang and rang. Cursing, she hung up, dialed one last time, and when she found it busy, slammed down the receiver and told herself she'd give it fifteen minutes and try again.

But four hours and three emergencies later, it was close to the end of her shift and the first time she'd had a chance to get back to her office.

She grabbed an apple from the basket on the corner of her desk and dropped into her chair. Releasing a heavy breath, she picked up the phone and waited for it, the low hum of the dial tone. But *nada*. Nothing.

"You have a very solid mind for a human."

Sara slammed back in her seat, the apple dropping to the floor with a dull thud. "Jesus Christ!"

"No. Alexander Roman." He stood in the doorway, taking up nearly every inch of it with his massive frame. He inclined his head, his fierce merlot eyes trained on her. "I apologize for startling you."

"How did you get in here?"

"Your door was open."

"On the *ward*," she pressed. "How did you get onto the ward?"

One corner of his mouth flickered up. "I find every door open to me these days."

"How convenient," she said, wishing her pulse would stop the whole racing routine.

His gaze shifted from her to the phone. "Making a call?"

"I've been trying to, but there's something wrong with . . ." She froze, looked up at him. "It's you, isn't it? You've been—"

His brows lifted. "As I said before, no police."

Fear flickered inside her chest. "You screwed with my phone?"

Alexander moved into the room, the door closing behind him. Unable to process the obvious, Sara pretended she had seen his hand on the wood, pushing it closed.

"Actually it was my brother Lucian," he said, coming toward her, the black wool of his coat snapping against his legs. "I couldn't leave the house until it grew dark—"

She stood up. Had to. Even with the anxiety snapping through her, she had to show him she wasn't about to cower. "Your brother's been watching me?"

"I had to make sure you were safe."

"If you really cared about my safety, you'd let me call the police."

"The police can do nothing."

"Spoken like a true renegade or a—"

He lifted one dark eyebrow. "Or a what?"

"Someone I should be treating with a good deal of meds."

He said nothing, just stood there, across the desk, dark as night, towering over her with a lethal grin playing about his mouth. Sara tried like hell to control her response to him, to that anything-but-sweet smile, but the traitorous, seductive heat that moved through her veins and sped up her heart was irrepressible.

"Do you really think the police can catch your skinny human?" he asked, coming to stand at the chair in front of her desk, his large hands closing around the metal top. "You think they're even going to look all that hard for him?"

Sara forced out a solid, "Yes." But honestly, she wasn't sure of anything at the moment.

"That little scumbag will not stop until you're dead," Alexander said. "And while he's trying, your officers will be pushing papers around their desks."

"You need to stop trying to scare me, Alexander," she said tightly.

"No, I don't think so. Sometimes fear is necessary to bring clarity to the mind."

"Where'd you get that? Oprah?"

He nodded to the wall of books behind her. "*Psychology in Today's Modern World.*"

Turning around, Sara glanced at the bookshelf, then faced him again, confused. "What?"

"Third shelf, halfway in, gold binding, page sixteen, middle paragraph."

She stared at him. "You've read that book?"

"Just now. The line jumped out at me. Seemed appropriate."

It took her a moment to process what he was saying, but when she did, she shook her head and said slowly, "No way."

His eyes held a bitter edge. "It's new to me as well." He reached out to her. "Come with me."

Sara's pulse kicked. "What? No!"

"I need to show you something."

She shook her head. "I'm not going to walk out of here with you to God knows where."

"All I wish to do is protect you."

"Protect me, kill me . . . potato, patato."

He was around the desk and in front of her in seconds, his voice low, menacing. "If I wanted you dead I could have done it back at my house, or at yours. And it would've taken an instant." He lifted his hand, touched her face. His palm felt warm against her skin. "I want you alive, Sara. And safe. I cannot allow that human to get close enough to hurt you again." His hand dropped to her chest, his palm resting just above her breast. "Just breathe now. Slow your heart. You have nothing to fear from me."

Sara wanted to hate herself in that moment, hate the feminine lust that ran through her blood and made her want to arch her back and touch her mouth to his, but instead she felt her heart slowing with each beat and warm desire filling her veins. If she tilted her chin an inch she could do it—feel his lips, maybe even the tips of his fangs. As she stared into his eyes, her breath slid into synch with his and her mind played back the events of that morning—how he'd protected her, how easily he'd lifted and carried her, how his fearsome manner only erupted when he spoke of the ex-patient who wished her harm.

She brought her hand to his cheek, let her thumb brush over the key-shaped brand. The surface of his skin was hot, rough, complicated—like him.

Alexander closed his eyes, sucked in air through his teeth, a low growl escaping his throat on the exhale. Sara couldn't stop staring at him, at his mouth, the one thing that was remotely soft about him. Would his kiss be harsh, demanding? Would his fangs cut her, scrape her bottom lip, draw blood? Would he grab the back of her skull, his fingers threading her hair, fisting her scalp as his passion grew?

"Come with me," he said in a husky whisper. "Now. Before I answer the question on both our minds."

Oh God. Her cheeks flushed and the quiver in her belly inched perilously lower. "I don't do this," she whispered in a pained voice. "Whatever it is we're doing here."

"I know," he returned just as softly, his breath a sweet, tantalizing breeze against her mouth. "Neither do I." He took her hand in his, opened the flap of his coat, and curled her body next to his.

As they left the office, walked down the hall toward the exit, Sara waited for the staff to notice her and the huge man with the brands on his face beside her, but they didn't. It was as if they were either invisible or shielded from view.

"Your doing?" she whispered to Alexander as they left the ward behind a visitor and passed by the nurse's station, again completely unnoticed.

"Nothing to explain this way," he said, guiding her into a waiting elevator.

Sara was silent as the elevator groaned and took off. Her entire adult life was built on rational answers to complicated questions, and right now she had nothing. Magic, invisibility, vampires—none of these things existed. And yet here it was . . . here *he* was . . .

The elevators opened abruptly, and through a blast of freezing night air, Sara saw that they were on the roof, the helipad and dark chopper waiting on the raised dais for an emergency call.

Alexander pulled her closer. "Come, Sara. It is very cold tonight."

But Sara eased away from him, stepped out of the elevator on her own, and embraced the cold air, desperate to clear her head—if only for a moment. She didn't like this—being out of control, allowing someone to lead her into the unknown and the potentially dangerous—even him. She turned. "Why are we up here?"

"I need to show you something," he said, walking calmly toward her, toward the edge of the roofline, "at your house."

"Cabs are down there," she said, backing up, backing away from him.

His eyes flashed. "This will be faster."

Sara barely had time to register the sudden, powerful strength of his arms around her or the comfort of his warmth. One moment they were at the edge of the roofline, the next they were airborne.

11

It took only seconds. From beginning to end, from what felt like stepping into the eye of a tornado, then being thrust out again.

Breathing heavy in the cold air, legs shaking, Sara stared at the front door of her apartment. "What was that?" she asked, unable to believe the reality of what she'd just experienced. "How did you do that?"

Beside her, Alexander released her and reached for the doorknob. "A simple mind request."

"As in, 'see my apartment door in your head and off we go'?"

He chuckled softly. "Something like that." He used no key, but the door swung wide for them anyway. "Shall we?"

As the wind whipped her hair about her face, wariness and fear gripped hold of every muscle in her body. She didn't want to go in there again. "Why are we here?"

"You need to see who and what you're dealing with." He gently nudged her forward. "Come, Sara."

Reluctantly, she stepped across the threshold and into the apartment, knowing that she had left the comfort of a rational existence somewhere back at the hospital. No matter how much she wished she could, it had become impossible to pretend that the man beside her was human or that she wasn't caught up in something impossible to understand and potentially life threatening. And the latter was proven the moment she caught sight of the interior of her apartment. She stared, openmouthed. The place was completely trashed and the smell of death was fresh. The living area had been turned into some kind of antivampire shrine with red paint slashed across walls, chairs, and on the couch. Crucifixes and garlic hung from light fixtures and picture frames, but most disturbing of all were the dozen or so mutilated bats positioned in a perfect circle on the floor with Tom Trainer's calling card—a small dead bird—in the center.

Unable to pull her gaze from the scene before her, Sara asked Alexander, "Do you know when this happened?"

"My guess is a few hours after we left."

"You've been here, seen this already."

"Right before I came to you."

She glanced up at him then. "I have to call the police, Alexander."

"They can do nothing for you. My brother Nicholas is a top-notch tracker. He will find Trainer. In the meantime, you need a place to stay. Somewhere safe."

She knew what he meant—where he believed that safe place to be—and she wasn't having it. "I'll stay with friends," she said quickly.

His brow lifted. "You want to bring this man to your friends?"

Sara's eyes narrowed. "You're playing dirty, vampire."

Alexander smiled. "It is how I play, woman."

The husky timbre of his voice, the predatory way he watched her made her insides quiver. "I don't get it. Why do you care so much?"

"What?"

Her voice dropped. "What is it you want from me? I'm not looking to be rescued."

In the silence that followed, an expression crossed Alexander's features, dimmed the fierce strength in his eyes; it was something achingly close to emptiness, and it made the residual fear that still remained in Sara's heart dissolve.

"You saved my life," he said softly, simply.

Sara's gaze locked with his then, a mutual understanding passing between them. He wished to do the same for her . . .

"But you will fight me," he said. "Why is that? Why are you so stubborn, Sara Donohue? Have you never let anyone care for you?"

His words made her throat ache, but she pushed the quick emotion away. "I don't need anyone to take care of me."

Alexander reached out then, brushed his fingertips over the quick pulse at the base of her throat. "Maybe not, but you will stay with me until this man is caught."

Sara fought for control over herself, but the heat of his touch mocked her resolve. *Goddammit!* For years—forever it seemed—she'd given her life over to one purpose, one goal, one person—and it had been a worthy path, still was. But Tom Trainer had forced his way into her world and she had to deal with him. After he was off the streets and no longer a threat, she could return to that state of normal, but for now, she needed to think about her own self-preservation. This man—this vampire who stood so close and touched her so tenderly—would keep her safe. She knew it. She knew it like she knew her own name.

Her gaze held his. "There'll have to be some rules."

"What rules are those?"

"I have a life, work, patients who need and depend on me."

Without another word, he left her and strode over to the door, which opened before he even reached the panel of wood. Once there, he turned to face her, his tone and expression grave. "Your work is your own," he said. "I swear I will not keep you from any of it."

She didn't move. "But you'll be watching me?"

The hard, possessive flash in his merlot eyes said it all.

As if forcing her to make a move, the stench of death inside her apartment grew suddenly worse. "All right, vampire," she said, walking past him and out into the frigid New York City night. "Let's fly."

12

Nicholas walked into the library, his stoic exterior masking the raging hard-on he had to rip out the jugular of the first beating heart he saw. Unfortunately, the only thing in the room happened to be not only pulseless, but family.

Seated in a huge leather armchair, legs splayed, eyes trained on his laptop, Lucian didn't even look up. "Is Trainer dead?"

"No," Nicholas said.

"Good, I don't want the Order up our asses any further than they already are. Is he at least scrubbed and put away for safekeeping?"

Nicholas paced the floor, pausing every few seconds to speak. "I couldn't find him."

"Well"—Lucian's gaze lifted—"that's unfortunate."

It was more than that, Nicholas thought. It was a first. In his hundred and fifty years, he'd never lost prey. "His scent is so weak to me now. He must be deeply hidden. But I will find him."

"I have no doubt."

"And when I do, he'll be begging me to end his life. The Order cannot detect torture within the Eternal Breed, only death."

Lucian grinned, impressed. "This human is bringing out a side of you I haven't seen since we were on the front lines. Up until now, you've quelled the animal buried within." Suddenly, his almond gaze changed from pride to unease. "Should I be concerned about this new development? Is there more? Has your hunger grown?"

"No. Nothing like that." But, Nicholas mused, he had felt a shift in himself as of late. Not hunger, but aggression and a burn for *gravo*, the poisoned vampire blood his mother had abused when he was just a *balas*, the drug he had gone to great and painful lengths to purchase for her before her death—the drug he had consumed in impressive quantities for several years afterward. He plunged his hands through his hair, attempting to rid his brain of the thoughts and images running through it. He caught Lucian staring at him, a suspicious frown playing about his mouth. He would do well to keep this new and slow burn inside of him a secret; no doubt it would pass in time.

He came around his desk and opened his own laptop. "Where are you with the Hollow of the Shadows?"

Lucian's frown deepened. "There's so little on the location of the Order. When I lived in the third *credenti*, I heard nothing of their whereabouts. From what

I've been able to find—which isn't much—they seem to live between worlds. Finding them won't be easy." He looked up, his eyes filled with disgust. "Alexander may indeed have to visit his old *credenti* and question his . . . *family* to get the information."

Nicholas stilled, his fingers twitching over the keyboard. It was a life, a reality they had sworn never to return to, and now the Order had forced them back in. "Don't text him, Luca. Let him come home and we will go together, find it together—stand together."

"He won't allow us to help."

Looking up from his screen, Nicholas raised one black eyebrow. "I don't care if he allows it. Do you?"

A slash of smile hit Lucian's full mouth. "Blood brothers we are, Nicky."

There was a knock on the library door and Evans entered the room. The servant looked from one brother to the other and said formally, "I am sorry to disturb."

"Not a problem," Nicholas said. "What is it, Evans?"

"A note has been delivered, sir."

"From Alexander?" Nicholas asked.

"No."

Nicholas stilled, glanced at Lucian, whose gaze was narrowed and fixed on the ancient Impure. Notes were never delivered to the house, not once in the sixty years they'd lived there. Business mail went to a box at the post office, and from time to time they would receive junk mail at the SoHo address, but nothing personal.

"From your human, Nicky?" Lucian quipped darkly. "Perhaps he's come out of hiding and is turning himself in."

Nicholas made a signal for Evans to hand him the letter, and when the butler placed the gray formal envelope with the gold seal in his hands, Nicholas's blood froze in his veins. *Kettler.* One of the highest-ranking families in the Eternal Breed, model citizens, purest of pure, and residing in the Boston *credenti.* His eyes found his brother's. "Kettler seal."

"What?" Tossing his laptop to the rug, Lucian jumped to his feet, his pale almond eyes now a blazing fire of gold. A growl . . . "No."

"From a Bronwyn Kettler."

"Fuck me."

Nicholas opened the envelope.

"It begins," Lucian said vehemently as Evans backed up to the door. "The Order has leaked our whereabouts. If one can find us so easily, the rest will follow."

Nicholas read the note once, then again. "She has called for a handfasting."

"You've got to be shitting me!"

"A traditional Eternal Breed handfasting. She wishes to live here, remain here all three weeks, in preparation for mating."

"With who?" Lucian demanded, coming to stand beside Nicholas, so he too could see the letter.

"Alexander."

"Well, thank Christ for small favors."

Nicholas shoved the letter in his brother's hand and returned to his laptop. He needed to feed. Soon. Something to calm himself and whatever was scratching on the inside of his brain, desperate to get out and pounce.

"She says she'll be here tomorrow." Lucian snarled, then turned to the butler still hovering near the library door. "Evans, send a return note; tell the *veana* to stop packing her bags. She will not be living here in preparation for mating with Alexander or anyone else. Tell her we are no longer part of the *credenti*—we don't play by their rules."

"No," Nicholas said quickly, his tone implacable and resolute. "Ready the sage room, Evans."

Lucian whirled on him, his fangs dropping a centimeter as he roared, "Are you insane?"

"Perhaps," Nicholas said calmly, "but no Pureblood *paven*, not even one who has cast off his species, can decline the call of a handfasting. It is a blood vow with our Pureblood females; it goes back centuries, even before the Order took power." He eased the envelope from Lucian. "Not to mention, it's really fucking rude."

"When have you ever given a shit about being rude?"

"Our blood dictates that we at least see her."

"Your blood, maybe," Lucian shot back, his fangs descending another inch. "My blood can go fuck itself."

"You can put those things back in your head now, Little Brother."

"We also made a vow, Nicholas. To each other—no humans, no *credenti.*"

Nicholas's frown deepened. Yes, and it had been so for a hundred years. The three of them living a life of solitude, living and building businesses in cities that allowed such reclusiveness, a life away from the abusive bonds of the *credenti* and the intrusive eyes of the Order.

Nicholas took a deep breath. "Times are changing, it seems."

Fangs fully extended now, eyes blistering with a hunger that had nothing to do with blood, Lucian snatched up his laptop and headed up the stairs to the second level. "Do what you will, Brother, but I am going to find this Hollow of Shadows before the Order seeps deeper into our lives and your etiquette-loving ass goes morpho too."

Deep in the clouds of his mind, Alexander willed himself to land. Sara was coiled in his arms, her hands gripping his waist, her nails digging into the flesh of his back. For a brief moment he wished he could stay in flight, have her tight against his body, her nails digging deeper into his flesh until she drew blood.

But in seconds, his feet hit concrete and the ice-cold salt air of the Atlantic rushed at him, whipping Sara's long dark hair against his face. He closed his eyes and his nostrils widened, taking in her blood scent. Normally, humans were cold, bland, lacking in spice, but not this one. She was scented with earth, a rich, hot blend that breathed desire into his lungs and, even though it was impossible, felt somehow familiar to him.

Beneath the half-light of the moon, Sara pressed herself closer to him and looked up, her stunning blue eyes curious, no longer wary. "It may be dark out, but I know this isn't SoHo."

As he gazed down at her, Alexander felt an ache run through him, from chest to groin. He wanted to stand on the icy path beside the tall beach grass and remain attached to her. He wanted her mouth against his, wanted to know what she tasted like. He could almost imagine it. She was a beautiful woman, yes, but it was her strength, her drive to be fearless in the face of something impossible and inhuman that made him crave her—made him want to crawl up inside of her and remain for days. It was a sensation he'd never experienced and it concerned him.

"Are we still in New York at least?" she asked, her eyes demanding the truth, yet promising to accept whatever the response was.

"We're in Montauk," he said.

"Long Island?" Her brows knit together. "Why?"

He reached up and touched her hair, her jaw. "A quick detour."

"For what?"

He wanted to drop his head, have just one taste of her, the drug that might grant him a few minutes of calm to do what needed to be done this night.

"Listen, Alexander," she said with a hint of frustration. "I'm here with you because I saw the logic in what you said back in my apartment, and because my number-one priority is survival. I'm admittedly scared of Tom, and I think you can keep him away from me. I'm not here because you're forcing me or holding me captive. I'm here because I trust you." She lifted one dark eyebrow. "I deserve the same."

Yes, she was fearless. No one but his brothers made demands on him. "How did you acquire such an attitude?"

"What attitude?" She tried to look both confused and put out. "I've got an attitude?"

He chuckled. "That wasn't an insult, Sara. You impress me with your candor. Where does it come from?"

"I don't know. I suppose from surviving on my own for so long."

"It made you strong." It wasn't a question.

"I think so. God, I hope so."

He shifted his gaze, looked out into the black water beyond the sea grass. "For some it would've broken them."

She laughed softly. "I've been broken, a few times, but I had something that kept me focused—*someone* who kept me going."

Alexander's head jerked back to her. "Who is this someone?" he demanded, his gut twisting. "A male?"

She nodded. "A man. Human."

Jealousy roared through him, the sudden emotion taking him by surprise. He'd never felt possessive over a woman, and this one should be no different. Why was it, then, that he wished more than anything to rip the head from the man she spoke of with such softness and care in her tone?

Reaching between them, Alexander took her hand and led her toward the very gates he had run from a hundred years before. For now, she was his and whoever this man was, he had no place in this moment, this time.

"We're here," he uttered, his body rigid. It was risky bringing her to this place, he knew that, but he couldn't help himself. He needed to keep her close. It was the only answer he had, and if he was forced to fight to keep her safe, he would.

"Here where?" Sara asked, looking from the iron gate before them to the eight-foot-tall and extraordinarily thick shrubbery that ran down both sides as far as the eye could see. "It looks restricted. Private property."

"It is," Alexander said.

Sara felt the misery in his tone, the weight of it. She looked up at him, his profile in the light of the moon. Easing pain came naturally to her, but what she saw etched in his features, the raw hatred there concerned her. Not for her own safety, but for the safety of whatever lay behind gate number one.

"Are you all right?" she asked him.

"Perfect," he said, lifting his wrist to his mouth and baring his fangs.

Sara stared at him, momentarily captivated by his beauty and those pinpointed fangs. Then everything changed. Without a word, he pulled in a breath and struck his wrist, puncturing his vein.

Sara gasped. "Stop! Jesus."

The blood that ran down his arm was the color of a beet. Sara watched it travel, utterly horrified. "What the hell are you doing?"

He moved closer to the gate and pressed his bloody wrist to one thick steel bar, ran it down the length. "Using my key."

He pulled his arm away, then displayed the gash to Sara's worried gaze. "Look now," he said. "No harm done."

His explanation did little to shut down the shock and panic running through her, but she watched as the cuts on his wrist sealed.

She released a breath she didn't realize she was holding.

His eyes flashed. "It pleases me that you care, Sara."

She frowned up at him. "You could've warned me."

He inclined his head. "I'm sorry."

There was a loud crack and Sara turned, watched as the gate opened at a snail's pace.

"Am I safe here?" she asked Alexander.

"You will always be safe with me." He eased her back against his side and together they entered the compound.

The first thing Sara saw was a snow-covered field that stretched so deep into the distance the moon didn't catch its ending with her light. Anxiety, brought about by the unfamiliar, knocked around in Sara's belly and she moved closer to Alexander as he guided them onto one of the dirt paths leading into a quiet wood.

It was a short walk through the cold, pine-scented forest, and when they emerged, Sara saw that they were in a little village. It was small, quiet, and so simplistically perfect looking that it felt as though they'd just walked onto a movie set. Sara was desperate to ask Alexander where they were and how this was possible, but she didn't speak, felt that if she did the entire thing would vanish.

They continued, taking the path that went straight through the town square. Oil lamps lit the front porches of modestly constructed homes and businesses. People dressed in simple, almost period costume milled about, riding horses or walking in and out of what appeared to be a general store. Sara jumped slightly as one young girl stopped directly in front of them and gave a small squeak of fright as she stared up at the both of them.

"Off you go," Alexander commanded softly, and the girl instantly turned away and took off down the lane, out of sight.

"What is this?" Sara asked, perplexed and fascinated at the same time. "Some kind of Amish town?"

"Not exactly. It's called a *credenti*, a vampire community."

Vampire community. The two extraordinary words rolled around in Sara's brain, looking for a safe, real place to land.

"There are *credentis* all over the world," Alexander continued, his voice devoid of all emotion now. "This is the one where I began my life."

Sara looked up at him, curious by this new bit of information. This was his home, where he was born, and yet he looked as though he would rather be anywhere else. Despite her own flirtations with anxiety at the moment, she curled her arm around his waist, offering him whatever support she could. He growled low in his chest and leaned in to her touch.

As they walked, Sara eyed the people around them. They were completely covered from head to foot in homespun clothing. "Why is everyone dressed like that?"

"They remain in their own time," Alexander said with a bitter edge to his tone. "The Purebloods and Impures that live within these walls and the walls of every other *credenti* are uninterested in the modern world and her conveniences. Simplicity is how they must live—it is in what they wear, what they see, what they talk about."

Sounded pretty restrictive to Sara, but she wasn't

the kind of person to knock someone else's choices. She gestured to men and women walking past them. "There's fabric wrapped around their throats and wrists."

"Yes."

"What's that all about?"

"All males and females embrace the ancient ways and texts of the Order."

"The Order?"

"The Eternal Order. Vampire law, vampire gods." He sneered. "They are responsible for this. They determine how a vampire should live to remain pure inside and out. And until a vampire's true mate finds him or her, the points on their bodies—neck and wrists—where blood is most commonly taken, are covered."

Sara was pretty taken aback. It was so primitive. "And everyone here goes for that? Abides by the law?"

"If they wish to have a peaceful existence they do."

"But you and your brothers—"

"Got the hell out," he finished for her.

They continued down the street, passing homes with farmland behind them. Men and women—male and female vampires—continued to stare, their gazes ranging from shock to disgust to fear. Just like Alexander, they could easily pass for human in the looks department, but unlike him, they were bone thin and noticeably shorter than an average human.

Sara wondered why that would be, but the thought

barely had time to register. Beside her, Alexander had stopped, his body frozen in place, a low feral sound erupting from his throat and filling the air around them. Sara had never heard such a sound; it was like an animal caught in a trap, and her heart suddenly ached for him. He was staring at something to his left and she followed his line of vision. There, a few feet away, standing in front of a small one-story home, was a male, a female, and a child, who appeared to be somewhere around twelve years old.

When she saw Alexander, the girl dropped her gaze to the snowy ground, but the male and female beside her stared at Alexander with looks of shock that quickly morphed into expressions of disgust. The November air chilled Sara to her bones, but it was nothing compared to the coldness that emanated from the two creatures before her. Every instinct, every nerve in her body screamed at her to run.

She dug her nails into Alexander's waist. "Who is that?"

"The *veana* who gave me life," he uttered, "and the *paven* who did everything he could to take it away."

13

It had been a hundred years since Alexander had laid eyes on his mother and her true mate, Theydon, and yet their scent still made him sick. It was the scent of hate, of abuse, of neglect, and its pungent stench sent a wave of fury through what remained of Alexander's soul. Had the Order set this up? Forced him to come here and prostrate himself at the foot of the very monsters who had driven him away?

Beside him Sara whispered, "They don't look happy to see you."

"This was a mistake," he uttered tightly, his nostrils flaring, releasing angry little puffs of air like a bull in the winter night. "I'm a selfish prick."

Sara looked up at him, her beautiful dark blue eyes confused. "What are you talking about?"

"I shouldn't have brought you here." The brands on his cheeks burned with an irritating pain. The need to keep Sara close and protected was nothing to this new need he had to keep her far away from the conversation he was about to engage in with his mother and her mate. "But it's too late for regrets."

"I thought you said I have nothing to worry about, nothing to fear," she said.

He looked down at her, feeling like a gigantic ass for scaring her. "And you don't," he said assertively. "They won't touch you."

"Alexander . . ."

"Come, Sara, let's finish this and get out." He walked, Sara beside him, toward the threesome. Just moments before he reached the porch, his mother leaned down and whispered something to Evaline, his little sister, and she turned and ran into the house.

Alexander pretended not to care. She was his half sister and he'd met her only once when he was a *balas*. No doubt she'd been poisoned against him by the *paven* who stood before him now.

Theydon was at least six inches shorter than him and possessed half the muscle mass, but the cruelty and evil he'd shown to Alexander as a *balas* still burned brightly in the older *paven*'s blue eyes. The instinct to kill was strong within Alexander—to protect the young *veana* inside the house and the beautiful human who stood beside him outside of it. But this was not the time for vengeance. The future of his brothers was crucial and he needed information.

"Alexander." Theydon's raspy tone curled around Alexander's neck and squeezed.

"In the flesh," he said with true menace.

"We thought you were—"

"Dead," Alexander finished for him, casting a quick glance at his mother. "Sorry to disappoint you."

Theydon stepped in front of his *veana*. "You don't belong here, *sacro*. What do you want?"

Alexander flinched at the ancient word for "filth"—the word Theydon had called him whenever he'd begged for blood through the bars of his cage. His fingers itched to wrap around the old *paven*'s neck.

"Why have you interrupted our nightly meditation—or are you just here to torment your mother?"

"I'll leave her torment to you."

His mother shook her head. "Really, Alexander, coming here after all this time, dressed that way, and bringing that 'thing.'"

"Impure *sacro*," muttered Theydon.

"You may address me in whatever way you choose," Alexander warned the old *paven*, "but say another word about my woman and I will rip your head from your shoulders, regardless of the sacred ground and consequences from the Order."

His mother gasped, put her head down, and started whispering an ancient plea to the Order.

Theydon put his hand on her shoulder. "Madeline—"

"He wishes to shame me. It has always been his greatest gift."

"His only gift. It is his father's blood that acts this way, not yours. Breeding Male *witte*."

Alexander smiled darkly. Yes, his father was an "animal." "And that animal is in me now, Theydon. So take care."

Madeline's brown eyes lifted to the brands on Alexander's cheeks. "You have gone through morpho."

"Yes."

Disgust saturated her gaze. "Yes. Your size, your eyes, the marks on your face and wrists—the look of the monster, the rapist . . . Though you will not become a Breeding Male, your father *is* within you."

Alexander heard Sara gasp beside him and he dropped his arm from her waist and went searching for her hand. It was the bond he needed, the strength he needed to stop himself from killing the pair before him. When he found her warm, willing palm, he squeezed it gently.

Theydon gestured to Madeline. "Go inside the house, *Madeline.* I will deal with your unwanted *balas.*"

With one last look at Alexander, Madeline turned and hurried up the steps.

When the door clicked shut, Theydon whirled on Alexander and hissed, "Why are you here, *sacro witte?*"

Dirty animal. Yes, indeed. "I seek the Hollow of Shadows."

Disgust gave way to fear and awe within the old *paven*'s pale eyes. "The Order?"

"I need their location."

"I don't know it."

"Don't play with me."

"Never. I do not wish to dirty my soul."

Alexander dropped Sara's hand and with the powers of morpho, shot forward, landing within a centimeter of the piece-of-shit *paven* who goaded him so easily. He spoke slowly and with deadly lucidity. "As you would have it, my hunger is never quelled, Stepfather, and when I look at you, the ache to rip you apart and feed on your unbeating heart is barely contained."

The old *paven* shuddered. "Do not threaten me, *witte*."

"There is no threat, only fact. An animal will kill to survive."

Theydon paused, seeming to consider his next move. "None of us can reveal the location of the Hollow of Shadows. We would be imprisoned for it. And I would never make such a sacrifice for you. You must find it on your own. Or not." His gaze fell on Sara and he sneered. "Now, your human is stinking up our air. Pray, take her back to where you came from and do not return."

Alexander's fangs dropped low enough for his stepfather to see, but the older *paven* didn't turn around and run. His steps were easy and calm as he made his way into the house, just as they had been centuries earlier as he'd left the outdoor cage and the starving, frozen *balas* huddled within it.

For Sara, the journey into the *credenti* had been a slow, vigilant one. The race out, however, was proving to be anything but.

Halfway through the woods, she stopped running, shrugged away from Alexander, and dropped at the waist, attempting to catch her breath. "I can't . . . You're going too fast."

His face implacable, Alexander said nothing, merely scooped her up in his arms like she weighed less than a pine needle and continued down the path at a hectic pace. Sara dropped her head against his chest and watched the blur of snowy farmland whiz past. She wasn't about to fight him or ask the dozen questions that licked at her curiosity after all she'd just heard. She knew he had to get out, breathe free again. It was an impulse she understood all too well.

When they finally reached the gate, Alexander bit into his wrist and slashed the gaping wound against the frozen iron. In seconds, the massive plates pulled back and Alexander flew through them, jetting across the roadway and into the thick beach grass. Clutching Sara tight against his chest, he faced the ocean and snapped his eyes shut. Before Sara could even take a breath, much less speak, they were off again, moving, flying, so high above the water the air grew ice cold, until—*CRACK*—they flashed downward and hit concrete.

Her heart beating with jackrabbitlike quickness, Sara lifted her head from Alexander's chest and glanced around. She gasped. They were on top of a lighthouse, sixty feet or more in the air, on a balcony overlooking a dark, wild sea.

"Not SoHo," Sara called over the wind and white curtains of crashing waves, her hair slapping against her cheeks.

"Not yet," Alexander called, then turned and carried her inside.

14

The round, glass room smelled faintly of mildew, and was sparsely furnished with two wooden chairs and a matching table.

Alexander set Sara down on one of the chairs, then stalked over to the window, spread his hands wide against the pane, and gazed out into the moon-brilliant night.

As Sara watched his muscles bunch and flex through his black sweater, she willed her legs to stop shaking. The mind-flying thing was going to take a while to get used to. "Are you all right?"

Alexander said nothing.

She tried again to engage him. "How long has it been since you've been back there, since you've seen them?"

Again, he remained silent.

Sara's heart ached for him. She'd never seen anyone treated so despicably in all her life and she knew he must be feeling humiliated and angry and embarrassed that she'd seen it all. And so she waited, gave him time to seethe, to think.

Finally, after many moments, he released a breath and said, "I escaped my *credenti* over a hundred years ago."

Escaped. A hundred years. Jesus.

"An older female," he continued, still facing the window and sea and the moon, "a teacher of mine who ran with me, told me about this lighthouse. We came here and hid. This is where I waited for my brothers to arrive. They'd escaped too and I watched their ships come in, the light from this tower guiding them to me, to our new life, free from the ones that birthed us and the ones who wanted to control us." He gave a bitter laugh. "Fuck the Order for forcing me to come back here." He pushed away from the glass, walked over to the empty chair across from her and dropped into it.

Sara watched him, the downcast expression, the silent, seething anger clinging to every muscle in his body. Within the six-foot-three, heavily muscled, branded badass, was a deeply hurt child and she wanted to run or fly or cut her wrist or whatever it took to get back into that *credenti* so she could kick his parents in their respective asses—vampires or not.

"Alexander," she said softly. "Hey."

His head came up, eyes too. They were large and scarlet and wounded. "Yes."

"Listen. The truth is . . ." She paused. What was the truth? Really? We can't choose our parents? He deserved better? What was the point? She shrugged and offered her best. "They're assholes."

He cocked his head to the side, no doubt wondering if he'd heard her correctly.

"They're assholes," she said again. "Plain and simple. It doesn't matter who or what you are—every species has them, right?"

It took a moment, but a hint of humor lit his eyes, his mouth too. "Yes. I suppose so."

She held his gaze, hoping the connection offered some molecule of strength. "And for whatever it's worth, I know how it feels to be haunted by the past."

"Do you?"

She nodded. "You know the man, the *male*, I was talking about before?"

The gentle smile on Alexander's lips disappeared.

"He's my brother."

Alexander's expression shifted in an instant. Shock now, interest too.

"When we were kids . . ." Sara paused, took a breath. God. Did she really want to go here? There were very few people in her life who knew the truth about her past and she liked it that way. But it was Alexander. He was . . . different. Unexpectedly, impossibly, surprisingly different. He needed something, and she had something to offer. She raised her eyes to his and prayed her tone would remain calm and even. "I caused a terrible accident, a fire that destroyed my home, took my father's life, and ruined my brother's physical and mental health." Her throat tightened and she swallowed. "My mother wasn't hurt, but she was destroyed too, in a whole different way."

"Oh, Sara . . ."

She didn't want to look up at him, afraid she'd see the same look of disgust that she saw every time she looked in the mirror. And so she hurried forward. "My father and brother were her world, you know? So when I did this to her—"

"Stop," Alexander interrupted fiercely. "Stop it right there. You did nothing to her. It was an accident."

"It was," she said, "but that didn't matter, you know? Something I did took away two people she loved. She may say it was an accident, that's there's nothing to forgive, that the past is the past, but I know it holds both of us hostage. I know in her heart I won't be forgiven until my brother's well." Tears pulsed at the back of her throat, but she wasn't going there. This wasn't her party. This was about helping him, getting him to understand that he wasn't alone. "My point is, my face isn't a welcome sight to my parent either. So I get it."

Alexander stared at her for a long moment, his eyes softening before he closed them and pulled in a breath. Sara wondered what was happening with him, if they were about to take off, fly somewhere that again wasn't SoHo, but then her chair began to tremble and jerk beneath her. She tried to jump up, but there wasn't time, the chair shot forward, pulled toward Alexander by an unseen force. Sara gripped the sides of the thick wood, then gasped as she stopped just an inch from his chair.

He opened his eyes, inclined his head. "Thank you for that, for telling me that."

She tried to catch her breath, slow her heart, but in this man's—this vampire's—presence it was nearly impossible. "It was just the truth."

His gaze moved over her. "You do something to me. You affect me in a way that's quite extraordinary."

"That doesn't sound like a good thing."

"It's a complicated thing. I should take you back to my home and yet . . ."

"You can't?" she finished for him.

"I won't."

He needed her. "Good." And she needed him. "I don't want you to."

A slow smile spread across his features, Sara's too. Then suddenly, he reached for her and pulled her onto his lap. Sara gasped at the sudden nearness, of the abrupt sexuality of his erection, granite-hard, pressing unapologetically against the back of her thigh. Instinctively, she pushed her hips forward, grazing the head of his cock with her backside.

Alexander's jaw went rigid and his eyes flashed with predatory fire. "I must have you near," he uttered. "I must know that you are well, that you breathe, that you smile."

His words, the low growl from deep in his throat

sent shivers up Sara's spine, made her skin tingle, her nipples harden. She could tell herself over and over that this wasn't real, that he wasn't real, that her feelings for him were nothing more than a delusion. But she would be lying. She wanted him, desired him.

His hands found hers, threading his fingers through hers and easing her arms behind her back, making her breasts jut forward. His gaze dropped to her mouth and his lips trembled, the tips of his fangs just visible.

She wanted to kiss him. She wanted to know what his mouth felt like, the warm wetness of his tongue and the thin, sharp jab of his fangs.

"What they said is true," Alexander said, his gaze, his voice, fierce with emotion and need.

"Who?" she asked, breathless. "Your mother and that jerk?"

He closed his eyes, dropped his head against her breast. "There is an animal in me and it is loose and hungry."

Heat pooled in Sara's belly, threatening to sink lower. "What is it hungry for? Blood?"

"You," he uttered, turning his head, nuzzling her nipple through her thick sweater. "I wish to mark you."

She shivered at his words, his desire.

He lifted his head, stared at her with eyes cherry black with desire. "I wish to make claim to you—let any male who comes sniffing around you know that you belong to me." He leaned forward, trailed the thin band of muscle in her neck with his nose, inhaling greedily. "You scent of blood and sex."

Her hips jerked against his cock. "How would you mark me?"

"It is like a tattoo, but the needle that is used is . . . well, in-house . . ."

She gasped as she felt two sharp canines dragging gently across her throat. Her thighs shook now and the little heartbeat hidden within her cunt throbbed.

"Would it hurt?" she asked.

He froze, then lifted his head and held her gaze. He looked deadly serious. "I don't know, but you're never going to find out."

"Why?" The fog in her brain, the raging desire in her body hummed too loudly. She hadn't heard him right.

"I must protect you," he said through clenched teeth. "From that little prick of a human, and from myself."

She eased back then, took his face in her hands—took in the fierce glare, the hard angles, the key-shaped brands, the full lips. "I don't need protection from you." She leaned in and brushed her mouth against his. It was the softest of kisses, and yet Alexander exploded with a wicked growl.

"Oh, fuck! No, Sara." He stood and set her on her feet, then walked to the door that led to the lighthouse balcony and opened it. Frozen sea air wafted into the room, making her shiver.

Bewildered, Sara stared at him, her body raging with both sudden cold and manic desire.

"The Order," he said, his voice as strained as the hard cock in his pants.

"I know," she said. She didn't argue or question. Whatever it was he had—that she'd felt on his lap, in his arms—whatever it was he resisted giving her, she wanted it. For now, she wanted it. "Let's go."

He opened his arms and she went to him, curled into his chest, and together they walked outside onto the balcony. With the waves crashing against the exterior of the lighthouse, Alexander closed his eyes, dipped into his mind, and once again, they flew.

15

For Tom Trainer, the pain of having fangs plunged into his skin and his blood drained to the point of near unconsciousness was horrifying in the extreme. And yet it didn't come close to the pain Dr. Donahue's rejection caused him.

The massive Impure, Mear, was kind to him, each touch a slow, sweet seduction to his flesh, while the half-breed assured him he was getting stronger and that the commander and his recruits would help him capture the woman who had spurned him and the *paven* who held her.

Tom shifted uncomfortably on the brown leather couch. They were in Mear's suite in the commander's home and it was his turn to drink. It was his third "meal" and he hated it, hated the metallic taste, the thickness of the liquid as it hit his tongue and slid down his throat. But it had already made him stronger, his brain clearer in his goal. His two canines were loose, and as Mear had told him, he would lose them within the month and fangs would begin to grow in their place.

He would be one of them. Almost. An *Imiti*, Mear called it. A human with vampire qualities. As long as he drank.

Mear turned to him, licked the remaining blood from his lips, and grinned. "Ready?"

Bile rose in Tom's throat, but he forced a nod, and when Mear slashed his own wrist with one sharp fang and held it to Tom's lips, Tom shut his eyes and drank.

Anything for her.

Anything.

16

Alexander stood in the middle of a football field, Sara's arms around him, gripping him possessively. This was not the location, the image, he'd pictured in his mind when they'd flashed a moment ago. He sought the Order, had tried to conjure their image in his head, but it had been pointless. Looking around him now, he had to acknowledge that he had no control over where he flashed and when. The Order had connected with him, and as he'd suspected they would, were messing with him.

He felt Sara's small, supple body shake. From cold, from desire, from fear? He wasn't certain, but he pulled her closer. Yes, he'd vowed to protect her, but there was something in him that warned that he needed protection too. A shift had occurred back at the lighthouse—his lighthouse, the one that had once been his salvation, had brought him back to life. A switch had been flipped when he'd heard her speak of her past, her pain, when he'd pulled her onto his lap and her body had responded so intuitively, so perfectly. The craving to mark her wasn't out of a desperate need to take her blood—that he could understand, he could deal with—*that* he was accustomed to.

No. The longing that pulsed within him now was something else entirely. He wanted her to feed him, fill him with something greater than blood.

She eased back then, looked up at him with those lovely blueberry eyes. "Any idea where we are, vampire?"

Yes, he thought, as his body pulsed with life, with need. He was well and truly fucked. This woman ruled his heart while the Order ruled his mind.

"Scotland." He glanced around at the campus, not so very different than it had been a hundred years before. "On the grounds of Creglock Academy."

"A school?"

"Lucian went here."

"A vampire school?"

"No. Hard-core military academy for rebellious, lawbreaking human children. His mother put him here when he was a *balas*, not even eight years old, then walked away for good. It was a nightmare. He was a vampire, so he grew slower than the other children."

Sara looked appalled. "His mother put him in a human school knowing he wouldn't grow like the other kids, and then never came back? She didn't even check on him?"

Alexander frowned. It was little wonder that Lucian

distrusted all females as he did. "He went from a small vampire *credenti* outside Glasgow to this. He was broken here, every bit of a young one's softness destroyed."

"His mother sounds like just as big a prize as yours."

"Yes."

"Did Nicholas have the same situation?"

"No. Nicholas's mother never punished him for his existence. He did it for her. Still does." Alexander caught her looking at him with that same expression of care he'd seen back at the lighthouse and he pulled the plug on the questions and answers. "What time is it?"

She glanced down at her watch. "One thirty."

"Shit. I need to pull my mind from everything and everyone and concentrate on the Order." Alexander closed his eyes and thrust every image away, every image but one. It was only his perception of them, but it was all he had to go on.

The familiar hum began at his feet, shot upward, and with a rush of wind, they were gone. This time, when they hit ground they were in the woods, outside a cave and it was warm, summer.

"Fucking hell." This was a battleground, long ago, for him and his brothers. It was where they'd learned to use primitive weapons, where Alexander's friend and teacher had gone missing. Why was the Order playing this game? Was it simply to humble him?

A growl rumbled deep in his throat. They'd be waiting for all eternity for such an event, and even after he was dust they could go fuck themselves.

Sara coughed, moved away from him, and went to the mouth of the cave, sat down with her back against the rock. She looked pale, tired, yet so fragile in her beauty. He went to her and knelt down beside her. "Are you okay?"

"A little nauseous."

"I'm sorry. I didn't think about what all the flashing would do to your system."

"It's okay. I'll be fine. I've never really been a solid flier."

He grinned.

Dropping her head back against the cool rock, she looked out at the brush. "Maybe it's me."

"What do you mean?"

"Maybe they won't see you because you're with me."

"Tough shit." But he'd wondered the same thing. "No doubt they're just playing with me." Controlling bastards. "If they want me bad enough to force my body through morpho before its time, then they'll take me any way they can get me."

"Morpho?"

"The time of maturity for a *paven*, a Pureblood male vampire."

"Is that what happened outside my apartment? The sunlight and the brands on your skin?"

"Yes."

"Why would they do that?"

"I don't know, but I will—" There was a loud boom,

like thunder against a mile of sky. Instinctively, Alexander started toward Sara, but an invisible hook wrapped his waist and pulled. He clawed at the air, but it was useless. He was sucked into a tunnel, seeing nothing but black, and seconds later, he was standing on sand and Sara was nowhere in sight.

"Welcome, Alexander, son of the Breeding Male."

Alexander dropped into fighting position, his eyes flickering around, looking for the origin of the voice and a weapon he could use against it. A sheet of sand whipped up in front of him, then just as quickly dropped to the ground as though weights were attached to each grain.

Before him, seated at a long glass table, looking remarkably like a modern version of the Last Supper were the ten ancient members of the Order. They were nothing like what he'd imagined them to be when he was a *balas*—even as a grown *paven*: ghostlike, otherworldly, paper thin, yet lethal to the core. No doubt the latter was true, but the ruling ten were as solid, as three dimensional as he was. They sat in their chairs, hands folded on the glass table, eyes trained on him. Each wore a red monklike robe, had a black circle, a perfect O, branded around each of their left eyes, and except for the three *veana* members, each had a full beard.

"Where is she?" Alexander growled menacingly.

The Order member at the far left, a *paven* with electric sky blue eyes and a black beard that tapered into a perfect point at the end, spoke first. "She is well. Asleep. She won't even realize you've gone."

Alexander's fingers twitched as he imagined them wrapping around the neck of each member of the Order and squeezing until their eyes popped as wide as their brands. "You'd better be right or we're going to have a serious problem."

The older *paven* grinned, displaying his set of brick red fangs—another symbol that he was Order, that his hunger had been completely fulfilled, that his long existence consuming blood was over. "Morpho agrees with you, son of the Breeding Male."

"How did you find me?" Alexander snarled.

"The human female you nearly devoured."

"Impossible!" Alexander roared. "I didn't take her life." Aside from going through morpho, killing was the only other way the Order could track either an Impure or a Pureblood outside of the *credenti*.

"No, but the Impure who watched you, then drank from the human after you left, did—he stopped her heart in under a minute." The older *paven* sneered. "Sloppy little *sacro* bastard. But his memories did lead us to you."

Alexander's eyes flashed at the black-haired *paven*. Once again, his uncontrolled hunger had imprisoned him. "What is it you want?"

"You've run from us for too long. It is time. You and your brothers must help your kind."

"Help?" Alexander released a bitter laugh. "You're

asking me to help the ones who tormented and tortured me? That's why you premorphed me?"

"You speak of one or two in the *credenti*, not the Eternal Breed as a whole."

"I speak of you."

"You accuse the Order of torture? Tread lightly, son of the Breeding Male."

A growl erupted from Alexander and he warned the male, "Call me that filthy title again and you will see how deeply I have morphed!"

The *paven*'s eyes narrowed and his hand came up in front of his face, ready for a mental battle. Beside him, another member of the Order, a *veana* with skin the color of clay and waist-length hair the color of snow, leaned toward him and whispered something. After a moment, the *paven* dropped his hand, but his irritation with Alexander remained. "We have a situation at several of our *credentis*," he said tightly. "An infiltration. Impures have broken into our communities, taken several of our *veanas*, impregnated them, then returned them to us. Thankfully, most of the *balas* never survived past the first month of swell, but the communities are growing scared. There is talk of families leaving, running away, hiding."

"Good," Alexander uttered flippantly. Did this asshole really believe he'd care if vampires were leaving the *credentis*? Hell, he was thrilled!

"You may have felt the need to run," the *paven* continued, "but this life is not torturous for others. These are families who are breaking apart."

"Perhaps they don't wish to be under your control any longer. I know I didn't."

"These are peace-loving, simple vampires. Most will not be able to survive outside their *credentis*."

"They'll be fine."

Nostrils flaring with irritation, the older *paven* turned to the others and muttered something in the ancient language. Alexander couldn't make it out, but he guessed it had something to do with his defiant attitude. He liked that.

When the *paven* turned back to him, his pale blue eyes flashed with ire. "You will help us. You will do your part in this war we find ourselves in."

"How? Protecting the *credenti*?" Alexander interrupted darkly.

"In a manner of speaking."

Alexander sneered. "Fuck you."

The *paven* shot to his feet, and as Alexander watched, he grew taller and taller until he was double Alexander's height. "Your insolent mouth will be your quick death," he roared. "Watch how you address the Order."

Alexander stalked toward him, stopped when he came within a foot of the table. "I will address the Order in any way I choose. It is *you* who want from *me*."

"Indeed" came the soft reply from the *veana* Order with the smooth, clay-hued skin. "Pray sit, Cruen," she said to the *paven* sitting next to her. "Let us be not only useful, but thoughtful." She turned to Alexander and inclined her head. "The half-blood Ethan Dare is the one who leads the Impures, who commands that they take our Purebloods and lie with them."

Though he remained aware of Cruen, Alexander turned his focus to his neighbor. "Why?"

"We believe his objective is to wipe out all Purebloods and turn the Eternal Breed into a race of only Impures. He wishes to defile us."

Alexander chuckled. As if the Eternal Breed wasn't defiled already. Honestly, he didn't give a shit if a vampire was pureblooded or not, and after all the years of treating its Impure citizens as unwanted embarrassments, an uprising wasn't much of a surprise. Then again, if the story the Order was pitching to him was true and females were being taken against their will and dishonored, swift and deadly action needed to be taken. "What do you want me to do about it?"

Seated once again, his pale face now a mask of indifference, Cruen spoke. "We know where you and your brothers went after leaving us. We know the skills you acquired in battle. The success you achieved." He lifted one black eyebrow. "We wish you to use these talents to bring down our new enemy."

"You want me to kill Dare," Alexander said.

Cruen nodded, and each member of the Order followed.

"And if I say no?"

"We will bring the second Roman brother before us."

Alexander's gaze tore into Cruen, who watched him in return, his lips lifting at the corners in a small smile, as though he knew exactly what Alexander was thinking. Yes, it was clear. Fucking crystal. If he didn't cooperate, give himself over to the Order's commands, Nicholas would be morphed next. Followed by Lucian.

Alexander lifted his chin. "Has Dare killed?"

"Yes."

"Then take him in. End his life."

"We have tried," the white-haired *veana* explained. "We cannot maintain a hold on him for more than a few seconds. It is an impossibility, and yet . . ." She glanced up at Cruen, who remained impassive, his eyes trained on Alexander.

There was nothing Alexander wanted more in that moment than to tell each of them to go fuck themselves because he was already screwed; he was already morphed. But there was Nicholas and Lucian to consider.

His teeth ground together, making his jaw scream in pain. "I will find and kill Ethan Dare, but I demand a blood oath that afterward the Order will forget that the Roman brothers exist. Nicholas and Lucian will morph in their own time."

A light flickered within Cruen's baby blues. "Bring his lifeless body to us, and we will give the oath."

"Fine," Alexander said. "Now I want the fuck off this plane."

He felt the pull, like a hook out of the world, then the tunnel into blackness. But before the world went completely dark to him, his eyes caught on another member of the Order, one he hadn't paid much attention to before, but who, though mostly covered by his hood, felt strangely familiar to him. The moment was over in an instant and when light returned to his vision, he was back in the woods, before the cave, and Sara was asleep on a tuft of grass, near the mouth.

She looked so soft, so fragile, yet he'd seen the fire that burned beneath her pale skin, had scented it, had wanted it flowing against the blood that ran in his own veins.

He knew he should wake her and leave the area immediately, but instead he lay down behind her and coiled his body around hers. The warmth she provided soothed him. He heard the blood in her veins moving freely, heard her breath leave and enter her lungs in an even rhythm. He closed his eyes and buried his face in her hair, desperate for the comfort he'd refused to take earlier, but receiving only a stiff cock and a dry throat.

She stirred, her shoulders lifting, her back arching; then a moment later, she turned in his grasp. "Hey . . ."

"Hey." He'd never seen dark blue eyes look so soft, so tender. He wanted to stay just like this, wrap his hands around her hips and pull her to him, let her know that he could no longer protect her body from his.

"Sorry I fell asleep," she said, rubbing her eyes.

"Don't be."

"I'm good to go now." When she sat up, he followed her.

"It's done, Sara. I saw them."

"What?"

"I've dealt with the Order."

"But how . . ."

"They took me—through my mind."

She took a moment to digest this, then asked, "What do they want?"

"What they've wanted for a hundred years," he said bitterly. "The control of me and my brothers." He stood and reached for her hand. "Come. Tuck in, now. We have to get home."

She took his hand and let him lift her, which he did, right into the curve of his arms. "The real home this time? SoHo?"

He grinned. "Yes."

"I have to work in the morning."

"I know."

"You—"

"Don't worry about me. I hate having you out of my sight, but I will not stop you."

He was entering a battle: with himself, the coming of his Pureblood female, his true mate, the Order, and an unknown assassin named Ethan Dare. He had no idea where it would end, but he did know that after a hundred years of freedom, his control had vanished.

Sara wrapped her arms around his neck and Alexander flashed, flew—the state of morpho so deeply embedded in him now that all it took was one quick thought.

17

Bronwyn Kettler stood outside the Romans' home, barely feeling the bite of cold that always spread across the city in November. Simply put, she was nervous. She wasn't at all sure of how she'd be received inside the building before her, the building that spanned an entire city block and rather brilliantly garnered little notice because of its weathered, unkempt brick facade.

She brought her gloved hand to the door and knocked again, this time with a little more force. It was rare for her to leave the Boston *credenti* for anything other than work. It was her home and she was at peace there with her family, but tonight another form of business needed to take place. Her future contentment depended upon it.

"Perhaps they're not at home," her assistant, Edel, remarked as she stood just behind her, engulfed in luggage and a week's worth of vampire genealogy work.

"They had warning of my arrival," Bronwyn said,

glancing over her shoulder at the older blond *veana*, who had outlived her true mate just six months ago when the *paven* had decided his long life was at an end and had walked out into the sun. Devastated by the loss, Edel had found a new way to be content, assisting Bronwyn in her work.

"Perhaps I should have left out the description of my appearance," Bronwyn said pointedly.

Edel nodded, her eyes softly twinkling. "Yes, the hook nose and the warts can be a turnoff to some."

"Not to mention my third eye and the way I snort when I laugh."

They both dissolved into laughter until Bronwyn heard movement behind the heavy wood door, and then the sound of locks retracting from their bases. The door pulled back and an older *paven* stood there, dressed simply, as though he had just come from one of the more rustic *credentis*.

"Good evening, Miss Kettler." He struggled to get all the luggage inside, then stood before them in the entryway and inclined his head. "May I take your coat and your companion's, as well?"

"Yes, thank you."

His eyes swept over Edel as she passed him her cloak, but he quickly looked away. He was a timid male, very unusual in one so seasoned, Bronwyn observed. Unless . . . She paused. Was it possible? Did the Romans have Impures working for them?

She and Edel followed him from the sleek foyer

through several living areas furnished in a modern design that fused beautifully with the ancient moldings and fixtures, then past a sweeping limestone staircase. She understood the wrecked exterior now. It wasn't just to keep their existence a secret; it was also to deter intruders of the sticky-fingered variety.

When the servant stopped before a large arched door, the nerves Bronwyn had wrestled with earlier bloomed into a full-blown anxiety. For a second, she thought about bolting, but her sister's face appeared before her and she stood up taller and prepared herself for whatever she was to encounter within the Roman household.

"He lied to us!" The male growl shot through the thick door, just as the old servant's knuckles lifted to strike. He hesitated. "The foolish bastard went to them without us," the *paven* behind the door yelled. "Without backup!"

"He didn't want us to have to go before them," came another male voice, a more controlled one, though still hypermasculine.

"That's bullshit and you know it! We protect each other. Blood stands with blood—it is the way it has always been."

"You look to the past far too much."

"And you still live there."

The old servant glanced back at Bronwyn and Edel and said, "One moment, please."

After a quick knock, he disappeared into the room

and left Bronwyn to wonder what she had gotten herself into. Descendants of the Breeding Male were rumored to be more aggressive than ordinary Pureblood *paven*.

And she was actually begging entrance to their lair.

"Miss Kettler is here." The servant's voice was barely audible through the door, unlike the one that followed.

"What?" came the annoyed bark of the first *paven*.

"Is she alone?" came the calm query of the second.

"No, sir," the servant said, his tone a loud whisper now. "An older *veana* accompanies her."

"Oh, Christ," shouted the first. "She brought her *tegga* with her. It's like the fucking Old Country."

Bronwyn glanced at the *veana* beside her and gave her a tedious smile. "He thinks you're my governess, Edel."

The *veana*'s mischievous brown eyes flashed. "If I may say, I hope that one is not your true mate."

"Indeed."

"Bring her," Nicholas commanded. "And you, Little Brother, had better watch yourself."

The door opened and the servant reappeared, his expression beleaguered. He gestured for them to enter. Bronwyn went first, her chin lifted to mask the fear that pulsed in her belly. She heard a curse, then a dark grumble. "First humans, then the Order, now simpering *veanas* from the *credenti* all descending on us like typhus-carrying rats."

No, Bronwyn thought as she entered the extraordinary two-story library, she was not the rat here.

"Miss Kettler. I'm Nicholas Roman."

The *paven* who stepped forward to greet her was very tall, very broad, and had eyes the color of the night sky. He was menacingly dark in both features and humor, and the moment she stood in his path she felt the true weight of his presence. Forcing her nerves to remain beneath the surface of her calm exterior, she waited for his gaze to move over every inch of her, before she spoke.

"Please, call me Bronwyn," she said. "Thank you for seeing me."

"Of course," he said, inclining his head, though his eyes went once more to the cloths covering her neck and wrists.

She tried not to be intimidated by him, but it wasn't easy. He was nothing like the *pavens* in her *credenti*, who were similar to her height and gentle in both action and tone. No, this *paven* was large and rough and no doubt breathed blood and sex, just as his sire had.

"You have brought a handfast?" he asked, his black eyes cool, though respectful.

"Yes."

"For my brother Alexander."

"Yes."

"Thank Christ!" came an irritated male voice from above.

It was the first voice she'd heard through the library

door and Bronwyn's eyes drifted upward, to the second floor of the library. She saw no face there, only dark blue jeans that housed long, thickly muscled legs and a pair of scuffed-up black hunting boots that were propped up on the wood banister. "Nice *tegga,*" the *paven* muttered down to her. "Do you still suckle at her tits?"

Beside Bronwyn, Edel sucked in air.

"Shut it, Lucian!" Nicholas snarled. "For fuck's sake." He turned back to Bronwyn and lifted his hands in the air, in a silent show of frustration. "I apologize for my brother."

Bronwyn's gaze lifted once again. So that was Lucian. The devil brother.

"Please ignore him," Nicholas said.

"I imagine that would be impossible," Bronwyn quipped.

Humor lit the *paven*'s black eyes. "Indeed." Then he sobered. "Bronwyn, I respect your call for a handfast, but why do you believe Alexander is your true mate?"

She hesitated before answering. Though she openly studied true mates, their histories, bloodlines, and the location of their marks on the skin, in the past year she had dipped into a strain of vampire lineage for a private client, lineage that was controversial and confidential. It was there that she had found her true mate, a son of the Breeding Male who, thankfully, carried no Breeding gene.

She looked up at Nicholas, who was watching her intently. She needed to give the *paven* something. It was only fair. "I study vampire genealogy. It's my life's work, my passion. I don't know how much you know about the subject, but when a *paven* or *veana* is born, they have three copies of each gene, one from their mother, one from their father, and one from their true mate. With either blood or skin samples, I can find any and all of these matches."

"And you believe that you and Alexander are a match?"

"I do."

"How did you come upon a sample of Alexander's blood?"

She hesitated, choosing her words very carefully. "The Order takes samples from every Pureblood at birth. The Order supports my work—they believe it could be vital in bringing mates together early to procreate if there was a devastation in the Eternal Breed."

"Do you have something to show me?" Nicholas asked. "A certificate? Concrete proof?"

She did, but the document also revealed information she couldn't share with anyone. "The law requires no such proof for a handfasting," she said quickly, "only a willingness—"

"There's no fucking willingness here, princess," Lucian called down, sarcasm dripping like lethal honey from his tone.

Nicholas sighed. "You are correct, Miss Kettler. You have your three weeks."

"Thank you," she said, relieved yet wary. "Where should I put my things?"

"How about back on the sidewalk?" Lucian suggested. "I'll give you a hand."

Without thinking, Bronwyn's gaze shot to the second floor and she said fiercely, "What is your problem, *paven*?"

But this time, there were no jean-clad legs, no boots resting lazily on the banister. This time, the devil himself stood there. Like Nicholas, Lucian Roman was tall, and alarmingly broad in the shoulders, but that's where the similarities ended. The youngest of the Romans was stunningly, terrifyingly good-looking, his jaw-length hair as white as an angel's wings, his almond eyes lethal and lustful, his face hard and chiseled. For Bronwyn, looking at him was like looking at the other side of death, and yet she could look nowhere but.

His gaze roamed over her, from top to bottom, in the most brazen of ways, like a tongue licking an ice-cream cone—like a *paven* who had removed many a *veana*'s purity cloth.

Beside her, Nicholas cleared his throat. "Evans will take you to your room, Miss Kettler."

"Thank you." Bronwyn ripped her gaze from Lucian's, nodded once at Nicholas, then followed Evans. She was nearly to the door when she suddenly stopped, turned back, and addressed Lucian one last time. "And by the way, Mr. Roman, I don't nurse from my business associate Edel, but I do let her wipe my ass from time to time."

Edel snorted from the hallway and a loud chuckle erupted from Nicholas, but Lucian remained impassive as he watched her—although his thick, blond eyebrows rose a good half inch from where they normally dwelled.

With a quick nod in his direction, Bronwyn turned and walked out of the library.

Alexander touched down near the back entrance to his home. Night had succumbed to the stillness and bitter chill of predawn, and every muscle in his body tensed, warned him to get inside and find shelter before the sun showed her merciless face.

The back door opened and without a word to Evans, Alexander carried Sara into the house. She was asleep, a delicious weight in his arms, her dark hair swinging from side to side as he moved. He wanted nothing more than to keep her against him, all day and deep into the night. But that was not possible, today or ever.

He took the back stairs two at a time until he reached the third floor, then stalked down the dark and quiet hallway until he reached his room. *LIGHT. DIM.* The mind command was as swift as the result, and he crossed the large suite and placed Sara on his bed, then covered her gently.

He stepped back. Yes, the woman looked right in his bed, beautiful, enticing.

She sighed in her sleep, turned her head, exposing the white flesh of her neck to his gaze. Saliva pooled in his mouth and his fangs vibrated with a sexual hunger he hadn't felt in quite some time. He could do it. Right now, he could mark her, score her with his fangs—a permanent tattoo that would keep any male fearful for his life away from her. He growled low, pained, the desire to act nearly debilitating. But it wasn't fair to her. She was human. She could never be his female, his true mate, the one who bore his mark.

There was a knock on the door and a firm whisper. "Sir."

With one final glance at Sara, Alexander left the room and went into the hallway. "What is it, Evans?"

"I have Dr. Donohue's room ready if you'd like—"

"No. She's staying here." *For now.*

"Yes, sir."

Evans's almost sheepish gaze dropped and Alexander released a breath. "Is there a problem, Evans?"

"While you were gone, there was a . . . development."

"What kind of development?"

Evans's gaze flickered upward. "You've been handfasted."

Alexander frowned. "What?"

"And she's in the room next to yours."

"What?" Alexander roared, his chest suddenly filling with air, his veins rushing with hot, irritated blood.

"Yes, Brother dear," Lucian called, coming around the corner, his almond eyes locking with Alexander's fierce gaze. "We've been invaded. First the Order and now the *credenti*."

"A Bronwyn Kettler, sir," Evans said quickly. "She comes from the Boston *credenti* with her assistant, and claims you are her true mate."

The madness he'd encountered this day was off the charts. He gestured toward her door. "Send her home."

"Can't do," Lucian said with a wry grin.

Alexander growled. "I don't have time for this bullshit, Luca."

Lucian shrugged. "Nicholas has given her the three weeks."

"Then Nicholas can have her! I've been to see the Order."

Lucian froze, his lip curling. "So you did it, then. Alone. You found the Hollow?"

Alexander turned to Evans and motioned for him to leave.

"I can't believe you went without us, without backup," Lucian accused when the servant was gone.

"I didn't go to them—they *took* me."

"I don't care!" Lucian roared, then shook his head and released a pissed-off breath. "What did the old fuckers want?"

"There's a threat to the *credentis* and to the Eternal Breed. They've been infiltrated by a rogue band of Impures and many *veana* have been taken."

"And? What?" Lucian chuckled bitterly. "They want our help."

"*My* help," Alexander corrected.

"You told them to go fuck themselves, right?"

"Not that simple, Brother."

It took only a moment for Lucian to get the clear picture. "Nicky and I go morpho if you don't do as you're told."

Alexander didn't need to confirm or deny, just lifted his chin. "I will take care of this."

Lucian was shaking his head. "No."

"Don't be stupid, Luca."

"I swear I will lock you up in that cage of yours and bury the key. You're not doing this again. We're brothers, partners. Just because you're the eldest doesn't mean you can make decisions about our future." Lucian arched one pale, severe eyebrow. "We made a pact to remain together, fight together. If we don't have that, we're based on nothing. We walked out of that life together, and we walk back in together."

Alexander hesitated, his jaw tight as a fist. He wanted to be harsh with Lucian, pull rank and refuse to see the reason in the young *paven*'s words. The love for his brothers warred with the pain of seeing them lose their futures.

"Together, *Duro*," Lucian said resolutely, then flashed Alexander a wicked grin. "Besides, I've been itching for a little recon."

Alexander thought of the blood oath the Order had given him. They would leave Nicholas and Lucian alone if Ethan Dare was brought in, and he would have a better chance of finding the Impure with his brothers' help. A low growl settled in the back of his throat. The Order had better come through with their end of the bargain. Because if they didn't, he'd have another battle on his hands, one he was only too willing to start. "Where's Nicholas?"

Lucian grinned, knowing he had convinced the alpha, his pack leader. "On that skinny human's trail."

"In-house or out?"

"Online. Downstairs."

"Good. Let's go."

Lucian flicked his chin in the direction of Alexander's room. "What about the female?"

"She's sleeping in my bed, and I don't want anyone disturbing her."

"I meant the other one," Lucian drawled. "The vampire female? The *veana* who thinks you are her true mate."

"Not my problem." Alexander started toward the stairs. "Let's go. We've got a rogue Impure to find and kill."

18

Sara awoke to the sound of muffled traffic and the scent of Alexander's skin. Disoriented, she lifted her head and glanced around the dimly lit room, a relatively bare space with pale gray walls and a white fireplace. Alexander's room, she was willing to guess. Alexander's bed. Obviously, he'd put her here after she'd fallen asleep last night somewhere over Jersey.

She dropped back onto the bed indulgently and pressed her face into his pillow, mindful of the bruise that still stung slightly. Oh God, she thought, breathing him in. He smelled so good, so indescribably good—like coffee, an earthy scent that was hard to describe but that made her feel warm and thirsty, and desperate to stay in bed. It was utterly impossible to deny her attraction to him, her desire for him now, and she wasn't even going to try. The irony of being caught up in a state of delicious insanity involving vampires, mind travel, and potential danger wasn't lost on her professional acumen. And yet she was willing to overlook it all if she could just feel that thing she'd felt in Montauk one more time. Tucked inside that ancient lighthouse surrounded by an angry sea, she'd felt completely and totally connected to someone.

It had been a long time.

Sensing the lateness of the morning even with the blackened-out windows, she glanced at the clock. It was nearly six thirty and she was on duty in an hour. She slipped out of bed and headed for the attached bathroom, which continued the minimalist style that Alexander seemed to favor. Gleaming white with chrome accents. For a second, she contemplated showering at the hospital, but her curiosity and her ache to remain close to him had her stripping off her clothes and stepping into the white limestone stall. She glanced around for the showerhead, but saw none. She twisted the faucet handles, hoping for an answer, and in less than an instant, hot water rained down on her from above. Startled, she looked up. The water was falling from a hundred tiny holes in the ceiling tiles. It was magnificent. As she washed her hair, she imagined Alexander beside her, engulfing her small frame with his massive one as the water sluiced over their skin. The intensity of desire that ran through her in that moment concerned her. Granted, fantasizing was a normal, natural part of being human, and for Sara not uncharted waters every other month or so, but the continuous, unbalanced need she had for this man, this nonhuman male, seemed excessive, and, frankly, out of the realm of what she considered normal. Maybe she was under some kind of spell. Vampire voodoo.

Grinning at her idiocy, she quickly finished up and left the bathroom. With a towel wrapped around her, she padded into the large walk-in closet attached to his bathroom, looking for a robe or something that would hold her until she could slip on yesterday's clothes again. But what she saw there made her pause, made her nearly drop her towel. Her clothes, every piece, every pair of shoes, was either hung up or folded on one side of the closest. He'd brought all her things here, put them beside his own. That intimacy, the sweet, uneasy promise of that gesture, sent a shiver of fascinated apprehension through her. How long did he expect her to stay? How long did he *want* her to stay?

In his room, his bed . . .

The clock on the wall screamed at her to hurry and she piled her hair on top of her head in a loose knot, covered the bruise on her face with a little bit of makeup, then slipped into a black pencil skirt, white sweater, and a pair of heels before grabbing her purse and heading for the door.

Outside in the hallway a young man was furiously working, installing several sets of rather unusual metallic window coverings to the windows. He didn't look up from his task and acknowledge her so Sara moved on, rounding the corner, hoping to find a staircase nearby. But in her rush, she ran straight into someone. "Oh!" She backed up quickly and apologized. "I'm so sorry. I—"

"It's all right. No permanent damage done."

Sara caught her breath enough to see the black-haired woman she'd nearly knocked down. She was a total stranger, but one of the most beautiful women Sara had ever seen. She looked to be somewhere in her early twenties and was a good five inches shorter than Sara, but her face and figure made up for her height. She had very pale skin, eyes the color of sunlit grass, pretty white scarves wrapped around her neck and both wrists, and a simple black dress that accentuated hips and breasts that would've made Marilyn Monroe jealous.

She smiled at Sara and stuck out her lovely, pale hand. "Bronwyn Kettler."

"Hi." Sara shook the woman's hand and returned her smile. "Sara Donohue."

"You're human?"

The question and its casual delivery made her laugh. "Yes. Which must mean you're not."

"There are days I wish I was. How's that?" The woman's smile deepened, exposing a lovely set of dimples and the tips of two ultrawhite fangs. "Are you going downstairs? I'll walk with you."

"All right," Sara said as they headed for the stairs. "So, do you . . . work here?"

"No. I'm here for a handfast with the eldest Roman."

"Handfast?" Sara repeated. The list of vampire vocabulary was growing at a steady pace. Starting a list might be a good idea, she thought.

"It's a vampire thing," Bronwyn said, shrugging her shoulders, which caused her very real, very perfect breasts to bounce. Sara had never been jealous of another woman's top half, but she really wouldn't mind possessing a rack like that.

"The handfast goes back many, many years," Bronwyn continued as they walked down the stairs. "You'd probably call it dating. Exclusive dating."

The captivated haze Sara had been in for the past two minutes abruptly wilted, and she rewound their conversation in her mind until she got to a point of confusion. She stopped on the last step and cocked her head to one side and said, "Wait a second. The eldest Roman?"

Bronwyn nodded. "Alexander."

Sara's smile, along with every intimate feeling she'd had in the past half hour, faded. "You're dating Alexander? For how long—"

"No, no," Bronwyn corrected quickly. "We've never met. We hadn't a need to. Until now. You see, in our breed, we have true mates—our destined one—and when a *paven* goes through morpho—"

Sara didn't wait for her finish. "You think Alexander is your true mate."

The woman lifted her chin confidently. "I do."

Electric currents of blind jealousy ran through Sara's

body, attacking every muscle, every soft spot of emotion, and her eyes narrowed on the woman she'd only moments ago thought sweet and charming. She'd liked guys before, even felt possessive a time or two. But this, what she was feeling now was altogether different. This had rage behind it, a true fighting spirit, and she wasn't exactly sure what do with the feeling.

Bronwyn's concerned gaze moved over Sara's face. "Are you all right?"

"Yeah," she mumbled. *Come on now. Get your shit together, Donohue.* Sara's gaze caught on the tips of Bronwyn's fangs and she inhaled deeply. She needed to get out of here, get back to reality for a while—*her* reality. Forcing a thin-lipped smile, Sara nodded at the woman. "Excuse me. I'm running late."

The woman smiled. "Okay. It was nice to meet you, Sara."

Right. Very nice. Normally, blurting out sarcasm in her head did wonders for her morale. Not so much today. Seemed she had competition.

Sara left the beautiful vampire on the stairs, walked across the foyer and out the front door into the sunlight.

Three hours later, she was embroiled in the dealings of the hospital: new patients, med schedules, group therapy checks, evals . . . Quite honestly, it was a welcome chaos. Here she knew the language, the rules—she ran the show.

"Gray? Are you listening to me?"

Well, not every part of the show apparently.

"Gray?"

Ignoring her and refusing to cooperate, Gray lay flat on his back inside of Walter Wynn's new high-resolution MRI scanner, while Sara sat on the other side of the glass, doing the job of an MRI tech. Moving in on the territory of other staff members wasn't standard practice in her hospital, but when it came to patients with PTSD and/or memory trauma, most of the staff understood her penchant for taking over jobs that weren't normally hers. Sara had to be on hand to witness every movement, every change, and today was no different. It was the first in a series of scans she was performing on three of her patients over the next seven days. As she recounted their traumatic memories, she was going to record the changes in the amygdala—the area of the brain that processed emotional and fearful experiences.

"I need you to hold your breath for a moment," she said again, this time with undisguised frustration. "Come on, Gray, please."

But not only did Gray continue to breathe normally, he slipped off his headphones and dropped them on his stomach. Cursing, Sara stabbed at the emergency-shutoff button and sank back in her chair. So, he was getting sick of this, of the tests, of the trials and the experiments? Well, so was she. Tough shit.

She reached out and pounded her fist on the console. What were their other options? Suicide? Sitting around staring into space, heavily medicated for the rest of his life? Not going to happen.

For more than three years, Gray had been a docile patient, wanting her to fix him and bring him back from wherever it was he mentally resided, but in the past six months things had changed—he had become sullen and uncooperative, as if he didn't want to get better. As if he'd given up.

She leaned in and pressed the button that released the table, watched as he slid out of the scanner, as he sat up and faced her through the glass. Their eyes locked. He was going to fight her—he was going to resist her attempts to help him.

She picked up the phone, dialed. "Tommy, I need a pickup in MRI. I'm done with him for today. I have Lotera and Mills scheduled for scans later this afternoon; you can bring them together."

When she looked up again, through the glass, Gray was holding the headphones. In under a second, he had them behind his head and in under two, he chucked them right at her. They hit the glass with a bruised thud and dropped to the floor.

Sara stood there, curbing the urge to run into the magnet room and scream at him as though he were an uncontrollable child. He wanted it too—she could see it in his eyes. He wanted her to get angry, to lose control.

He wanted her to fail.

Thankfully, Tommy arrived. He came in to the magnet room and took over. Sara left the console room before them and headed over to the juvenile wing, her nerves frayed. It was part of the job, failures and successes. Couldn't have one without the other—couldn't recognize one without the other, but it was a hard truth to accept.

"Hey, Jerry," Sara said, coming down the hall and pausing outside the door of one of her new patients, Pearl McClean.

The short, stocky male nurse looked up from his charts and smiled. "Doc."

"How's she been?"

"Real quiet night. Took her meds. No drama."

Something Sara always liked to hear. "Any visits?"

"No."

And something she didn't. It was another tough truth, but kids who consistently acted out at home, self-mutilated, lied to their parents and were in and out of treatment tended not to have too many visits. Mom and Dad stayed away for a while, to catch their breath and regain their sanity.

Sara pulled back the door and walked into Pearl's room. She saw the girl right away, lying on her bed, looking up at the ceiling, her straight, pale hair spread around her head like the rays of the sun. At first glance, she appeared peaceful, but as Sara drew near, she noticed that the girl's body was tense.

Sara sat down on a chair next to the bed. "Hey, Pearl."

The girl said nothing, kept her eyes skyward.

"How are you feeling today?"

No response.

Sara glanced down at the girl's chart, checking to see if labs were back and if there had been any communication between Pearl and the nurses during the night. Nothing on the former or the latter, but Sara did see a note regarding the impressive physical improvement of Pearl's cuts.

"I'd like it if we could talk for a few minutes," Sara said, reaching out and touching the girl's shoulder gently. "What do you think about that?"

"Don't. Touch. Me." Pearl yanked her arm away, turned her head, and pinned Sara with a venomous stare.

"No problem." Sara said the words calmly, as though she'd said them a hundred times before. And she had. She gestured toward the girl's legs with her chin. "I understand you're healing nicely."

Pearl's eyes lost all of their fight and she looked very sad. "How do you know that?"

"The nurse who checked you this morning."

Pearl's light brown eyes filled with tears.

"You don't want your cuts to heal?" Sara asked.

"No."

"Why not?"

The girl shook her head, but said nothing.

"Pearl," Sara began, her tone gentle, calm. "Do you want to talk to me? Tell me what happened."

"No."

"I know you must be feeling scared—"

"You don't know shit."

Wow. Okay. Sara shrugged. "I know you're angry."

Pearl turned away, fixed her eyes to the ceiling once again.

Sara continued. "I just want to help you."

"I don't want your help."

Sara sat back, tried a different tack, one based solely on the truth. "Just for the record, I know what it feels like to be alone and scared, yet have to keep up some hard-ass front so you don't look weak." She saw Pearl's fists unclench. "I know how it feels to hurt—and honestly, being hurt by someone you care about is—"

"What is it, Dr. Donohue?" Pearl interrupted, turning to look at Sara again.

Sara shrugged, but her tone was all seriousness. "It's wrong, and it's not your fault."

Something flashed in Pearl's eyes, but Sara didn't stop to analyze what it was. She was getting somewhere, getting through the girl's metal-hard exterior and she needed to stay on the path. "You didn't cause this or ask for it," Sara said evenly. "I know it may feel like that, but—"

The girl's laughter halted Sara's attempt at a dialogue. "You're embarrassing yourself, you know that?"

"Really?" Sara asked. "How am I doing that?"

Grinning, though her eyes remained cheerless, Pearl lowered her voice to a whisper. "These." She reached down, ran her hands up her thighs in an almost blissful sweep. "These are my emancipation."

"Your emancipation from what?"

"Life."

That was the look in her eyes, Sara realized. *Pleasure.* Those cuts on her legs had nothing to do with punishment or releasing pain. They were all about creating pleasure.

"Pearl, did you cut yourself?"

The girl's grin widened. "Not telling."

"If you talk to me," Sara assured her, "tell me who did this to you, I promise I can keep you safe."

"I am safe." Pearl's brows lifted. "But if you push me any more on this, Doctor, I'm not so sure about you."

Sara exhaled heavily, grabbed the file from the side table, and jotted down a few notes. Threats were a common form of mental illness in teens, even on the smallest of scales. Gaining Pearl's trust would take time, as it did with most.

After she left the room, Sara headed back to her office, making a quick stop at the nurse's station to get the number of Pearl's social worker. "Can you get Melanie Abrams on the phone for me?" she asked one of the nurses. "I don't have her direct line at my desk."

"Of course, Doctor."

Sara barely had the time to take in the quiet solitude of her office before the call came through.

"Ms. Abrams on three, Doctor."

"Thank you." She picked up the receiver and punched in line three. "Hey, Mel, it's Sara Donohue over at Walter Wynn. I wanted to see if you might be coming by this afternoon."

But the voice that came through the receiver was not female. "Sara."

No. It was all male: deep and sensual and so comfortingly familiar that her shoulders relaxed down into their proper place for once.

"You left without saying good-bye, woman," he growled.

Sitting back in her chair, Sara couldn't help but smile. "You were gone from the room when I woke up."

"Duty called," Alexander said, his tone regretful. "I wish I had been there with you, beside you. I wish I was there with you now."

Me too.

"But have no fear, there is someone watching over you."

Sara sat up abruptly, her shoulders back up near her ears once again. "What?"

Alexander chuckled. "Just to make sure you're safe in my absence." His voice dropped. "Sara?"

"Yes?"

"I miss you."

Sara closed her eyes and inhaled. She had patients, charts, phone calls to make, but she was pretty sure that if he kept talking like that she was going to forget them all and enjoy the sound of his voice for the next ten minutes.

"So," she began, very consciously egging him on. "What's your next step with this Eternal Order?"

19

It was close to sundown when the brothers descended the stairs that led to the tunnels beneath SoHo. They had spent the day strategizing, attempting to locate Dare's hideout, and mapping out several sections of the city. It was a far cry from the captains-of-industry gig they'd been living for the past seventy years. Building companies and acquiring enough funds to last a hundred lifetimes, they were content, pleased even, to give up the day job and return to the battlefield once again.

Alexander dropped to the bottom step with an exaggerated thud, and breathed in the familiar cold, dusty scent. He itched to turn right and head for his cage. He needed to feed before they went aboveground, and like it or not, he could never get cow's blood down unless he was inside that steel piece of shit.

He scowled. He really was like a fucking dog, wasn't he? Addicted to his abusive metal master.

"It's been a long time since we've shed blood in the

name of war," Nicholas said, coming up beside him and dropping a hand on his shoulder, steering him away from the tunnel leading to his cage.

"Too long," Lucian muttered, moving around both of them to take the lead down the dark passageway.

"I'd hoped we'd find a way to get back on the front lines," Nicholas continued. "Just didn't think it would be in the service of the Order."

"The only ones we serve are ourselves," Alexander said.

Up ahead, Lucian chuckled. "Yeah, you keep telling yourself that."

A rare growl erupted from Nicholas. "Listen, Luca, once we engage in this fight, Alexander is your commander and you will come to heel."

Lucian turned then, started walking backward, one pale eyebrow raised. "I thought this was a democracy, boys."

"I'm not bullshitting you, Little Brother. Disrespect will not be tolerated. And we'll deal with you as we did the last time we went to war."

"What was that, then?" Lucian stopped, his brow furrowed. "First World War? With the Aboriginal trackers? Damn fine and bloody time that was." He turned and began walking down the tunnel again, calling back, "You did wield that spear with perfect accuracy, Nicky, if my ass recalls it correctly."

Shaking his head, Nicholas chuckled softly, then caught site of Alexander, who remained impassive as he stalked past the guards. "Has the hunger returned, *Duro*?" Nicholas asked. "You look ready to spring."

There was hunger there, Alexander thought, taking a quick inventory of his mood, but it was not just for blood—it was a hunger for her, the woman. And a weakness perhaps, as though he didn't feel entirely whole when she wasn't around, when he couldn't hear her voice . . . even across a phone line. "I'm worried about Sara," Alexander said, his tone as tight as the fists at his side. "If something happens . . ."

"You have someone on her?" Nicholas asked.

"Yes."

"Who?"

"Dillon."

Nicholas uttered a grunt of surprise, his breath visible in the frosty air of the tunnels. "How did you make that happen?"

"There was a debt I requested be paid."

"Isn't Dillon working for that human senator from Maine?" Lucian called from up ahead. The vampire had impeccable hearing when he chose to. "Running his security detail?"

"They brought in a temporary replacement," said Alexander, picking up his pace, stalking past another set of guards and down the final passageway. He needed to get there, feel the cool metal weapons in his hands, feed his need to hunt in the only way that was available to him.

"Here we are," Lucian announced, placing his palm

against the keypad and waiting for the identification system to read his print.

There were two loud buzzing sounds and then the metal door slid back and the brothers walked into the ten-by-ten room. Their gazes were quick as they checked each shelf to make sure their weapons stockpile was intact. Guns, knives, swords, bayonets, ammunition—from ancient world to modern world, there was everything and anything needed to extinguish the heartbeat of either human or Impure.

Alexander palmed an ancient Egyptian dagger, a favorite of his, and slipped it into his waistband, then grabbed two Glocks and turned to his brothers, raising an eyebrow. "Pick your poison, *duros,* and let's get to work. We need to find Dare ASAP or the both of you are going to be sunlight intolerant and bugged by the Order for all eternity."

"Nicely put," Nicholas said, loading himself down with ammunition.

"And no fucking pressure at all," Lucian muttered as he slipped a handmade tribal spear into the waistband of his jeans.

Sara rode the elevator to the lobby, wondering what, if anything, would be waiting for her when she stepped out of the metal box. Alexander had said she was being watched, but that was only during daylight hours, right? Did that mean he might show up to take her home? Be in the lobby, holding a bouquet of flowers like guys did at the airport sometimes. *Get a grip, Donohue. Jeez.* Sara laughed to herself and shook her head at her juvenile thoughts. Yeah, flowers and a ride home because they were both in junior high . . . The door to the elevator opened and she and several others walked out into the lobby. First thing she saw was the red blaze of sunset streaming in through the windows and hitting the white tiles on the floor. *Sun isn't down yet, girlfriend.* Even if he'd wanted to, Alexander wasn't going to be waiting for her.

She moved through the crowd and headed for the doors. So where was he, then? Home, chatting it up with the hot little vampire in the room next to his? And if he was, she thought, pushing through the double doors, could she blame him? Beautiful, great personality, same species, and believed they were destined for each other. Throw in the killer breasts and she was really the perfect girl.

The blast of winter air hit her square in the face and she quickly pulled her coat closed at the neck. For one moment, she contemplated not going back to the house in SoHo, making it easy on all of them. After all, she wasn't a drama-loving kind of girl and the thought of engaging in some sort of love triangle just screamed pathetic, desperate chick. But she couldn't go home. It would be stupid and irresponsible, two things she was not. She could get a hotel room—but then again, what protection did that offer? She wasn't a fool. It was either Alexander's way or going to the police, and she'd missed the window on the latter. If she went to the cops now they'd call her a nut job and kick her vampire-loving ass out onto the street.

She walked to the curb, ready to hail a cab, but before her hand made it into the air, a sleek black car pulled up in front of her. She moved away from it, farther down the sidewalk, but kept glancing back to check on its progress. Suddenly, the back door opened and a woman got out. She looked like a lawyer or maybe someone who worked on Wall Street. She was dressed in business clothes, and had shoulder-length auburn hair, nicely curled under at the bottom. Her face was pale and oval shaped, and when she turned her gaze on Sara, her hazel cat eyes narrowed. "Good evening, Dr. Donohue."

Sara had her purse open and pepper spray in her palm in under five seconds. "Do I know you?"

"I'm assisting Alexander Roman."

As the woman walked toward her, Sara was grateful for the heavy street traffic. "Assisting him with what?"

"You."

"You're the one watching me?"

She clipped a nod, then gestured toward the town car. "Please. Get in."

Sara laughed, but the sound held little humor. "Yeah, like that's going to happen."

The woman lifted one manicured eyebrow. "You're not going to give me trouble, are you?"

"I might."

The woman's face remained impassive, but her hazel eyes hardened.

"Listen," Sara began, releasing her NYC-tough-bitch attitude on the woman, "whoever you are—"

"Dillon."

"Okay. Dillon. You're a woman, right?"

"Veana."

Great, another female vampire. "Whatever. How smart would it be for me to get into a car I don't recognize with someone I don't know?"

"You take cabs all the time, don't you? Same thing."

No. Not the same thing at all. Sara put her hands up and shook her head. "Thanks, but no thanks. I'll walk."

The *veana* cursed under her breath. "Alex didn't tell me what a pain in the ass you were."

Alex? How friendly were they? "That's too bad. Could've saved you the trouble of coming here."

Sara turned and started down the street, the icy wind finding its way inside her coat. For several seconds she heard nothing but street noise as she walked, then behind her, near her left earlobe, came the hushed words "Don't be a fool."

She stopped, whirled around, her heart pounding like a mouse with its tail caught in a trap. The female stood in front of her, breathing slow and easy.

How the hell?

Dillon cocked her head to one side and said in a low, deadly voice, "My assignment is to bring you back to the Romans' compound and I always complete my assignments. So if you're thinking of going anywhere else but there tonight, think again."

Fear pulsed in Sara's blood. Calm and dignified, with nary a hair out of place, Dillon didn't look all that big or tough, but Sara knew in her gut that she was as lethal as a gun to the head.

"You and Alexander . . . ?" Sara began, but Dillon knew where she was going and cut her off.

"We are nothing."

"Friends?"

"No."

Sara didn't buy it. "Then why are you doing this?"

"I owe him."

"He save your life in 'Nam?"

"No. Spanish Civil War."

"What?"

Dillon's face hardened. "Let's go, Doctor."

Sara didn't know if the female vampire was lying or telling the truth, but it didn't really matter. Her main objective was getting through any and all potentially dangerous situations so she could care for Gray. If she was gone, Gray's treatment would be put in someone else's hands, and she would never allow that to happen. This *veana* in front of her was on a mission to keep her safe, and apparently the vampire would not be dissuaded from it.

"Fine," Sara said, lifting her chin. "I'm going back to SoHo."

"Wonderful," Dillon muttered, turning around.

"But," Sara called out, "not in that car."

The female vampire stopped, growled, "Fucking New York women," then headed for the black town car.

After repositioning her shoulder bag, Sara turned and resumed her walk down 12th Street toward SoHo. Behind her, the gentle hum of a car's engine reminded her that Dillon followed at a snail's pace.

20

Ethan Dare had a love affair with the mafioso. He thought the ways they did business, carried on relationships, and handed out punishments were perfection personified. And so when he'd hatched the plan to bring down the Eternal Order, he'd adopted many of their traditions, one being their particular way of dealing with a problem employee—or in Ethan's case, a problem recruit: dark restaurant, large table, hidden weapons.

"You have two objectives," Ethan began, his gaze connecting with each of the six recruits at his table. "To find and recruit other Impures. And to impregnate humans, Impures, and, if we're very lucky, Purebloods. My question is: Why isn't the latter happening with greater speed?"

One recruit, Grevon, a short half-breed with black hair and eyes the color of snow downed his scotch and soda before answering, "Pureblood DNA repels our own."

Ethan pinned the little shit with an ice-cold stare. "That's because you're not keeping them in a state of desire for the moments following release."

"You have granted us some power, Commander, but it is nowhere near as strong as yours. At the moment of release we are weakened, and we cannot hold on to the control we had over the *veana*'s mind."

A large male recruit to Ethan's left grunted into his plate of rigatoni. "Speak for yourself, Grevon."

Grevon hissed at the male. "I am, and for several others sitting here." He turned to Ethan and shrugged. "We need more power, Commander. We need you to give it to us if you want this job done with greater speed." The male crossed his arms over his chest. "I suggest you go to the Supreme One and—"

The shot was barely heard over the evening restaurant chatter, and Grevon had the courtesy to drop ever so swiftly headfirst into his veal piccata, so that no one but the five remaining recruits noticed the hit.

It was a thing of beauty.

Ethan smiled at each one of his remaining Impures, reveled in the barely hidden fear that lit their eyes. "I want more Pureblood females and I want them in *swell*. If anyone here is too lazy or too chickenshit to make that happen, I suggest you leave right now."

No one moved, not even a muscle twitch, and Ethan grinned. They were either willing to do whatever he asked of them or not about to stand up and show him their backs. To be honest, Ethan didn't care which it was, he just wanted blind devotion, and with the example before them—a fellow recruit's head lolling in his plate—Ethan was willing to bet he'd have a few Pureblood females in his house by tomorrow night.

Dinner and drinks with the boys was damn good fun.

He was about to slide the gun he held between his legs into his coat pocket when he scented something among the perfume and the tomato and garlic. He was an Impure, true, powerless for most of his life, but when he'd joined with the Supreme One, drank from the *paven*'s ancient vein, ingested the pure and powerful blood, he'd been granted powers beyond his station, and sniffing out the enemy was one of them.

Ethan cocked his head to the side and inhaled deeply. There were *pavens* near, Pureblood, old blood, and if he wasn't mistaken, one of them was morphed and on the hunt.

Hidden in the shadows near the back entrance of Cipriani's Italian Restaurant, the Roman brothers gathered, ready to spring. His hand on the Glock at his lower back, Alexander watched as Dare and several of his recruits sat at a table chatting it up like they were having a tea party.

"This should be an easy kill," Lucian muttered.

Alexander glanced over at his brother. "You sound disappointed."

"I am," Lucian snarled. "I was looking forward to . . . I don't know—this is bullshit."

"What?" Nicholas asked in a harsh whisper. "What is it you want, Luca? An epic battle?"

"Hell, yes!" Lucian hissed.

Nicholas shot Alexander a beleaguered eye roll, then turned back to his younger brother. "I'll engage you in a little blood sport later, all right? Let's just end this Impure jackass, drop him at the feet of the Order, and get our lives back."

Lucian frowned. "Fine."

"On my signal, then, boys." Focusing all of his attention on the room before him, Alexander was about to lower the lights and change the mental frequency of the patrons and staff in the restaurant, when it was suddenly done for him. On alert, he whirled back to his brothers, but even before they shook their heads Alexander knew it hadn't been them. Time slowed and the mélange of scents that hummed in the air ceased to exist. Crouched and ready for whatever was coming his way, Alexander locked eyes with Dare, who seemed to know right where he stood in the shadows.

Beside Alexander, Nicholas spotted something, someone, in Dare's group and let out a feral growl. "How the hell did he—"

"Move in!" Alexander commanded. "And don't touch Dare. He's mine."

In a rush of muscle and movement, the three advanced on the scene, Alexander in the lead, his speed unmatched by his brothers. Time barely existed, and the minds of the patrons were temporarily shut off as Alexander stalked forward, disengaging the safeties on the Glocks in his fists. But before Alexander hit tableside, Ethan Dare pulled his own gun and fired. He hit the eldest Roman in the shoulder with a sharp rip of flesh.

"Fuck. You." Alexander raised the Glocks and fired—one, two, three shots, straight at Dare's heart. But the strange Impure was quick—eyes shut, arms spread-eagle style around his crew, and in a breath, he was gone—Alexander's bullets hitting leather.

"What the hell just happened?" Alexander roared, staring at the now empty table.

"Trainer was with them," Nicholas said, nostrils flaring. "Did you see him?"

Alexander didn't answer. As long as Trainer stayed away from Sara, he didn't give a shit about who the skinny human hung out with. He was more concerned with Ethan Dare's abilities. "Where did they go?"

"*How* did they go?" Nicholas said, his gaze still focused on the chair Tom had been in only moments ago. "Only morphed Purebloods can flash like that. And only outside."

"Dare *is* an Impure, isn't he?" Lucian interrupted, glaring at Alexander like he'd left something out of the battle plan.

"I don't know what he is," Alexander uttered, motioning for them to follow as he headed for the back door of the restaurant, his shoulder leaking blood. "But this job just became a helluva lot more interesting."

"Well, there you have it, Luca," Nicholas said dryly as Alexander dipped into his mind and returned normalcy to the restaurant, staff, and patrons. "Seems as though you'll get your epic battle, after all."

21

Sara had been home all of thirty minutes, and after changing her clothes and running her freezing hands under warm water in the sink in Alexander's room, she headed downstairs to find something to eat. Instead, she found Evans dusting a pretty cherrywood table in the entryway.

"Good evening, Doctor," said the old *paven*, inclining his head. "Is there anything I can do for you?"

Sara's stomach chose that exact moment to alert not only herself, but Evans, of its emptiness, and she laughed at the odd sound. "I am pretty hungry."

"Oh my, yes, of course you are." Evans's expression changed dramatically, from reserved to highly embarrassed. "Please follow me."

He led her through a few rooms that were large and windowless and appeared to be office space before finally going through a set of double doors. Sara took in the enormous well-lit living room they entered, a living room that just screamed MEN LIVE HERE. The walls were painted in a dusty red and gold, and the dark wood floor was draped in contemporary ivory and green hand-knotted wool rugs. At one end of the room, a pool table and a few black leather club chairs were set up. At the other end, a grouping of comfortable leather couches sat facing a massive flat-screen TV positioned a few feet above a beautiful river-rock fireplace. The room was masculine to be sure, but not in an off-putting way.

Evans turned around to face her then, looking a bit sheepish. "This used to be the kitchen, but when the Romans moved in . . . well, there was really no need for it."

Sara understood his meaning at once, and was surprised at herself for not thinking of it sooner. "Sure. Of course." She shrugged. "It's no problem. All I need is a menu for some good Chinese and a phone."

There was a sudden movement behind her, a whoosh of paper, and then a sober female voice that uttered, "No deliveries."

Sara whirled around, saw Dillon seated on a couch, her nose deep within the pages of the *Wall Street Journal*, and sighed. Had she been there the whole time? Sara wondered. Lying down or . . . hidden? And why was she still in the house? "I thought you were gone," Sara said.

"Unfortunately not." Dillon's face remained hidden in the paper.

Sara glanced over her shoulder at Evans, who appeared uncertain about what to do next, or how to deal with his new guest. "No worries," Sara told him. "I'll go pick up something."

"No," Dillon said harshly, flipping a page of her newspaper.

Sara turned back to face the irritating female vampire. "So what do you suggest, Dillon? Starvation?"

She shrugged. "Not my problem."

"What is your problem, then? I mean besides being a huge bitch?"

Unfazed by Sara's anger, Dillon stated evenly, "Bring you here. Keep you here."

Sara took a deep breath and let it out slowly. "I'm hungry. As in, my gas tank's on empty. I need food, and I'm sure as hell not going on your diet, so—"

"I'd be happy to share what I've brought with me."

Both Sara and Dillon turned to see who had spoken. Standing in the doorway, dressed in skinny jeans, a long, pale gray wool sweater, that same white neck scarf, and high-heeled boots, was the vampire perfection known as Bronwyn. Smiling boldly, she entered the room with a black travel bag dangling from one petite, scarf-wrapped wrist.

Evans inclined his head. "Miss Kettler."

The black-haired beauty came to sit on the couch opposite Dillon. Sara watched as she took out what appeared to be a bento box, opened it, and began to assemble a meal.

Confused, Sara stared at her. "You eat food?"

"Certain foods," Bronwyn explained, spooning what looked like a squirrel's diet onto her plate. "In the *credenti*—our community—these basic staples—grains, berries—come from the earth and help us keep clarity and strength of mind, while keeping our bodies pure."

From behind her newspaper, Dillon snorted.

"Not everyone's into that kind of thing," Bronwyn said with no embarrassment, no censure.

Fascinated, Sara came to sit between both the *veanas* on the third couch. She wondered about Alexander. Did he eat like this too? "Is this all you have, or do you still drink . . ."

"Blood?" Bronwyn finished for her.

"Yes."

"Yes, it is blood of the Order, extracted and placed in small vials, then rationed out to the citizens of the *credenti*."

A hum of unease moved through Sara. The Order. That group seemed to have their hands in everything—everyone's lives, everyone's futures.

"We don't drink from each other," Bronwyn continued, taking a bite of some kind of seed bar. "That honor is saved for our true mate."

Unease changed into a perfect storm of irritation and jealousy within Sara. Bronwyn was waiting for her true mate—Alexander—waiting to drink from him, fill her body with his potent red blood.

Sara stared at the beautiful vampire. The idea of

taking another's blood into her mouth, swallowing the metallic liquid and wanting more should've made her nauseous to say the least, but it didn't. Not with the picture she had of Alexander in her mind—his naked chest, massive shoulders, and long, thick, waiting neck.

She glanced over at Dillon, who remained headfirst in her paper. "Are nuts and berries what's for dinner at your house?"

"Fuck no."

"Why not?"

Dillon ignored her, but Bronwyn quickly offered an answer. "There are some who don't agree with this way of life and its benefits. Some who think our breed should live on blood alone."

"What happens to them?" Sara asked.

"They decide to leave the *credenti.*" Bronwyn chewed her food, but didn't seem to enjoy it much. "They walk out and choose another life."

Sara wondered if it was really as simple as all that. She eyed Dillon again, who remained still and silent behind her paper. "You walked, Dillon?"

"No, human. I ran."

Bronwyn shrugged as though this were no big deal. "Like I said, the lifestyle doesn't suit everyone."

"No," Dillon growled, thrusting down her paper and eyeing the vampire across from her. "The prison time doesn't suit everyone."

A muscle in Bronwyn's cheek twitched, but she kept

her cool. "For some, it can feel that way. For others, it's a wonderful, happy, complete existence."

Studying human behavior had always been a passion for Sara, but this—studying vampire behavior and vampire cultural differences—was thrilling, to say the least. She sat forward, looking from one *veana* to the other. "So the ones who leave the *credenti*, can they exist among humans and not be detected?"

Bronwyn nodded. "For a while, if they're discreet in their appetite."

"How long is 'a while'?"

"When morpho hits for a *paven* and meta occurs for a *veana*, one is forever changed, and living among humans becomes impossible."

Sara sat forward in her chair. "Why?"

"A *veana* goes through meta at fifty years, far earlier than a *paven* goes through morpho, and though she can still remain in sunlight, the urge to find her true mate and grow large with swell is intense. It's wise for her to remove herself from human male company and return to the safety of her *credenti*. For a *paven*," she continued, "sunlight becomes the enemy of the body and like the *veana*, the need to find his true mate becomes impossible to deny. He can become rather like a hunter in his quest to find his *veana*."

Morpho was what Alexander had been through at her door, Sara mused. That's what she'd saved him from, the burns and the pain. So if one followed the other, that would mean he was on the hunt for his true mate, or soon would be. She looked at Bronwyn. "Are you, or members of the breed, tempted by human blood?"

Holding a plate of seeds and brown plantlike cakes out toward Sara, Bronwyn said, "We don't crave human blood, only the blood of other vampires."

Her eyes trained on Bronwyn, Dillon snorted again.

Sara declined the plate with thanks. "So you learn to suppress yourself and the need for blood until your true mate comes along."

Bronwyn nodded. "Exactly."

"What if you can't?" Sara asked.

"There are consequences to every choice, aren't there?" Bronwyn's gaze suddenly shifted over to Dillon, whose jaw looked so tightly clenched Sara worried that she'd crack a tooth, or a fang.

Dillon stood then, said caustically, "I think we're done talking about this."

"Why's that?" Sara asked innocently.

Dillon glared down at her. "Thought you were hungry, human."

Sara's brow lifted. "You gonna make me something, vampire?"

It was over in a split second, but Sara could've sworn she'd seen Dillon smile. "If you like your steak tartare, yeah," she said dryly. "If not, I'd better go out and get you something before the boss gets back."

Bronwyn interjected, "I forgot to ask before, but

why are you here, Dillon? I'd heard you were helping guard a human politician or something."

"I took a short break to help out Alexander, protect his lady of the moment here." She nodded toward Sara.

Bronwyn stopped eating her plant cake and looked over at Sara, this time like a bird inspecting a juicy little insect. As a slow dawn of understanding came across her face, a low, feral growl emanated from the back of her throat. She said nothing, but her eyes changed from their benign and beautiful pale green to a raging sea of emerald.

Truly afraid, Sara sat back in her chair. Coming to stand beside her, Dillon chuckled humorlessly. "Did I say something I shouldn't have?" she asked, her brow lifted as she looked at Bronwyn. "Remember, Miss Kettler, we're all responsible for our choices."

Before Bronwyn could say a word in response, the doors to the living room burst open and a chorus of loud male voices entered. All three females turned to see Alexander, Nicholas, and Lucian stalk in and head straight for the leather club chairs, Alexander leaning on Nicholas for support.

"Get blood on my pool table, *Duro*," Lucian snarled playfully at Alexander, "and I'll take a shot at that other shoulder of yours."

"Blood should be the least of your worries in regards to that table," Alexander returned dryly as a worried and anxious Evans fussed around him.

Nicholas chuckled, dropped Alexander onto one of the chairs. "True enough. If I had a pint for every time you scratched and pocketed the eight, I'd be a satiated *paven*."

"Yes, Luca—you need to learn to control your *balls*," Alexander declared, causing all three brothers to break into laughter.

"What happened?" Sara asked, running over to them, Dillon behind her.

Alexander sat in one of the club chairs, his shirt off, a thick towel pressed against one massive shoulder. For Sara, it was impossible not to stare at the impressive cords of muscle that stretched taut against his smooth skin. Never in her life had she seen such perfect masculine beauty. He captured her gaze then and his eyes were soft with pleasure and his full mouth curved into a smile. Sara's heart fluttered in her chest and she itched to run at him and jump in his lap.

"We went in ready to play and win an easy game," Nicholas was saying. "But the rules have changed."

"Who did this?" Dillon demanded. "Ethan Dare?"

Behind Sara, a gasp sounded. *Bronwyn.* Sara tore her gaze from Alexander and raised a brow at Dillon. "Who's Ethan Dare?"

The *veana*'s eyes narrowed. "A piece-of-shit vampire with a cause."

"An enemy of the species," Bronwyn added, coming to stand beside Dillon, her tone thick with unmasked revulsion. "An Impure who wants to destroy the Eternal Breed, turn it from purity to poison."

"A little late for that," Lucian muttered under his breath, unloading his weapons and tossing them on the pool table.

Ignoring his brother, Nicholas turned to Sara and said, "Your skinny attacker was with him."

Shock and fear rippled through Sara. "You saw Tom? What was he doing there?"

"We weren't sure at first, but it looks like he's become a recruit for Dare."

"That doesn't make any sense," Sara argued. "How could that happen?"

Nicholas shrugged. "Not sure. But he is with Dare and"—he ventured a worried glance at Alexander, then returned to Sara—"he's no longer fully human."

Sara's eyes shifted to Alexander. "Talk to me."

"There is vampire blood in him," Alexander said softly. "*And* there is vengeance. We scented it. Which means you are in far more danger than I thought. Either Dillon or myself will be with you 24-7."

Sara was too shocked to immediately protest, but she knew there would be a discussion later. She wasn't about to be controlled by Alexander or by the psychotic actions of her ex-patient.

"Oh, shit," Nicholas muttered, nodding at Alexander's shoulder. "It's bleeding out again."

Following his line of vision, Sara gasped. "Oh my

God!" The towel that Evans now held to Alexander's wound looked like an overturned can of red paint, fingers of blood spreading in every direction.

Alexander glanced down, yanked off the towel. "More towels, Evans."

"Yes, sir. Right away." The old servant was off like a shot.

Sara stared at the bullet wound carved into Alexander's powerfully muscled shoulder, and the blood, a good deal of it leaking from the hole. She'd seen plenty of blood in her time, worked on the brains of cadavers in med school, and yet seeing Alexander with a hole in his body made her sway on her feet.

"Hey there," Alexander said to her gently, "don't go soft now."

"It looks bad."

"It's nothing. Human inflicted. The bullet's already been removed and the wound will fade in a few hours."

"No. It will fade now," said the resolute feminine voice behind Sara. There was a whisper of fabric and Bronwyn moved past her to Alexander's side.

"Stop!" Sara blurted out, following the *veana*, grabbing her by the wrist. "Don't touch him." She couldn't help herself, the strange urge to protect him guiding her actions.

"Easy, Doctor," Nicholas said, coming to stand between her and Bronwyn, forcing Sara to release the *veana*'s wrist. "It's a Pureblood *veana*'s pleasure and her gift to heal a *paven* or *veana* if she can."

Bullshit, Sara thought. Not if the *paven* was *her paven*. Sara looked at Alexander, waited for him to respond, to tell Bronwyn to back the hell off. But he didn't. He nodded.

Ready to spring, ready to punch the wall, Sara watched the beautiful vampire female inhale deeply through her nose, then part her perfect lips and blow on the ravaged and bloody skin of Alexander's shoulder. Shivering, Alexander closed his eyes and let his head drop back. Bronwyn repeated the act several times until Alexander released a sigh of satisfaction, and before Sara's eyes, the hole in his skin began to close.

The jealousy, the hatred that rushed through Sara in that moment, reminded her of the early days of junior high and a boy she'd loved who had only noticed her when she was with her incredibly hot best friend, Penny Mathews, or when he needed help on his biology homework. Watching Bronwyn heal Alexander, Sara felt odd, competitive, unsure if she could stop herself from ripping the *veana*'s arm off if given the chance.

When the hole was completely closed, Bronwyn stepped back and Alexander opened his eyes and looked up at her, nodded. "Thank you."

She smiled, an irresistible smile. "Anytime."

Jaw clenched, Sara glanced over at Dillon. The vampire was watching her, a curious expression on her face. Sara wanted to shake her, yell at her, *You're a* veana *too! Why the hell couldn't you be the one to fix him?*

But this wasn't about Dillon. This was about Sara and all that she lacked and being no match for something with fangs. So, trying not to appear as though her tail hovered between her legs, she lifted her chin and announced to the room, "It's sleep time for the human. Night, everybody." Calmly, coolly, and without looking at either Bronwyn or Alexander, she walked out of the room.

22

Alexander stood outside Sara's bedroom door—the bedroom she'd moved all of her things into sometime after leaving the living room an hour ago.

The bedroom that was an entire floor away from his.

Pressing his head against the wood, he flared his nostrils and inhaled, splitting her scent into physical and emotional fragments. His mouth pulled into a frown. She was still awake, yes, but she was pissed off, distracted, turned on, jealous, and . . . very worried.

He lifted his hand to the wood and knocked, the heady anticipation of seeing her running wild through his veins. Christ. Why was he so taken with this woman, so driven to protect her and see her happy? What did he even know about her besides the story of that horrific accident that would've broken anyone else but had only made her stronger, more determined, living to heal the brother she loved before she even thought about healing herself? What did he know about her besides the fact that she was the kind of human who had helped drag a vampire animal inside her home and out of the sun when she could've easily kicked him aside?

Perhaps that was knowing enough.

He heard her footfalls coming toward him, scented her unease, and when she finally opened the door, he was prepared to give her the food he'd brought, ask if she needed anything else, and leave her to sleep. But then he saw her: barefoot, her dark hair, thick and soft, falling around her beautiful face, and wearing a white silk bathrobe that caressed her luscious frame as his own hands would if given the chance. She looked like a goddamn angel, and he wanted nothing more than to bury his head between her breasts and feel her wings close around him.

"It's late." She stood in the doorway, her blueberry eyes weary as she barred him entrance.

He stared at her, his covetous gaze unwavering. "Why aren't you in bed, then?"

"Who says I wasn't?" she returned softly.

"Are you having trouble sleeping?"

"A little."

His voice dropped to a whisper. "It's probably because you moved out of my room."

Her eyes flashed with sudden heat. "I never moved *into* your room."

He shrugged. "Technicality."

She paused for a moment, her gaze sweeping over him, resting on the large brown bag in his hand. "What do you have there?"

"Dinner." He raised his brows suggestively. "Best Chinese in the city."

"How would you know that?"

"What do you mean?"

"I heard about your eating habits, the lack of solid food."

"Dillon talks too damn much," he grumbled.

"It wasn't Dillon," she told him, her eyes revealing the sadness and frustration she wouldn't say aloud.

Alexander leaned against the doorjamb, hovering just inches from her, and inhaled deeply. "Let me in, Sara."

Sara stared at him, her insides melting, not at the words he'd uttered, but at the reverent, vulnerable, teasingly pained way he'd uttered them. Perhaps both of them wished they could just walk away from the imaginary string that connected them, that demanded they remain close and pretend they were unaffected by each other, but that seemed an impossibility. Sara pushed away from the door and allowed him to enter. It seemed that no matter who was in the house, or what they claimed to be, she would still open her door and her heart to Alexander—just as she knew that he would not stop caring for her, protecting her or pursuing her.

She watched him as he crossed the room, carrying a small table under one arm as though it weighed less than a feather. He was so beautiful. The way he moved, those long, terrifying yet graceful strides, made the muscles around her heart contract.

"What's all this?" she asked as he placed the table by the window, pulled two chairs to meet it, then began drawing out linens and silverware and a wineglass from the larger bag he had slung over his shoulder.

"You didn't think I'd have you dining on the floor, did you?"

Her gaze moved with him, reveled in the peculiar sight of him—this branded, skull-shaved, six-foot-three linebacker of a vampire—fluffing out a snow-white tablecloth and waiting patiently for it to land on the glass tabletop. "Not the floor, but the bed would've been fine. I'm all good with the room service."

He turned and flashed a predatory half smile. "Eating in bed shouldn't involve food, woman."

A searing wave of desire moved through Sara and her gaze ran the length of him, from black boots to black thermal, every inch of him blazing hard lines and thick muscle. It was juvenile, but she hated that another female had even gotten close to him tonight, much less healed him, and she knew that when this thing between them finally went south her feelings of possessiveness were going to cost her big-time. "How's your shoulder?"

"Fine." He continued to set the table.

"I'm kind of surprised Dillon didn't rush in to help you—being your friend and all."

"Dillon enjoys seeing me in pain."

Sara had a feeling Dillon liked to see everyone in

pain—physically and emotionally. "Well, it was a good thing Bronwyn was there."

"Yes, she was very helpful."

Sara frowned, and a muscle twitched near Alexander's mouth as he placed a red cloth napkin across her stark white plate. "Your jealousy has a scent, you know."

"What are you talking about?"

He glanced up at her. "It's exquisitely strong."

"Is it now?" she tossed back. "Does it smell like kung pao chicken?"

He laughed—a deep, rich sound that played about Sara's skin like a lover's kiss.

"Listen," she said with a frustrated sigh, walking over to the window. He was so near she could scent the warm blood spice of his skin. How, she wasn't exactly sure, but her mouth ached, watered . . . "I'm not going to be that girl."

"What girl is that?" he interrupted casually, following her every movement with his dark cherry gaze.

"Going after some other woman's man. Acting like a jealous asshole. That's not my style."

Again, his mouth twitched with humor. "What is your style, Sara?"

She shrugged. "I don't know; for starters, maybe going after someone who's unattached . . ."

He nodded. "Very wise."

". . . someone with a good soul, a good heart."

"Well," he said, reaching for her hand, drawing her to him. "That won't do, as I believe I have neither."

A flush of heat moved up Sara's neck, sent her pulse racing as he pulled her closer, crushing her against his hard chest. His touch was electric; every time, a shock of sweet electricity went straight to her nerve endings and all she wanted to do was yank off her robe and feel his hands on her skin. But she attempted to remain sane. "My point is," she uttered, gazing up at him, at his striking, fearsome face, "the whole true-mate thing—it seems inborn and unbreakable, and deeply a part of your culture. And, well"—she lifted one yielding brow—"she's lovely."

Alexander cupped her chin and forced her eyes to his. "Listen to me, Sara, for this is truth. Bronwyn is not for me."

Between her legs, a muscle long forgotten began to tremble, to clench. "She thinks she—"

"No." His eyes were like two garnets, blazing with heat.

She shook her head. "It's really none of my business."

"Sara." He brushed his thumb over her lower lip and she felt his cock stir hard and thick against her belly. "Please"—his voice was low and pained—"before I press you back against this window and take the meal that *I* desire . . . sit now. Eat."

His words, a delicious threat, made Sara's heart pound, and for a moment she didn't move. She was starving, yes, but not for the food on the table. She wanted to remain where she was, protected and safe, the hard muscled planes of his chest pressed against her breasts and the strange and delicious, spicy blood scent of him filling her nostrils.

And she wanted him to take from her, whatever it was that would satiate his hunger . . .

"Come," he uttered, husky and slow as he broke their connection and led her over to the table, releasing her into a chair. He took the one opposite and began opening containers of food and piling her plate three inches thick as though she were a lumberjack who hadn't eaten in days.

Sara watched him, waiting for his eyes to meet hers and give her some clue as to how he was feeling. Was it the same as she was? Nervous and vulnerable, yet desperate to know how his naked skin would feel against hers.

But though his jaw pulsed and clenched, he remained focused on the task of getting her fed. He poured some wine, then grabbed a pair of chopsticks and ripped off the paper with a little too much force. His thick knuckles were white as his hands gripped the wooden chopsticks just as they'd gripped her waist only moments before, and with one crack, a lone chopstick jumped from his grasp and went flying across the room, hitting the wall with a dull click.

"Fucking human utensils . . ." Alexander muttered before pitching the other wooden stick after it.

Sara bit her lip, trying to hold back laughter. "Uh, Alexander?"

He cursed again, his eyes narrowed on the wall. "What?"

"If you don't mind, I think I'll just use a fork."

His gaze lifted then and she saw the beginnings of mirth in his eyes. She couldn't help herself, she laughed, and in moments the ire in his expression died and he joined her, chuckling low and easy.

Fork in hand, Sara dug into the mound of food. After the first bite, she nodded enthusiastically. "This is good, very good. Spicy."

"You like heat on your tongue, do you?"

"It can be intense sometimes," she returned playfully, "but yes, I do. What about you? Like your blood spicy?"

His gaze moved over her face, then dropped to her neck. "I think I would enjoy it very much."

Sara's body responded instantly, heat and pressure building between her thighs. She crossed her legs, but that only made the sensation worse. She wondered what the night would bring if she could barely contain her desire through dinner. She forced a bit of chicken down her dry throat, then said, "Bronwyn said that your kind doesn't crave human blood."

Alexander sat back in his chair, crossed his arms over his splendid chest. "Our kind craves every kind of blood."

Sara frowned. "Then why would she say . . ."

"In the *credenti*, the Eternal Breed is expected to resist what is not pure."

"And human blood is—"

"Unclean, impure, powerless."

"Wow. I suddenly feel the need to shower."

Alexander laughed, an enchanting rumble of thunder that moved seductively down her neck and back. She shivered.

"What about you?" she asked, watching his expression carefully. "Do you think human blood is . . . dirty?"

"No, but then again, I like all things dirty."

She laughed softly. "Have you ever had human blood?"

"I left the *credenti* a hundred years ago. To survive, I took food wherever and whenever I could get it."

"What about now?"

"I believe I am more discriminating now."

"So does that mean you haven't drunk blood from a human lately?"

He arched one dark eyebrow. "What's lately?"

She rolled her eyes, said impatiently, "Alexander."

Grinning, he nodded toward her plate. "So that kung pao's pretty good, eh?"

She cocked her head, playing along. "Best I've ever had. Sure you don't want a bite?"

"Depends."

"On?"

"What surface I get to eat it off of."

Cheeky bastard. She eyed him. "Would you take blood from me? If I offered it?"

His eyes darkened, the brands on his cheeks too. "No."

Her heart seized with his vehement tone. "Why not?"

He shook his head. "It's not a good idea."

"Because of my unclean blood?"

"No. Hell, no. I don't believe in any of that horse-shit."

"Then why? Are you afraid it would turn me?"

He gave no answer, but his gaze dropped to her neck.

Her meal completely forgotten, Sara pressed him for answers she wasn't sure she desperately needed to have. "Would you be afraid to turn me into what you are?"

He shook his head. "Not possible."

"But you said Tom was—"

He cut her off. "That's different. He's not a vampire. A human can never become a vampire. Vampires are born, not made. However, if a human drinks the blood of a vampire they can change into an *Imiti*."

"What's that?" Sara asked.

"Something that resembles a vampire—something that has lost all of its humanity—something corrupt. Not something to be loved."

A slow, unsettling reality came over Sara in that moment. The desire, the need, the pull—it was all there between them, unstoppable and undeniable. And yet it meant nothing more than an acknowledged understanding. Desire, yes. Love and a future together, no. She put down her fork. "So this . . . you and me . . ."

His gaze held hers. "Impossible."

Her appetite died right there and her body went cold and numb. The impossibility of her and him was barely a shock and yet she felt bereft at hearing him concede to it. Angry as well. She'd let herself think there might be a way, a place for them to exist, to know each other better between two worlds. She pushed away from the table, stood and went over to the door.

Alexander watched her. "What are you doing?"

"Kicking you out."

His eyes softened. "Sara . . ."

She shook her head, hand on the doorknob. "No, there's not going to be any of that. I heard what you said, and I know what you meant by it, so let's just call it a day. I have enough impossibilities in my life right now. I don't need another one."

"Sara, come back to the table."

"I won't deny my attraction to you, Alexander. You know it. I know it. And sitting around here flirting and one-upping each other with witty sexual innuendo is fun and all, but it's going to become real painful real soon."

Sara never saw him move. It was like sensing wind before the gust hit, and in the space of a mere breath, he was standing before her, his eyes feral in their unquenched need. "It's already pretty fucking painful."

His arm went around her waist and he gathered her

close, his head lowering, his mouth finding hers in a kiss that was neither sweet nor soft. It was hard and urgent and hungry—just as he was, and Sara felt unable to resist him or her own curiosity, her own desperation to taste his mouth, his skin. She wrapped her arms around his neck, her fingers gripping his hard, nearly shaved skull.

"You are mine," he uttered, thrusting his tongue into her mouth, possessing her, lapping at her teeth, groaning as he found the wet heat inside. "An impossible future," he uttered, pulling back just a breath. "But now—right now—I cannot deny what my unbeating heart desires."

With his free hand, Alexander untied the knot of silk at her waist and dragged the robe from her shoulders and hips. "Hot skin," he growled as the white silk landed in a pool around her feet. "Beautiful Sara."

The cool air hitting her naked flesh warred with the hot touch of the vampire who held her so close. Yes, she could pretend as well as he could. She was his. For now she was his.

Alexander ground his erection against her belly and raked his fangs across her bottom lip. Yes, that was what she wanted. *Draw blood. Taste.*

The muscles between her thighs quivered at the thought, of the image in her mind—her blood on his tongue—and she reached down, gripped the edges of his shirt, and yanked the fabric over his head. The black thermal flew to the bed just as Sara's gaze landed on Alexander's chest. Wide shoulders and thick biceps gave way to yards of lean skin over waves of muscle. Her hands, her touch, began at his throat and drifted lazily downward before sneaking between their bodies. A low, fearsome growl erupted from Alexander's throat as Sara's hand closed around the heavy cock in his pants. *Mine,* she thought, feeling the pulse of his shaft against her palm. *Mine. For now . . .*

She squeezed him, and with her free hand fumbled with the zipper of his pants. Alexander sucked air between his teeth, pulled back, and stared down at her. "Careful now, woman." His eyes blazed with lust and his fangs elongated before her eyes. "Release me or blood will be spilled."

A warning.

He wanted to bite her.

Sara's fist clenched tighter around his shaft, showing him how badly her cunt wanted to do the same.

"A dangerous game you play," he hissed, his eyes turning black cherry. He gathered her in his arms and carried her to the bed, sat her down on the achingly soft bedspread. He lowered to his knees before her, his even gaze roaming her naked flesh, the trimmed curls between her thighs that glistened with moisture, her flat stomach rising and falling with each heavy, desperate breath, and her sensitive, distended nipples that ached to be suckled.

His fangs quivered. "I have a need to torture myself, can't breathe without torturing myself."

Her cunt ached, clenched with a need to be touched, to be filled. "This is torture? Touching me? Kissing me?"

He leaned toward her, his large hands encircling her waist, his mouth closing in on her left breast. "Sweet, painful, exquisite torture." He latched on to one ridged nipple and suckled deep.

Sara arched her back, giving herself to him as a mother to her child, feeling the tips of his fangs scrape enticingly against the dusky circle surrounding her nipple. Wetness dripped from her core to her thighs and her breathing turned ragged and strained as the early pulls of orgasm hummed within her.

Alexander left one breast for another and fed deeply, his tongue flicking over the aching bud until Sara was panting, her brow glistening with sweat. "Please . . ." she moaned. "I need you . . . Please, Alexander."

"You never have to beg, Sara." Alexander grabbed her ass, pulled her to the edge of the mattress and whispered, "Open for me."

Splaying her thighs, Sara glanced down, her gaze foggy, dreamlike. She saw Alexander's head poised before the entrance to her body and she saw his cock, jutting out from the confines of his pants. She licked her lips, wondering what he tasted like, wondering if she would ever get the chance to find out.

"Open yourself wider," he uttered, his hands gripping her inner thighs now. "I want to see all of you . . . yes, every pink, swollen inch."

"What are you doing?" She knew. Yes, she knew—hell, her body knew. She just wanted to hear him say it.

Alexander traced one long finger down her center, making her hips jerk. "Feeding from you in the only way I can."

As he said the words, clear fluid leaked from Sara's cunt and she moaned. Alexander saw it too. He lowered his head and lapped at the sweet moisture, groaned as it traveled down his throat. "Oh, sweet love. So hot, so wet. Your taste . . . It will haunt my days, stretch my cock at night."

"Alexander, please . . ."

"Yes," he whispered, penetrating her with two thick fingers, "ending your torment will be my greatest pleasure." His dark head disappeared between her thighs, and he licked at her flesh, flicked his tongue over her clitoris, grazed her swollen lips with his fangs. Just as he'd suckled at her breasts, Alexander milked her clit, gently and rhythmically. He slipped a third finger inside her and went deep, curving his fingers to hit the sweet, hidden spot of pleasure.

"Oh God. Alexander . . ." Sara gasped, bracing her hands on the bed, and she thrust her hips up, forward, pressing herself tighter against his mouth. As he played her body, Sara's mind cleared of all thoughts, leaving only sensitized, electrified skin and muscle.

Her legs began to shake, her thighs too, and she felt tears well at the corners of her eyes. He made her feel this way, only him, for however long it lasted, and she would take this memory with her into every night she was without him.

Heat and electricity surged within her and she bucked against his mouth, everything gone, nothing remembered—the only thing that focused her was climax. Her thrusts became wild, unchecked, and she gripped his head as he flicked her clit over and over with his hot tongue. And then she gasped, stiffened, the walls of her core clenching around his fingers, bathing his fingers as rocketing pleasure coursed through her.

"Yes . . . oh God, yes," she cried out, riding the waves, riding his mouth, each electric current more intense than the last until finally the world slowed and stopped spinning, and her brain was cleared of the fog of passion and everything returned to the way it had been before.

They gripped each other at the same time, holding on tight as sex scented the room, as Sara caught her breath. She wanted him inside of her, but she didn't want to let go of him either. She opened her eyes and saw the curve of his neck and the shoulder that only hours ago had been ripped into by a bullet. She stared at his skin, blinking to clear the remaining fog in her head as she noticed that the wound had opened again, just a tiny sliver. And it was leaking blood. She licked her lips, ran her fingers over the healed section of his injury.

He hissed.

"I wish I could've done this for you," she said softly. "Healed you."

"It was nothing."

"It was everything."

His hands went to her waist and he eased her back from him. The absence of his skin gave her a cold, lonely feeling that she despised, but the sweet sincerity in his merlot gaze cut her heart deep. "Please understand my meaning. Her power was nothing to me—meant nothing to me. You are the one I want."

She believed him and knew that their impossibility plagued his heart as much as it did hers. But she couldn't help herself, she wanted to give him something. She leaned down and kissed his wound.

Alexander froze, his eyes growing wider as he seemed to feel something. "What? What the hell was that?" He cursed, jerked away from her as though she'd burned him.

Sara's heart started to pound, and she shook her head. "What's wrong?" She'd never seen him look so panicked, not even in the *credenti* standing before his family. "What did I do?"

He turned his head, stared at the wound on his shoulder. "It opened—how is that possible?"

Sara fought for an answer as she wondered why this seemed so important to him. "Maybe when we were together, when you were—"

"No! Nothing should be able to open that wound

after a *veana* has healed it." His eyes flew to her face. "Did you get anything on your mouth?"

"What?"

"Blood?" he nearly shouted. "My blood—on your mouth? Did you ingest it?"

She shook her head, confused, troubled. "No. I don't know. I don't think so."

"Be sure. What do you taste?"

"Nothing."

The relief that spread over his face, the way his shoulders dropped with eased tension scared her, perhaps even hurt her a little. It was clear that he wanted no part of himself inside her . . .

He stood, grabbed for his shirt. "I have to go."

"Why?" Sara asked him, then demanded, "Where?" Just moments ago, he'd given her the most perfect pleasure of her life, while taking nothing for himself. She didn't understand that, didn't understand him. She knew he was in need of release—for God's sake, his cock was still stiff in his pants.

He pulled the thermal over his head. "I have business with the Order, then training."

"Alexander—"

He stalked over to the door, looking like something a linebacker would fear, but Sara knew . . . she knew him, she knew the heart he swore he didn't possess. His hand on the doorknob, he paused and muttered, "Shit." His voice dropped, went as gentle as he could manage. "I apologize for my harshness, I—"

"It's okay," she said, though she wasn't entirely sure she meant it. After all, he wanted to run from her, escape the desire that rushed through him like a tidal wave, and yet it seemed he couldn't stop himself from coming back for more.

"If I've finished before the sun is up, before you must leave for work, I will return—"

Neither could she. "Okay."

"—to your bed."

"Yes." How could she ever refuse him? "Be careful."

"Good night, Sara."

When he was gone, the room felt cold and empty, and Sara slipped on her robe again and went over to the window. Black sky and city lights. She doubted she would sleep tonight as her fatigue had all but disappeared.

Turning away from the window, she sat down at the table and stared at her plate of uneaten Chinese food. For a moment, she toyed with the idea of eating, but stopped herself. She would have no interference. Wrong or right, sick or sane, Sara wanted nothing to take away the little bit of Alexander that was inside of her—nothing to quell the hint of sweet metallic that hovered on the tip of her tongue.

Blood.

His blood.

23

Alexander returned to the battleground he and his brothers had once fought on and stood at the mouth of the cave that Sara had slept near and waited for the Order to pull his ass into their sandy little world again. He wasn't sure if this was how it worked—if the commanding ten would see him without an invitation this time, but it was worth a shot. The mission they'd sent him on had a design flaw and he had to know if those bastards had been aware of it or not—if they'd sent him in cocky and blind. And why.

He closed his eyes, breathed deep.

I'm ready, fuckers.

But when he raised his arms, nothing happened. He remained grounded, the frigid wind pulsing around his body. Behind him, a trio of birds took off and flew over his head, squawking, mocking him.

Goddammit, he wanted to be back in bed with Sara, his arm around her waist, pulling her impossibly closer against him until they fit, locked.

His cock twitched, his shoulder warmed—the open wound she'd touched her lips to an hour ago, now closed again. Another thing unexplained.

He shut his eyes once again and tried to focus. *Come on, you bastards. I know you can feel me.* He waited, let the moments tick by, but nothing happened. They were playing with him, he just knew—they loved playing with him.

Unable to stand still any longer, he walked to the edge of the small cliff and looked out over the snow-covered valley. He cursed the ruling ten. A hundred years of existing in a world without them and now he was practically begging to go before them.

Full circle had never tasted so goddamn bitt—

His thoughts died in his mind and as he felt himself being yanked from the mountainside, he grinned with satisfaction. They'd felt him.

The flash was quick. He was pitched about in darkness for a couple of seconds, then anchored to the ground.

It took him a moment or two to get his bearings, get his mind solid, but once he did, he crouched down into a fighting stance, his hands up, his eyes working to take in everything at once. But it was not as he remembered. No sand, no ruling ten sitting behind a table, their eyes trained on him. He was in his old *credenti*, in Montauk. And it was summer.

What the hell?

At first he wondered just what game was being

pulled on him—was he being cast back in time or something equally irritating—but then he realized that the Order might, in fact, be here. Several times a year, the Order would travel, visiting *credentis*, lecturing and teaching on the proper ways for a Pureblood to live, eat, mate. The Triba, it was called. And to startle a community, demonstrate their oh so great power, the Order would abruptly change the season, usually to the opposite of what it was—fall to spring, winter to summer.

Alexander turned and started toward the field that only a day ago had been ankle deep with snow. Now, beneath trees heavy with leaves and air scented with the nearby beach, it was a picturesque stretch of red and purple flowers. As Alexander walked, he saw Impures working in the field, weeding, picking the delicate blooms and putting them in baskets. They glanced up as he passed, then looked away, but their Pureblood neighbors, who sat in groups of ten or so under the shade of the many thick-leafed trees bracketing the field, completely ignored his approach. Each Pureblood was listening to a member of the Order. All but one, anyway. Alexander spotted his little sister, Evaline, sitting with her mother and Theydon under a willow tree. All three were cross-legged, their backs pole straight as they listened to the white-haired female member of the Order. Evaline gave him a small smile, but was quickly reprimanded by her father with a swift yank of her chin back to face the Order.

Alexander's lip curled. He had protective feelings for the girl, a connection of blood that was hard to ignore. But he would do just that, because no matter what interest she showed him now, with the council and training of her parents, she would grow to revile him in time.

"Back so soon?"

Alexander turned to find Cruen standing behind him, his red robe brilliant in the sunshine, his startling blue gaze accentuated by the single black circle brand around his left eye—the one that proclaimed to all the world "I am Order."

"We have a problem," Alexander told him.

"We?"

"Did you know that Dare can flash?"

Cruen glanced around at the other members of the Order who were busy with the Triba, unable to hear their conversation; then he sniffed and uttered, "Impossible."

"It happened before my eyes," Alexander said. "And he took an entire table of Impures with him."

For one moment, Cruen appeared thoughtful; then he shrugged and offered a flippant gesture with his hand. "It was a trick. Human magic, no doubt."

"That's bullshit, and I think you know it."

"I'm surprised at you, Alexander Roman. I had heard you and your brothers were great warriors in battle, keen observers—but you have fallen for a parlor trick."

"This wasn't a fucking Vegas lounge act, Cruen. I know the difference. This was Pureblood flashing."

"Silence," Cruen hissed. Behind him, the other members of the Order were ending their sessions. "You will return and fulfill our agreement. And next time, *we* will summon *you*. Understand?" His blue eyes flashed and he hissed low and ugly, "Son of the Breeding Male."

Fangs flashing, Alexander lunged at the *paven*. But even with his quick mind and shocking speed, he made no connection with Cruen. The *paven* was gone in an instant, and Alexander was yanked out of the *credenti* by an unseen force, thrust into the now familiar blackness and dropped beside the mouth of the cave.

Seething, he snatched up a large rock from the ground and threw it against the cave's wall. It shattered into a hundred tiny pieces, and Alexander couldn't help but wish it had been Cruen's arrogant, thick head.

Cursing into the cold mountain air, he clamped his eyes shut and flashed home.

Thirty minutes later, he was sitting in one of the brown leather chairs in the library, a stockpile of weapons on the table beside him and a vampire physician, who had come to check on his shoulder wound, pacing the floor in front of him.

"So do you have an answer for it?" Alexander asked, his conversation with the Order pushed to the back of his mind. For now.

Leza shook her head. "I'm afraid not." She stopped

in front of him and ran her hand over the smooth skin of his shoulder. "Are you certain the wound was open?"

"Of course I'm certain!" Alexander returned gruffly. "I felt it, saw it—saw the tears of blood weep from it."

"Well, it has healed itself again."

Alexander cocked his head to one side. "Don't look at me like I've lost my mind, Leza. Sara saw it too. In fact, she . . ."

"She what?" the physician interrupted, her eyes narrowing with curiosity.

The look made Alexander pause. He wasn't about to go there, reveal the details of Sara's unfortunate, unforgettable kiss to his shoulder. If he did, there would most certainly be a lecture coming his way, not to mention a suggestion for testing to be done on the human female. And after what he'd just endured with Cruen the Prick, he was done listening to reprimands.

Leza's gaze bore into him, suspicious about his silence. Jaw tight, Alexander stood and went over to the table, started loading a magazine into his pistol. "Sara witnessed the open wound, that's all."

But Leza didn't buy it. "If we connect the dots, this change in your wound happened while you were with Dr. Donohue. She might be a part of it."

"No," he said simply.

"You have never been one to ignore the realities nor the probabilities of a situation, Alexander Roman."

Alexander slammed the bottom of the mag well until it clicked into place. "The reality is—no amount of exertion should be able to break that seal."

"True." Leza shrugged. "I've never seen it or heard of it happening. A *veana*'s healing power has always been impenetrable."

Alexander continued loading weapons, but his mind returned to Sara's bedroom and her soft eyes and sweet mouth. If she was the catalyst to his wound opening again, what would be the reason for it? Did she have some kind of power over him? Something he couldn't understand? Or was this just a random act, a fluke? Was it possible that a *veana*'s breath might be too weak to truly heal the son of a Breeding Male?

He tossed the loaded Glock onto the table. Whatever the answer, he needed to keep his mind on the blood of another today. Within the hour, he and his brothers were going into the tunnels for a training exercise and a strategy session to make sure there was no escape for Dare and his recruits next time.

He lifted his gaze to Leza's and said resolutely, "Perhaps I saw something that wasn't there."

Leza didn't say anything for a moment; then her eyes softened and she nodded. "Perhaps."

Alexander returned to his work just as a knock on the library door echoed through the room. "Come," he called.

Leza was packing up her medical bag when the *veana* entered. Along with the strips of fabric tied around her throat and wrists, she was dressed in jeans, a white sweater, and had a lovely, obliging smile affixed to her face. She was admittedly beautiful, and if Alexander sensed it correctly, had a sharp brain as well. But she might just as well have been dim and unappealing for all it mattered to him. The woman with the blueberry eyes, yielding heart, and damaged soul so like his own possessed him now.

The *veana* inclined her head and smiled confidently. "Alexander?"

He inclined his head. "Hello, Bronwyn."

Leza glanced from one vampire to the other, then slung her bag over her shoulder. "Alexander, if there are any changes, send for me immediately."

Alexander nodded. "Thank you for coming."

When Leza left the room, Bronwyn went over to the couch and sat down. "Sorry to disturb you."

"It's no disturbance." Alexander noted that the *veana* didn't seem at all nervous holding his gaze. She wasn't for him, that was certain, but it didn't stop him from feeling a good deal of respect for one with such a strong backbone.

"I assume you know why I'm here," she said, crossing her feet at the ankles.

"You think we are true mates."

"I do."

"Nicholas told me of your work with bloodlines, genetic codes, DNA—how you believe we are a match. He also mentioned that you have nothing to show us that documents this claim."

"Actually I do"—Bronwyn sat up taller as she explained—"but the document also reveals information I've collected for a private client of mine. I'm not able to share it with anyone at this time."

"How interesting and inconvenient," Alexander said.

"I know, but I assure you our blood, our genes are a match. I wouldn't be here, come here without seeing the proof on paper."

Alexander lifted his chin, showed off the brands on his cheeks. "You see my mark?"

"Yes."

"And you have this mark on your skin?"

Her eyes dimmed, just a hair. In fact, if Alexander hadn't been studying her so closely, he never would have noticed the chink in her confidence. "I haven't found it yet. But that means nothing. As you know, *veanas* can develop their marks later, or sometimes the mark is so hidden—"

"I feel no connection to you, Miss Kettler."

Bronwyn stilled, her gaze locked to his.

Alexander sighed. "I apologize for my bluntness. But you must understand, I won't be mating. Ever."

"May I ask why?" she said tightly.

"A true mate is responsible for giving love, sex, blood, yes?"

"Yes."

"I don't believe that the first exists, the second I can have without mating, and the third . . . Well, let's just say that after years of being starved, having to beg for even a drop of blood, I would never allow anyone to have that kind of control over me again."

She took a moment to digest this; then she stood up, nodded at him. "I understand. But regardless of your strong feelings, I still ask for these three weeks."

Alexander nodded. "Of course." Perhaps he was more like Nicholas than he thought. The old laws were deeply imprinted within him as well.

"And maybe in time you will come to see—"

Lucian busted in then, cutting off Bronwyn's words with his mere presence. His gaze searched out his brother, completely unaware of who else was in the room. "I hope you've loaded us down because after that show at the restaurant I've got a real hard-on for that Impure."

"Hello, Lucian."

The pale, cruelest Roman brother turned at the sound of Bronwyn's voice. His lips pressed together in a thin line as his almond gaze moved over her. "*Puritita,*" he muttered.

Bronwyn flinched and said tightly, "Don't call me that."

"Maybe you should remove the cloth from your neck and wrists, then."

"You know I cannot."

"Right," Lucian drawled evilly. "The *credenti* has a tight hold on its *virgini*."

"Shut it, Lucian!" Alexander commanded, but Bronwyn didn't need his defense.

She stalked over to the terrifying albino, all six-foot-five, two hundred and twenty pounds of him, and stabbed her finger into his rock-hard chest. "Just because we want to hold on to the traditions of our kind, care for our families, and save ourselves for our true mates, does not mean we're unenlightened idiots."

Lucian's mouth curled into a mocking smile. "Actually, that's exactly what it means, princess."

Bronwyn muttered something, then turned away from him and faced Alexander once more. "Thank you for speaking to me. If you'll excuse me, I need to get back to Edel. We have work to finish."

"Of course." Alexander watched her go, banking her visceral response to his brother—no fear in those emerald eyes, only the heat of fury and the scent of sexual interest.

Lucian was already at the weapons table, sharpening a long blade and complaining. "I fucking despise the *Puritita veanas* of the *credenti*."

"Well, don't despise her too much," Alexander said, thrusting a Glock into the waistband of his pants. "I need you to stand in for me with this handfasting thing."

Lucian jerked to face him, knife poised in his fist. "What?"

"You heard me, *Duro*."

"No. Hell no."

"Lucian—"

"Get Nicholas to do it," Lucian said brusquely.

"He's good with propriety and society. I swear he still has ties to them, emotional or something."

Alexander shook his head. "Nicholas is busy."

"Doing what?"

"Tracking Trainer and Dare."

"Screw that!" Lucian roared, plunging his knife into the table. "I'll find the location on those two assholes and Nicky can take the *veana*."

The blade stuck there, swaying, as Alexander spoke low and slow. "I need your help and you *will* do this for me."

"Why? So you can fuck the human?" Lucian sneered. "You're as bad as Dare."

Alexander was in Lucian's face in under a second. Chest to chest, nose to nose, two sets of fangs bared. "You speak of her to me in that manner? To me? A morphed male?"

"No," Lucian said. "I speak that way to my brother, who has shit for brains, as of late."

"Watch yourself, Little Brother, before your tongue grows entirely too wicked to remain in your mouth."

Hissing, Lucian pushed Alexander off of him and returned to his knife, yanking it from the table. Brawn to brawn was not Alexander's preferred way of dealing with his younger brother, but despite the fact that the *paven* had become too defiant for his own good lately, times had changed. They were no longer a democracy. The Order was back in their lives and they were at war—fighting a battle against a new race of vampire, and he, Alexander, as eldest of their family, was running the show.

He pointed at Lucian with his favorite Egyptian dagger. "You will do this for me. Watch out for her, protect her."

Slightly more conciliatory now, Lucian grumbled, "She's a pain in the ass."

"Good, then you won't touch her."

Lucian snorted. "Yeah, like that's ever stopped me."

"You will not touch her," Alexander repeated.

An evil grin spread over Lucian's features. "What if she touches me first?"

Alexander shook his head. "You're still such a fucking *balas*, you know that?"

"'Evening, ladies." Nicholas walked in, joined them at the weapons table. He grabbed two guns, sank them into his waistband, picked up a tribal spear, and said, "Ready?"

"I know I am," Lucian said, heading for the door.

"Did you get a location on Dare?" Alexander asked Nicholas as they followed. He'd decided to keep his meeting with Cruen to himself. No new information had been given and with how his brothers felt about him going to the Order alone, he wasn't about to drop that bomb if he didn't have to.

Nicholas grinned. "Better. A possible residence."

Alexander flashed his fangs. "Nice."

"Yes," Nicholas agreed. "But don't forget. The human is mine to kill."

Out in the hallway, Alexander corrected him. "Our main target is Dare."

Lucian snorted.

Nicholas narrowed his gaze on Alexander as they headed toward the entrance to the tunnels. "Why does it seem that you wouldn't be all that pleased to have Tom Trainer executed?"

"Because he wouldn't," Lucian muttered.

"Shut it, Luca," Alexander growled.

"What's the deal?"

"Get a clue, Nicky," Lucian said, pulling the door to the tunnels wide and barreling through.

Nicholas stopped Alexander before he could enter. "Alex?"

"We're going to be late," Alexander said through clenched teeth.

"Duro?" Nicholas pushed.

Waiting for them a few feet ahead, Lucian exhausted a breath. "The human's dead and Alexander has no excuse for keeping the woman here."

Alexander's jaw tightened.

Nicholas let out a defeated breath. "Shit, no. Alex, you can't keep her. She doesn't belong with you—or to you. She will be your downfall. And possibly ours as well."

Eyes blazing with fury, Alexander let loose. "Kill the

motherfucker, Nicky. Rip out his jugular and feast, for all I care. I'm just saying Dare needs to be the priority. Now, if you're both done busting my balls, let's move," he said, stalking past them. "Dillon will throw a shit-fit if we're late."

Nicholas hesitated for a moment, then shrugged his shoulders and took off after his brother down the dark passageways lined with Impure guards, as always, their eyes trained on the stone floor.

Sara was dreaming. And in her dream, Tom Trainer was sitting beside a very large, very handsome man on a sofa she didn't recognize in a room with blue walls. Tom's mouth was buried in the man's wrist, and his cheeks pulsed as he took deep pulls from the man's vein. As if he'd heard something, Tom released the man and sat up. Blood stained his lips and chin. To Sara's sleep-infused mind, her former patient looked different—older, chiseled in feature and more clever around the eyes.

Beside Tom, the large man moaned a little, as if he were in pain—but a sexual pain, and he pulled Tom toward his chest and kissed him tenderly on mouth.

Suddenly, the focus on the dream lens in Sara's mind expanded and she could see the entire room. Now the blue walls displayed photographs of couples having sex, but they were not inanimate, they were alive, moving. On the rugs surrounding the couch and Tom and his lover were men and women engaged in sex. Sara watched as after one female had finished being serviced by her male another female took her place.

Sara's body responded to the images. Heat pooled in her belly, then drifted lower, and her legs began to tremble. With a flash, like lightning to the mind, the room disappeared and Tom's face sat before her, his features larger than life. When his mouth opened no sound came out, though his voice seemed to echo in her head.

I will fuck you, Dr. Donahue. Then I will kill you.

With a gasp, Sara came awake. Sweaty and disoriented, she sat up and looked around the room, saw the chair against the table and the uneaten food, and the view of the city lights out her window. *Oh God. Thank God.* Alexander's house. SoHo.

"Sara? What is it?"

She turned and breathed a sigh of relief. In the dark, she hadn't seen him, hadn't known he'd come back. But there he was beside her, his large body so near, ready to protect her both in body and mind.

She lay down, her arms going around his neck, her face burrowing in his chest. "Hold me. Jesus. Just hold me tight."

She knew why she was dreaming about Tom; it was normal for her fears of him coming after her to be worked out while she was asleep. But the sexual nature of the dream had felt so real. Her lower half ached with it.

"You're shaking." Alexander wrapped his arms around her and pulled her even closer against his warm chest. His shirt was off and he wore sweats on his bottom half, but it did little to stop her from feeling his erection against her belly, stiff as marble and pulsing. Her skin tingled, desperate to be touched, and she arched her back. Alexander's hand slipped from her lower back to her bottom, gathering her against his hip, and when it did, he felt something there that made his cock jump.

"Not fear that has you calling out, is it?" he growled against her neck. "Were you dreaming about me?"

Sara didn't know what to say. She didn't want to tell him about her dream, not now, not yet, not when it was so fresh. The conflict her body was under made her irrational and selfish and all she wanted to do was to have his hands on her, in her.

She pressed her hips forward, her core squeezing against his thigh. "Alexander . . . please . . ."

Alexander gave a soft chuckle as though she'd just affirmed his query, and he kissed her ear as he slid his fingers from her backside all the way down the soft, wet trail to the opening of her body. "Is this what you want?" he whispered, his fingers finding the sensitive spot his tongue had lapped at hours earlier.

Sara moaned softly. "Yes."

"Is this what you need?" he asked, his two fingers making lazy circles over her clit.

"God, yes . . . please . . ."

His mouth was on her neck, then her ear. "Is your cunt aching to be filled, Sara?"

"Yes." *With you*, she wanted to call out, but before she even had a chance, Alexander drove three fingers so deeply inside of her that his knuckles disappeared and her breath, her words, were caught in her throat.

"No more dreams," he uttered against her neck, his mouth suckling at the skin over her vein as he slid another finger inside her.

24

Pearl McClean sat on the edge of her seat in the visitors' room wishing she had a mirror. She knew she looked like shit and it made her crazy. Alistair was here, the one who watched over her for Ethan—the one who'd seduced her mother so he could remain close to Pearl.

Dammit. She wished Ethan could come and see her. It was so boring here. No fun, no blood. She lowered her lashes over her large brown eyes and used her little-girl voice. "I want to go home."

"I know," Alistair said, staring out the window at the cloudy winter morning. "But it isn't safe. You need to stay here until everything is complete."

Pearl watched him at the window, tall, lanky, his long, brown hair framing a rock-star-like face. In fact, when she'd met him and Ethan at a Slayer concert six months ago, she'd thought they were part of the band. She smiled, remembering that night. Before the band had even gotten to their second set, Pearl had offered

Ethan her virginity, and a few weeks later, when she'd found out what he was really a part of, she'd offered him her life too . . . and her womb.

"They're giving me pills," she told him, unease in her tone. "They watch me to make sure I swallow them."

He shrugged. "It won't affect your *balas.*"

"Ethan's balas," she corrected him gently. "Ethan's child."

"Yes." He turned then, giving the city his back, and grinned at her, his black eyes sharp. "Once you release it from your body, it will belong to the commander."

A wave of distress moved through Pearl. She didn't like when he called the baby "it."

Alistair must have sensed her concern because he went over to her immediately and sat down, spoke to her with a soothing tone. "Once the *balas* is no longer within you, you and the commander can be together again. You'd like that, wouldn't you? If this *balas* survives, you will become a very important human to him."

Pearl swallowed thickly. She wanted more than to be important to Ethan; she wanted him to change her into what he was. She wanted to feed from him, then let him take her vein as he took her body. It had taken seventeen years to realize that she wasn't meant for this life, this human existence. And this life had no need for her either.

"Can you ask him to come?" she begged him softly. "Just once."

For one moment, a look of annoyance crossed Alistair's face; then something stole his attention. The black in his eyes blurred with gray and he froze, cocked his head to one side. He looked as though he was listening to something, but Pearl didn't hear a thing. Suddenly, he stood up. "I have to go."

Pearl's heart dropped. "What?"

"She's here," Alistair hissed harshly.

Pearl stopped protesting. "Who?"

"Your nosy little doctor. She's just walking into the hospital now."

Sara took the fire stairs two at a time, energy racing through her blood. For the first time in her career, she was both late for work and not sorry about it. She grinned, shook her head. Screw the "impossible." She was going to live in it for a while, for as long as it felt like this. Last night and early this morning, something had been turned on inside her, a fresh wave of passion she hadn't known she'd been missing.

She threw back the door and headed onto the fourth floor and to the keypad on the wall leading to the adult ward. She'd closed herself off all these years, turned herself off completely, maybe because she'd felt she didn't deserve passion or release or anything that gave pure pleasure until her brother could have those things as well.

Whatever the answer, tonight, instead of going home to an empty apartment and an empty bed, she would go home to Alexander. And anyone who had an objection to that could just suck it.

She was down the hall and nearing her office when Claire stopped her, motioned for her to come over to the nurse's station.

Sara walked over, grabbed her messages from her box. "What's up, Claire?"

"You said you wanted to know when Pearl McClean had a visitor."

A strange sensation coiled through Sara. "Yes."

"About thirty minutes ago."

"They're still here?"

"He," Claire corrected, popping a Certs in her mouth. "He's still here."

"The boyfriend?" Sara asked, her body on alert now.

"Yep."

Shit. Dropping her notes on the desk, Sara turned and headed back toward the juvenile ward. What was the mother's boyfriend doing visiting the girl alone? Did the mother even know about it? As Sara hauled ass through one ward into the other, she knew this wasn't about pseudostepfather types in general—this was about this particular man. Everything in her gut told her something sketchy was going on with that relationship and she should've blocked the man from visiting without the mother, even if it got her in some legal hot water.

When Sara arrived at the visitors' room and saw that it was empty, she cursed and headed over to the nurse's station, asked the male nurse behind the desk, "Pearl McClean's visitor? Is he gone?"

The man nodded. "Left about five minutes ago. She's back in her room now."

Sara released a breath of frustration. Great. "Can I have her chart?"

"Sure thing." The nurse thumbed through the stack on his desk, pulled one and handed it off. "Here you go."

"Thanks." Sara took a quick look-see. "There are no labs in here."

The nurse shrugged. "Maybe they're backed up downstairs."

"They're always backed up downstairs," Sara said with a grin, pushing away from the desk. She wanted to get a look at the girl's blood—see if anything was low, see if any drugs were in her system. When she got to Pearl's door, she knocked once before heading in. Pearl's roommate wasn't around, and Sara was grateful for the moment of private time. Pearl was lying on her bed facing the wall, her body coiled up like a shrimp, and Sara went over to her and sat on the edge of the bed.

"Pearl?"

Nothing. She didn't even move.

"Pearl?" Sara repeated, a bit more forcefully now. "I need to speak with you, and the longer you ignore me and don't say anything, the longer you're going to remain under my care."

Again, the girl lay silent and still. For a moment, Sara wondered if she was actually sleeping. Then in a low, angry tone Pearl muttered, "Why did you have to come in today?"

"It's my job," Sara said evenly.

"Well, you ruined everything."

"Why? What happened? Was it your mother's friend? His visit?"

"Yes."

I swear, if that piece of shit touched her . . . "Can you tell me what it was that upset you?"

"You," Pearl uttered with a true bite to her tone. "You upset me."

Sara shook her head, trying to connect the pieces. "I don't understand."

"Can't you just leave me alone?"

"No, I can't. I think you're in trouble and hurting, and it's my job to help you." Sara placed a hand on the girl's shoulder. "Please let me help you find a way out."

Pearl jerked her shoulder away, and still facing the wall, fell silent. For a full twenty minutes, Sara sat at the girl's side hoping she'd reveal something more, but she didn't. Finally, Sara left the room and headed for the stairs. She had a date with some brain cells in the research lab next door to the hospital, another patient who'd had serious past trauma. But as she headed into the stairwell, her mind wasn't far from Pearl and the anger the girl had for what she believed was

Sara's interference in the relationship she had with her mother's boyfriend. Sara made a mental note to call Melanie, Pearl's social worker, and to try the mother again, get her in for a session ASAP. And if that didn't fly, she mused, walking down the stairs, she was going to go to the residence. Home visits weren't policy, of course—but rules rarely stopped Sara when she was looking for an answer.

Aboveground, the sun was attempting to push its way through the clouds and melt the snow on the sidewalks. Belowground, huddled inside his cage, naked and cold, Alexander fed on warm cow's blood until he felt his insides clog. The blood tasted like battery acid and did little to curb his hunger, but he refused to give in to what he truly required—what he truly desired. Even during bouts of intense hunger, before his body went through morpho, the cow's blood had sustained him well enough, given him the amount of energy he needed to live and work unfettered among the humans.

But now . . . his body required so much more, not to mention someone else entirely.

He let his head drop back against the stone. He needed rich, ancient, life-sustaining blood—he needed to drink from his true mate and he wasn't sure how long he could hold out without finding her. It was how he was constructed, and if he continued to go against his nature he would either starve to death or lose his shit completely and hunt down any female unlucky enough to cross his path. Including Sara. He knew he should speak with Bronwyn, search her skin and see if her claims were true, or just ask her for a pity feed. But he just couldn't do that to her . . . to Sara.

His insides coiled in pain, in desperation, crying out that he had no loyalty to Sara, no promise to keep himself away from another's vein. After all, he could feed from one and please the body of the other, couldn't he?

But Sara would never accept that. He knew her now. He'd seen her desire for him, felt it as her hand had fisted his cock in the ultimate display of ownership. She wanted all of him.

Fucking hell. Didn't she get it? She was human and could never feed him or feed *from* him, not if she wanted to keep her soul and her heart pure. His body stirred, his cock too, at just the thought of her with her own set of fangs, puncturing his skin, drinking straight from his heart, taking long pulls of his blood into her mouth as he nuzzled and suckled at her sweet cunt.

His jaw clenched to the point of pain and he got up, pulled on his clothes. He was done here—until the next feed, whenever and whatever that may be. Maybe Nicholas and Lucian had a point, he thought as he left the cage. Maybe Sara needed to go, just as much for her own protection as his sanity. But even as he said the words in his head, he knew he'd never allow it.

He ran down the tunnels, causing the Impures who were on guard to thrust their heads down. Once inside the house, he went up to her room and sat in the darkness the heavy, custom-built shades provided.

As the luscious scent of the orgasm he'd given her just hours before drifted up from the bedsheets to his nostrils, he dropped back into his chair and closed his eyes. He would only stay a minute or two, he mused, his hand sliding down between his legs, wrapping around his prick.

Tonight was the night that Dare would die, that his brothers would be freed of the Order, that Tom Trainer would see hell, and if he, Alexander, allowed it, the night his beautiful woman left his life for eternity.

25

"Even as adults we are constantly growing new brain cells. The sample of this man's cells showed that as his doctor attempted to suppress his past trauma with certain noninvasive treatments, a heavy collection of youthful active cells were provided to the brain. I want to try this with you, then get you back in that MRI for the seven days."

Sara stood at the edge of Gray's bed, her coat on, bags over her shoulder. It was late and she was tired, but she was hoping her words, her request would have some effect on him. Even just a hint of hope in his hopeless expression would do it for her right now. Unfortunately, as Gray stared up at her, there was nothing but frustration in his eyes.

"Don't you see," she said, trying like hell to sound enthusiastic. "If enough new, young cells were created, perhaps they'd tamp down the memory, or rewrite it."

He looked down at his fire-ravaged hands and

shook his head. A boulder of despair rolled through Sara in that moment.

"You just don't care anymore, do you?" she said, glancing out the window at the black night and the lights of the city, then back again to her brother. "Well, that's fine. I'll just have to keep caring for you."

She saw his jaw tighten, his fists too, and she nodded.

"Okay, I'm going. I'll see you in the morning."

She left the room and headed for the elevators with a heaviness around her heart she hadn't felt since those early days after the fire. Sure, she'd always experienced anger and frustration and guilt during her school years and into the first years of Gray's therapy, but it fueled her study and gave her reason to be optimistic about her abilities.

Lately this feeling of impending doom, possible failure hovered in the air around her . . .

Night loomed cold and black as she walked out of the hospital. When she spotted the town car at the curb, she headed straight for it, relief filling her, a grateful smile playing sadly about her mouth. It had been a long, difficult day, and the thought of going home to Alexander filled her with a deep sense of hope and pleasure.

The driver nodded as she climbed inside and took the seat opposite Dillon, who was wearing a white shirt, charcoal gray pantsuit, and black leather heels, and was, as usual, neck deep in the *Wall Street Journal*. The *veana* clearly loved the news.

"You're getting smarter by the minute, human," Dillon drawled.

Sara settled back against the leather seat and yanked off her scarf. "Gee, thanks, Dillon."

"Don't get me wrong—I admire your commitment to being a pain-in-the-ass renegade, but not having to force you into the car makes way less work for me."

"Well, I aim to please."

"Really?"

"No."

Dillon snorted, then tossed the paper on the seat beside her. "So what do you do in that hospital all day? Shrink heads?"

"That's a human joke. You sure you want to fall that far?"

"Can't help it. It's the company I keep these days."

"Well, you're watching me. You see what goes down, what I do."

Dillon shrugged. "Looks like a lot of pushing paper and pill-popping nut jobs to me."

Sara cocked her head to the side, narrowed her eyes. "Where are you actually going when you should be watching me? Starbucks?"

The *veana* grinned. "The one on 34th and Lex makes a mean carotid frap."

Sara laughed. "Nice. Vampire humor. I like that."

Dillon's grin flickered. "You do spend a lot of time with that man."

"What man?" Sara asked, glancing out the window as they passed one of her favorite delis.

"The young one," Dillon continued. "With the dark blond hair and impatient eyes."

Sara turned back. Normally, people described Gray by the burns on his hands, never by the expression in his eyes. But then again, Dillon was neither a person nor normal. "He's a patient, and some patients need a little bit more of my time and attention than others."

"That all it is, huh?" Dillon said, her tone casual.

"Of course. What else would it be?" Before Dillon could speculate, Sara changed the subject. "So, how's the training going?"

"With the guys?"

"Yeah."

She shrugged again, looking bored. "They're not totally inept."

Sara laughed. "That's good. So did you work the whole time or did they have some downtime? Do they get breaks?"

The *veana*'s eyes narrowed. "The Romans don't require 'breaks.' "

"Okaay. Good to know."

"They stopped to change weapons, however."

Sara brightened. "Any chatting going on during that time?"

"Chatting?" Dillon repeated, pronouncing the word like a high-class Brit. "Sure there was chatting. It was during teatime and right before instruction on skipping."

The heavy sarcasm in Dillon's tone made Sara smile and shake her head. "I just wanted to know if he said anything about me, okay?"

"Who?"

"Alexander."

"Oh, fuck me." Dillon dropped back against her seat as the car made a quick stop at a light. "I don't owe him for this."

Sara put up her hands in surrender. "Forget it. Sorry I asked. And before you even go there—*yes,* I am ten." She turned away, stared out the window.

They drove the last five blocks in silence, and when they came to a halt in front of the house, Sara got out quickly and hightailed it up the sidewalk. Dillon followed. When they reached the door, she released a weighty breath. "Hey. Human."

Sara glanced over her shoulder. "What?"

The *veana* shook her head as though she couldn't believe she was actually about to say what she was about to say. "He said, 'Let anything happen to her and I'll shackle your fangs and leave your ass in Mondrar for the next century.'"

"What's Mondrar?"

"It's like jail for vampires. Controlled by the Order." She shook her head and uttered tightly, "It's not good."

Sara grinned with pleasure. "Really? He said that? He said he'd do that to you?"

Dillon snorted. "As if he could manage it."

"Thanks, Dillon," Sara said with a laugh.

Cursing, the *veana* pushed past her and opened the front door. "You know, you're both fools," she muttered, waiting for Sara to enter. It wasn't a question.

"Yes, I know." Sara lifted her brow as Dillon shut the door. "See you later?"

"Not if I see you first," she called back, heading into the living room.

At nine o'clock that night, Brooklyn hummed with traffic and pedestrian life, but on Clark Street in Boerum Hill the only ones driving or walking past Ethan Dare's residence were prostitutes and those looking to score drugs. His three-story town house appeared to be a boarded-up crack house, complete with pipes, plastic baggies, and dirty spoons that littered the snow-covered front yard.

Alexander stood across the street in the shadow of a cherry tree admiring the half-breed's ability to not only vanish with a group of dinner guests, but to mask the exterior of his home so well. How the little Impure prick was managing something only a morphed Pureblood was capable of was anybody's guess—maybe he'd ask him before he killed him.

"I say we go in weapons drawn," said Lucian, who was beside him. "I doubt anyone on this block would give a shit."

Nicholas snorted. "Might even think we're cops."

"We go in fast and quiet," Alexander said in a clipped, authoritative whisper. "One goal. Ethan Dare. I want his body brought before the Order tonight."

Jaw tight, Nicholas nodded.

Lucian too. "Yes, sir."

They nearly flew across the street. Avoiding the front of the house, they hustled around to a side window, where Nicholas made quick use of his blade, cutting through a thick layer of cardboard. He yanked the brown paper back, revealing a wall of wood planks that looked damn sturdy. He growled low in his throat. Yes, this would keep the crackheads out and the vampires in . . . He gestured to Lucian, and when Nicholas stepped back, Glock at the ready, the pair kicked the shit out of the boards until they had a hole wide enough to get through.

In a flash, Nicholas had the head of his gun inside the hole, ready for whatever lay in wait. Detecting heartbeats, Alexander twisted his mouth into a wicked grin and he gestured for his brothers to follow him.

"Aim well and spare all innocents," he whispered as he stalked, hunched over, through the crawl space and into the room. Courtesy of his species, his eyes quickly adjusted to the darkness, his retinas flipping on their internal light.

"Un-fucking-believable," Lucian uttered, taking in the art-deco room with its polished fixtures, expensive furniture, and crystal chandelier. "Just like our place. Wreck outside, palace inside." He turned to glare at Alexander. "How is this possible? Dare's got to be getting help from a Pureblood."

Alexander agreed, but he didn't have time to toss out ideas right now. He was sensing activity, slow heartbeats above him. Purebloods had no pulse, but Impures did. And humans too—he could scent them. He motioned to Nicholas. "We take each floor together; cover me. Lucian, take Nicky's back."

Grabbing the Glock from the small of his back, Alexander took the lead as they inspected each room on the first floor, just in case Dare was hiding. When they found nothing and no one, they headed for the stairs. Yes, Alexander mused, his fangs twitching as he climbed, heartbeats and scent were stronger this way. His finger hovered near the trigger. He was a perfect shot, no way could he miss unless Dare and his recruits pulled another disappearing act.

Silent as shadows, the brothers moved up the stairs. When they hit the second floor, they ran smack into a large Impure. The male was so damn shocked to see them, he turned to run, but Lucian grabbed him by the arm and knocked him unconscious before he had a chance to react or call out a warning to his buddies. Unfortunately, the sound of his body hitting the floor reverberated down the hall, and in seconds, there were three Impures hauling ass toward them.

Come on, then, Alexander mused darkly. *Let's see what you can do without your commander.*

Lucian and Nicholas took off in opposite directions,

while Alexander aimed and fired directly at the large black-haired Impure who was descending upon him, a sword in each fist, slashing at the air. But just seconds after Alexander's finger touched the trigger, the Impure vanished. *Flash. Gone.* Just like at the restaurant.

A growl ripped from Alexander's throat, but it died there. Someone was breathing near his shoulder. He whirled around. A fist slammed into his nose and he jerked back. The Impure had reappeared! *How the hell were they doing this? And inside the fucking house!*

Quick, intent rage took Alexander's mind and, completely unconcerned with the racket he was about to make, he reached out for the Impure, who had his sword pulled back over his shoulder, ready to plunge the blade into Alexander's heart. In less than a second, Alexander's hands were around the male's throat, snapping his neck. He let the body fall where it had stood and glanced over at Lucian. The fierce albino had an Impure guard in a headlock, knife drawn, ready to slash his throat.

Flash. Gone. The Impure disappeared.

"They're flashing!" Alexander shouted. "Quick kills!"

Circling around behind his brothers, Alexander covered them, ready to spring when the next Impure surfaced. A moment later, Lucian's Impure reappeared just behind Nicholas. Alexander shoved the head of his Glock into the Impure's back, firing. Heartbeat extinguished, the Impure dropped to the floor like a bag of rocks, joining his comrade in death.

"Thanks, *Duro*," Nicholas said, his black eyes flashing with bloodlust.

Alexander grinned. "Anytime."

The brothers turned and saw Lucian slash the wrists and throat of the third Impure, then haul him to the ground, conveniently forgetting the orders to provide a quick kill.

Grabbing the male's throat, Lucian stuck his palm over the deadly slash, managing to slow the thick ooze of blood as he said, "Where's your boss, Impure?"

The male blinked up at him. He was clearly in deep pain, but his eyes remained defiant just as his tongue stayed mute.

Lucian sneered. "Not going to tell me? Big mistake."

The Impure spoke through a bloody gurgle. "You'll . . . never get him, Pureblood *witte*."

"We will get him, Impure. Unfortunately, you will not be around to watch." Lucian pushed the male away and stood, watched as the blood flowed thickly from his neck, watched as in seconds, the light died in his eyes.

"Upstairs," Alexander ordered. "Search every room for Dare."

Music, soft and seductive, met them as they reached the top floor of the house. To Alexander the music seemed to be coming from every closed door, filtering out of every crack and crevice, into the hallway as though it were a solid, living being. No Impures blocked their way this time, and the brothers moved with pantherlike quickness down the hallway, stopping at every room, checking every corner for Dare. But there was no sign of the half-breed.

At the last door, Alexander paused. He scented both human and Impure and something else that felt druglike in its powerfulness. Weapons drawn, he nodded at each brother. With a grunt, Lucian kicked open the door, then crouched, ready for action. But what the brothers found on the other side of the wall made them stop and stare.

"Holy shit," Nicholas muttered under his breath, lowering his weapon. "What kind of party is this?"

Lucian snorted. "Fuck party. This is an orgy."

"Is Dare in there?"

Alexander shook his head, his cock stirring at the scene before him. Males and females—easily twenty or so, Impure, Pureblood, and human alike—were naked and coiled together, some asleep, some moving together in a rhythm as timeless as the dance of sun and stars, and all completely unaware of the Roman brothers' presence. In fact, Alexander thought, studying the lack of movement in their eyes, they seemed to be in some kind of trance.

Alexander's gaze shifted to several females sleeping alone on beds off to one side. Their bellies were in different stages of swell. "He's making more Impures . . ."

"What?" Nicholas asked, his eyes lust-filled as he watched the show.

"He's raising an army, just as the Order said."

"To fight for control over the *credentis*? Or to completely destroy the Pureblood breed?"

Alexander shrugged. "Perhaps both."

Lucian sneered. "Well, whatever he's doing, at this rate, it'll be a century before he succeeds."

"The question is what do we do now?"

"Find and kill Dare," Lucian stated flatly. "That is all we are contracted to do."

True. And yet . . . Alexander lifted his chin toward the crowd and the pregnant females asleep on their beds. "What about them?"

"They're having a hell of a lot more fun than we are," Lucian muttered.

"They're barely coherent, Lucian," Nicholas said, his tone one of disgust.

Alexander nodded. "Some of them have been torn from their *credentis* and brought here to be either pestle or mortar."

Lucian shrugged. "Not my problem."

Alexander and Nicholas said nothing.

They didn't have to. Lucian's gaze was traversing the room, resting on the females and their bellies. His lips thinned. "Dammit! I don't do rescue . . ."

Alexander knew that Lucian hated the idea of further assisting not only the Order, but members of the *credenti*, but he also understood firsthand what deep pain a forced swell and an unwanted *balas* wrought. With a grumble of annoyance, he pushed past Nicholas, who was now staring unblinking at the orgy in front of him, and tried to get to the females on the other side of the room. Not even halfway there, he froze, cursed. "I can't get to them," he called back. "There's something blocking the air around them."

Alexander closed his eyes and attempted to take down the invisible shield with the power of morpho, but he could sense nothing there, nothing in Lucian's way. His lips curled back as he opened his eyes. This wasn't the mission he'd agreed to, the mission he'd been forced into. He rubbed a hand over his face, felt his brands grow hot. No matter how much he despised his species and the Order who ruled them, he could not turn his back on those innocent females and the *balas* they carried.

"Fall back," he ordered, pushing away from the door and heading down the hall and toward the stairs. His mind jumped and devised. He knew what had to be done. Tonight, he would dive deep into his mind, and though it made his skin twitch with revulsion—though Cruen had warned him against it—he would attempt to connect with the Order once again.

The study had been on rats, but what the hell, Sara reasoned, curled up in a chair on the second floor of the Roman brothers' library, there was always a jumping-off point. Shock treatments to induce fear, followed by a drug to bring about temporary amnesia, followed by a new, gentle memory to take its place. A little thrill ran through her. What if this was the answer? Or at least got her infinitely closer to it? Sara glanced at the clock on the wall. It was close to midnight. Tomorrow she would run the idea by Pete, get his thoughts. Gray's memory of the fire would need to be reinforced somehow, simulated, which would be pretty hellish, but then again, so was the life he was living now. The amnesia, she thought—would she have to go with hard drugs? She didn't want to go the drug route again, not yet. She could use hypnosis or sodium Amytal, but would either be strong enough to calm the fear center of the brain? Her gaze scanned a row of books on the wall in front of her, not really seeing anything but ancient cloth spines. Hypnosis was a thought, but then again, Gray always fought the relaxed state—hell, he was fighting everything these days. He still refused to get inside the MRI machine . . .

Sara stilled, cocked her head to one side as though she'd heard something. But there was nothing there, nothing her ears picked up anyway. Suddenly a wave of anxiety moved through her, a feeling of dread so powerful she stood up and ran to the top of the stairs. For a moment, she wondered if her reaction was about Gray, the thoughts on testing and drugs, and the ever-present fear that every one of Gray's memories would die off along with the memory of the fire and he'd be left with a blank history. But then, just as quickly as it came, the anxiety faded away and a heady sensation of pleasure wrapped around her body like a blanket.

Alexander.

She practically leaped down the stairs and ran out of the library. She saw Evans hustling out of the living room and down the hall, and she called after him.

He stopped and turned, looking a bit preoccupied as he said, "Dr. Donohue?"

"Is Alexander home?"

"No, but he should be returning soon enough. Anything I can help you with?"

Disappointed, she shook her head. "No, no, thanks."

He looked relieved and quickly turned away, started down the hall again.

"Wait a sec! Hey, Evans?"

She caught up with him, noticed that his eyes held a bit of frustration in their depths. "Yes, Doctor?"

She sighed. "I don't know how I know this, but Alexander's here. In this house."

Evans paled. "What?"

"I can feel him . . ."

Shock registered in his eyes.

Sara rushed ahead. "I need to see him."

Evans shook his head. "I'm afraid that's not possible."

"Why?" She shrugged, her eyes imploring him for answers. "What is it? Why can't you tell me where he is?"

It took a moment for Evans to give her an answer, as though he were searching for the right one. "He wouldn't wish it."

Her heart squeezed in her chest. "Did he say that? Did he say he didn't want to see me?"

"Please, Doctor. He will come to you when he's ready."

Sara opened her mouth to respond, but stopped herself. She read people very well and she knew when it was time to ease off—knew better than to keep pushing a loyal employee for answers that might get him into trouble. She pressed her lips together in acquiescence and nodded. "I'm sorry. You're right, Evans. It's no big deal. I'll see him tomorrow."

He gave her a grateful smile. "Very good, Doctor." Then turned and resumed his course down the hall.

Sara watched him go, and when he was far enough away not to hear her footfalls, she followed him.

26

The Order.

The motherfucking Order.

He couldn't get to them. No matter where he'd flashed to, no matter how hard he'd called to them in his mind, they had ignored him. Maybe all that talk about "innocent members" of the *credentis* being taken was just that—talk. Maybe it was all about what it had always been about with them—Pure Blood.

Alexander dropped his head back, exhausted. The bars of his cage felt cold and soothing against his naked skin. Between the battle at Dare's and the hours of failed mind travel, his veins were as dry as winter leaves and his belly ached for the rich, power-inducing blood of a *veana*.

He closed his eyes, lifted his chin, and sniffed the air as an Impure entered the room. A growl hummed at the back of Alexander's throat. "You bring the scent of Dr. Donohue with you tonight, Evans."

"Yes, sir."

His eyes remained closed. "You wish to drive me mad, then?"

"No, sir. I'm sorry, sir. She stopped me in the hall, wanted to speak with me."

"What did she want?"

"You, sir."

Alexander's eyes opened and he searched out the face of his servant. A soft, sad smile lit the old Impure's eyes as he stood there, on the other side of the bars. He too understood the pain of an unfulfilled desire. Alexander wondered what Evans would think if he knew what Dare was promoting. Would he join forces with the half-breed? Would Alexander blame him if he did?

As another wave of Sara's scent drifted into Alexander's nostrils, his mouth watered. He slammed his fists against the bars. "Have you brought me something besides the scent of a blood I cannot taste?"

"One of the Impures is fetching your repast, sir."

The blood of a cow. Alexander sneered. Just the thought of it turned his stomach. He gripped the bars, wishing he'd ordered spikes to be placed on the steel poles, their sharp points stabbing into his palms, replacing one pain he couldn't quell with another he could.

"The hunger grows worse," Evans said, observing him.

"Take the pity from your eyes, Evans," Alexander growled.

"Sir. Miss Kettler could—"

"No."

"She is pure."

"Cease!"

"Even if she is not your true mate, her blood will fill you, give you time—"

Alexander's hand was through the bars and around Evans's neck. "Say another word and *your* blood will fill me—impure and weak though it is."

Hanging a foot above the ground, Evans stilled, his jaw trembling, his eyes popping with fear. After a moment, Alexander released him onto the stone floor below with an irritated grumble. "Leave me."

Sara was lost.

Twenty minutes ago, she'd followed Evans into a remote part of the house, through a door, and down some steps into what she'd assumed was a cellar, but what had turned out to be an entire secret world beneath the SoHo streets.

She looked behind her, down the length of tunnel that was high and relatively wide and lit every ten feet or so by torches. It went on forever, branching out in several directions. It's how she'd lost Evans. Fear of what might be lurking in the shadows beyond had made her question her decision to follow the servant many times, but the drive and curiosity to explore, mixed with the unshakable feeling that Alexander was near, kept her in pursuit. As a doctor, she questioned the base, raw instincts that pushed her to find him; as a woman, she ran blindly.

She wove her way through the tunnels as the air grew colder and colder and she could see her breath. Just as she was wondering if anyone but the Romans used the tunnels, she spotted something ahead and froze. A man—short, stocky, and definitely not Evans. He stood against the wall, perfectly still, his chin lifted. As quiet as she could manage, Sara turned around and hurried back the way she came, veering off onto another leg of the tunnel, one she'd rejected earlier. She kept running, growing warmer with the exercise, not slowing down until she saw another light ahead, and a voice she recognized. Her heart jumped into her throat and she sprang ahead, into the light and a cold, cavelike room.

But her excitement died a quick death. Cut into the rock wall was a cell, a cage, its steel door shut. As she approached, she noticed there was an opening in the top of the door, three iron bars that revealed one lonely prisoner. *Alexander.* Her gut pulled at the sight. In the dim light, she saw him on his knees, nude and shaking, huddled over the body of a cow. His fangs were bared and he was about to strike, about to feed . . .

"Oh God." Her breath rushed from her lungs.

Alexander's head came up with a jerk. His eyes were bloodred and menacing as he stared straight into her. He looked utterly inhuman at that moment—like a starving wolf, ready to kill anything that came near his untouched meal. He lowered his chin and growled at her, his fangs fully extended now, twin blades of instant death.

Disturbed and confused, Sara turned and ran from the room, down the hall, her heart slamming against her ribs. The scene played in her mind, over and over, and suddenly she couldn't catch her breath. She stopped at the apex of the tunnels and gripped the rock wall for support. What was happening to her? Why was she stopping? Why wasn't she running for the front door, terrified, desperate to get away from him? Why did she, even now—even after what she'd just seen—yearn for the beast in him to search her out?

"You saw me."

Sara gasped and whirled around. Naked and aroused, nostrils flaring and fangs bared, Alexander towered over her, his mere presence forcing her back against the stone wall of the frigid tunnel.

"You saw what I am," he snarled.

Her breath coming heavy and uneven, Sara locked eyes with him. "Yes."

"An animal that seeks blood."

"Yes."

He leaned closer, his warm breath on her cheek, his spicy blood scent filling her nostrils, his cock hard against her belly. "An animal that hovers over its dead prey—"

"Stop saying 'it'!" she broke in passionately.

He leaned in closer still. "—Ready to sink *its* fangs into the animal's vein."

"You're not an 'it,' goddammit!"

"Am I not?" he roared back, the sound echoing through the cavernous tunnels. "You saw me in that cage! What the fuck am I, then?"

Sara didn't move, just stood her ground, chin lifted, staring into his belligerent merlot eyes. "You are the one I . . ." Her tongue refused to say it. She couldn't. It was too soon. He wasn't ready or able to hear the truth from her.

Alexander dropped his head, his mouth just inches from hers. "You are afraid."

"Yes."

He cursed. His jaw looked tight enough to crack and he pushed away from her. "Go now."

"Alexander . . ."

"Go now, because if you remain I will take you—your body and possibly your blood as well."

Sara barely hesitated. "Then do it." She started to unbutton her shirt. "Take me!"

Alexander's eyes flared with panic-laced desire. "No! Sara, stop."

But Sara wasn't listening. She was done with this shit. She wanted her shirt off, wanted to be naked like him—wanted his hands on her and his cock inside her, and she didn't care about the consequences.

"For fuck's sake, Sara, stop!" He reached out and grabbed the two sides of her shirt and held them together. "No matter what I am, I would never take a female who fears me."

She tried to push his hands away. "I'm not afraid of you, Alexander."

"Bullshit," he growled. "I heard what you said before, and I scent your fear now—"

She locked eyes and growled back, "Listen to me, vampire, and listen well. The only thing I'm afraid of is *me*! That's it. Afraid of what's happening inside of me. Things I want, things that don't make any kind of sense for a human to want." Her voice cracked with emotion, but she kept going. "I'm afraid of being without you, never feeling again the way I feel when I'm with you. I'm afraid of never seeing your eyes again or your mouth, or hearing your voice. I'm afraid you'll never allow yourself to fill the emptiness in my heart, my soul, or my body—"

Sara never finished her thought. Alexander crushed his mouth over hers, his kiss so warm and intense that Sara felt utterly helpless and heart-shatteringly thrilled all at the same time. With a moan of pleasure, she wrapped her arms around him and kissed him deeply, her tongue playing with the tips of his fangs. Suddenly, a fragrance so rich, so intoxicating, floated into her nostrils and she opened her eyes and stared at him. Then she saw it. The wound on his shoulder. It had opened again, just a millimeter, but she saw two tiny tears of blood on the surface. How was this happening? she wondered, her tongue dry, her throat parched. She had no answer, only the cry her body refused to silence, and she hugged him close, let her tongue sweep over the two sweet red droplets.

* * *

Alexander's skin blazed with a sudden and intense heat. It had to be forty degrees at most in the tunnels and yet his body burned as though it had been pitched into the epicenter of a forest fire. *Sara.* Paradise and hell pressed sweetly against his cock and his chest. His arms tightened around her. She was everything—his desire, his tormentor, his sparring partner, and his savior, and if he was going to burn for this, so be it.

He pulled his head back and found her mouth again, kissed her hard and furious and hungry, tasting her sweetness and something else he couldn't describe but that made his cock weep at the tip. He prayed to all who looked down upon him that he could control his need for her blood, that her mouth and her eyes, her words and her honey-sweet cunt could satiate him enough not to go for her vein.

In his history, mating and feeding had never gone together: one was for pleasure, the other for sustenance. With Sara, that custom was for shit. He wanted both, he wanted his cock inside her while he suckled from the spot below her left breast.

On a growl, he eased away, looked at her with her back against the wall, her face tipped up to him, her long lashes fluttering, her blueberry eyes heavy with lust. She was so beautiful, his heart ached to have her—to claim her—completely and always. He smiled at her then, and when she smiled back, he reached for her unbuttoned shirt and splayed the material wide, pulling it down off her shoulders. Then he dropped his head and cut the fastening of her bra with his fangs. Sara's breasts sprung free, the large, perfect globes lifting and lowering with each breath she took. Alexander stared with shameless hunger at her nipples, pink and rigid. They called to him, as a grown *paven* and as a *balas* who had never been allowed the closeness and care of his mother's bosom. Her sweet tits begged him to suckle, and he did, drawing on the hard tip, flicking one with his tongue while his fingers played at her other breast.

Sara moaned, arched against him, gripped his scalp with her fingers. "Feel me," she whispered, taking his hand and placing it between her legs. "Feel what you do to me. How ready I am . . ."

She was hot and damp, even through the heavy jean fabric. Alexander nearly lost it. His cock strained, pre-come beading at the head, desperate to find its way into the hot tunnel of her body. He yanked at her jeans, the zipper, pulling the whole mess down to her ankles, growling as she quickly stepped out of the unwanted fabric and stood naked and glorious before him. His mouth found hers again as his hand slid between her thighs. He palmed her, held her in his hand, cursing at the feeling of hot, wet curls tickling his skin. He couldn't help himself. He let one finger slip between her lips, run lazily over her clit, then slide home, so deep into her cunt her body jerked and she sucked in a breath. Oh God. To be here, he thought, to be buried here for days . . .

"The guards," she uttered against his mouth, reaching between their bodies for his erection.

Fuck. Alexander moaned, pumping himself against her hand as he slipped another finger inside her. "They will not. Our scent will keep them away. No male would approach another male during mating, and if they tried, it would be their death."

"I want you." Sara reached behind his shaft, cupping his balls. "Now. Inside me."

Alexander released a feral cry. He could take no more of this play. He lifted her up and placed her down on the head of his cock. The hot slide into her cunt was pure, unimaginable pleasure and his fangs lengthened and pulsed with an all-new flash of desire to feed—like nothing he'd ever experienced before. For a moment, he just held her there, closed his eyes, fought for control over his hunger and let her muscles clench around him. "We're going to hell for this," he uttered against her neck, her vein that throbbed with life.

"Good," she said, clinging to him. "I love to sweat."

Alexander drew back and took her mouth again, kissed her hard and demanding as he gripped her buttocks and started to move. Slow strokes at first, but as she moaned into his mouth and arched her back, grinding her nipples into his chest, he cried out again and thrust deeper into the slick mouth of her cunt. Her breath was coming quick now and her hot muscles stretched and hummed around his cock. And then he heard her gasp, felt her nails dig into the flesh of his back, and he pumped harder, his mind going numb as her body shook with climax.

As the hot wash of Sara's orgasm flooded his erection, Alexander knew the true pain of hunger. The starvation of his youth and the intense pain of premorpho was nothing compared to this—his hunger for her. He glanced down, saw his cock disappearing inside her body, saw his balls slam against her ass, felt her muscles convulsing around him. His mind screamed for her blood just as his own rushed through his veins and pooled into his scrotum.

He would come. And when he did he was going to bite her.

"Fuck! Sara . . . Fuck, I need you!"

"Take me, then," she uttered, jerking her hips against him. "All of me. I'm yours."

He pushed back, desperate to see her eyes when he exploded inside her. Under heavy lashes, her eyes were blue-black and filled with rapture as she held his gaze. Alexander's hands tightened on her buttocks, his fingers wet with her come as he drove into her. Over and over, moving with frantic speed, filling her until he thought his mind would explode. And then it did. His jaw went wide, his throat released the call of mating, and he thrust into her so deeply she gasped. Hot seed poured from his prick, and Alexander turned away from the beautiful female in his arms and bit down into the flesh of his own wrist.

27

Sara felt drugged, sensations and emotions whipping through her at a clipped pace as she tried to figure out what had just happened. Alexander was still inside of her, hard and pulsing, and yet her eyes remained on the gash in his wrist.

"What happened?" she asked, licking her lips as her mind conjured images of closing that wound herself.

"It's no good."

"What?"

"It's not working. Your blood. I have to have it . . ." He pulled out of her, panting, his eyes cherry black and ravenous.

Without him, she felt so cold. "In the cage, the meat . . ."

"It's too late." He was backing away. "It won't hold me now. Something's happened. Something's been triggered." He shook his head. "This was . . . a mistake." He doubled over, gasping. "Fuck."

She started to go to him.

"No!"

He turned on her, his eyes blazing. His gaze fixated on her breasts, on her nipples still hard and glistening from his kiss. Then his gaze dropped, to the curls between her thighs, wet from his come. His fangs dropped and he roared a painful cry. "Go. Back to your room. Now. Before I bleed you dry."

Tears pricked her eyes. She grabbed her clothes and ran. She hoped she was going in the right direction, was wearily thankful when she saw the staircase and the door leading to the main house. At the base of the stairs, she dressed at lightning speed, then dashed up the steps and through the door.

Dillon stood there, right in her path, an unreadable expression on her face. "Have fun?"

"Fuck you," Sara uttered, pushing past her and hustling toward the stairs, wishing she'd never followed Evans, yet at the same time hoping Alexander would come after her again. God, she was stupid. By the time she got to her room, the anger had downgraded into something resembling pathetic despair. Her body felt so empty, her mouth dry. What the hell was happening to her? She pressed her head against the wood, listened to her heart knock inside her throat. The blood. His blood. *Shit*. Had she triggered something inside the both of them by ingesting it? Even those tiny drops?

She brought her hands up, palms splayed on the door. Oh God, she scented him. He was near. Her mouth watered. *No. no.* She pushed away from the door and ran down the hall. *Up*. She needed *up*. She took the stairs two at a time, her breath coming quick. At the top, she turned and ran down the hall toward his room. But something stopped her in her tracks—a figure, crouched near the wall. She began to walk slowly toward it, realizing the closer she got that it was Alexander huddled there. He was outside Bronwyn's door, his hand gripping the handle. He looked desperate, ravaged, like an injured animal.

Tears welled in Sara's eyes and she shook her head. "Just do it."

He looked up at her, his eyes unnatural, filled with a passion that had nothing to do with sex. "You don't understand," he uttered hoarsely.

"No?" She moved closer, until her feet were nearly touching his. "Tell me, then."

"The hunger is too great." His eyes rolled back as he sniffed the air. "What happened between us destroyed my control."

"So you want to fuck me and feed from her."

"No." He shook, his muscles rippled. "I want only you."

She stared down at him and whispered the word "Impossible."

"Sara . . ."

"Remember that word? Impossible? It's how you thought of us."

Before she had a chance to take another breath, Alexander reached out, grabbed her wrists, and pulled her down to him. He looked at her, every inch of her face until he held her gaze. His words had an edge to them, a bitter growl. "There's nothing I want more than to be inside you again, so deep you can barely breathe." He may have been on his knees, but he was still a creature to be feared. "I want to drink from you while I make you come again and again." His grip on her tightened; his mouth inched closer, just inches from her own. "But if I feed from you, I won't be able to stop—not until I've consumed every drop of your blood, not until I've quieted your heart. With all that you care for in this world, are you willing to take that risk?"

Sara held her breath, tears falling from her eyes onto her cheeks as she fought the need of her body and her heart with the promise she'd given long ago.

"Are you?" he demanded coarsely.

She shook her head.

He leaned in, brushed his mouth against hers. "Impossible."

Sara pulled away from him. "I can't stay here."

"Sara."

"I won't stay here and watch while you go into another female's room and feed from her." She backed up, tears streaming down her face. "I'm a fool, but I'm no masochist."

"It's a feed," he called after her. "It's nothing. It's you going into your kitchen and taking a steak from the—"

"No!" She shook her head. "It's not."

She turned and walked away. She wouldn't glance back. If she saw Bronwyn open her door and touch him, she wasn't sure what she'd do. It was impossible to deny. Since ingesting Alexander's blood, a change had occurred within her—just as he had said it would. But the change wasn't into a corrupt *Imiti*—not yet anyway. It was into a female who felt entirely too comfortable with the idea of slamming her fist into the face of anyone who got too close to her vampire.

She started to run, didn't stop until she was inside her room. She packed her things in a haphazard manner—wet toothbrush with dry underwear. She didn't care. She had to go. The danger inside the house had just become greater than the one that waited for her on the outside.

Bags in hand, she left her room and walked down the hall, praying she didn't run into anything with fangs on her way out.

28

Lucian leaned into the spray. He liked it hot. Burning-the-skin kind of hot. Made him wonder if morpho would dissuade him from going in the sun or encourage him. Grinning, he shut off the water and grabbed a towel, wrapped it around his waist.

He was one step inside his bedroom, one foot on the hardwood floor, when his skin twitched violently. In a flash, he reached behind the Hockney on the wall, grabbed his gun, and aimed it at the *veana* standing beside the massive Chinese Evergreen in the corner of the room.

"You almost got your head blown off, princess."

"That would've been most unfortunate," Bronwyn said, walking toward him, looking imperious and completely unruffled by the weapon in his hand.

Why the hell wasn't she afraid of him? Lucian mused with irritation. Maybe she knew about his agreement with Alexander, the vow he'd made to keep an eye on her during this handfasting period.

"Coming into a *paven*'s room without his consent, and without a *tegga*." Lucian clucked. "The *credenti* would not approve."

"Edel is sleeping, and"—she shrugged—"I did knock."

"Yet when you got no answer, you decided to break in?"

"It was vital I see you."

His pale brow lifted. "Was it? How much of me did you wish to see, princess?"

She looked down her nose at him. "Don't be crude, *paven*. I've come to tell you that your brother's gone."

Lucian stared at her.

"Alexander," she said. "He's not at home."

"And?"

She walked over to the window. Lucian followed her with his eyes. Those high-heeled boots and jeans she had on were really working for her. "He was outside my door with the human woman, Sara," she said, her back to the window now, to the heavy snowfall outside. "They were arguing about his need to come to me, drink from me."

A thread of covetousness moved through Lucian, but he discarded it instantly.

"I heard her say she was leaving for good," Bronwyn continued. "Alexander seemed very upset about it."

"And did he?" Lucian asked brusquely. "Did he come to you?"

Bronwyn's lips pressed together and her gaze dropped to the floor. "No."

Lucian narrowed his eyes. There was shame in her scent. Had she told Alexander he could drink from her and he declined, rejecting her? Or was there something else? "When was this?"

"Twenty minutes ago."

He glanced at the clock. An hour until dawn. What the hell was Alexander playing at? "You checked the house?"

"Evans conducted a search."

Maybe he was still in the tunnels, hiding, Lucian thought. Maybe the cage. "I'll take care of it." But even as he said the words, he knew in his gut that his brother had gone after Sara.

He headed into his closet.

"I'd like to help if I can," Bronwyn called after him.

"Why are you so concerned?" he called back.

"What?"

He grabbed some jeans and a heavy sweater and headed back into the room. "Why do you care about Alexander? He doesn't care for you. He wants nothing to do with his true mate—none of us do."

"How lucky for you," she muttered.

He tossed his clothes onto the bed. "What?"

"You're all very lucky you can choose to reject your true mate like that." She crossed her arms over her splendid chest and regarded him with a vicious stare.

"So easy. No care for the *veana* and what becomes of her life, her future. What nightmare awaits her if you choose not to search for her, claim her, mate with her for life. For some of us, it's about survival."

Lucian said nothing, but his gaze held hers. She was something, this *veana*. A controlled beauty and a real pain in the ass. But if she thought he was going to feel sorry for her, she could think again. "Everyone has a sad story to tell, sweetheart. But yes," he added, dropping his towel, "I am lucky."

He waited for her to gasp, cover her eyes, curse at him for standing before her with his cock hanging out. But she didn't. "Not going to run screaming from the room, princess?"

She held his gaze. "I've seen my fair share of *paven*."

His brows lifted.

She shrugged. "Just because I remain intact doesn't mean I don't have the need for it. When the time is right, I will go after what I want, what I need."

Lucian's cock stirred, and Bronwyn's gaze dropped.

He made the mistake of watching her watch him.

She licked her lips.

Shit. He turned away and yanked on his pants. "On your search through the house, did you happen to see Nicholas?"

"No."

"Course not," he muttered. His brother was disappearing too damn much lately—time for an intervention.

Dressed and a little cock heavy, Lucian strolled past Bronwyn and walked out the door.

"You're welcome," she called after him.

"Oh, yeah. Thanks, princess." He didn't turn around. "You're a real ass-saver."

Ethan scored the skin of Pearl's belly, lapped at the droplets of blood, then lowered his head to listen. She had only a gentle swell, but Ethan could hear the slow thudding of his newest recruit beneath her pale skin.

"The *balas* is doing well," he said, lifting his head. "You are a solid host, my sweet Pearl."

Pearl smiled and moved closer to him on her bed. "I would do anything for you, you know that."

"I do." Ethan had used the powers of the Supreme One to get into the hospital undetected and to keep Pearl's roommate asleep and unaware. Pearl had begged to see him and though he had not the time or interest to look in on her, he didn't want her to start yapping to the doctors and nurses about what grew inside her womb.

Noticing the annoying look on her face, Ethan asked, "What is wrong, Pearl?"

"I hate it here," she said with fake tears in her tone. "The doctor won't leave me alone. I can't do anything. Ethan, when can I leave? I want to be with you."

"Soon, my love," he said. "But for now, the *balas* must be protected above all things." He heard her woeful sigh and chuckled. "What do you need from me, sweet one?"

"A taste of you. To feed your *balas*."

Ethan raised an eyebrow, moderately impressed. Pearl McClean was no innocent. She knew well how to play him, as he played her. They would do well together in future, his seed implanted in her every year until she could give him nothing more. Then he'd toss her back where she came from.

"It can be for only a moment," he said. "Then I must go."

She nodded, and when he ran his fangs across his wrist and presented it to her, she eagerly licked her lips, then lowered her head.

29

Sara glanced at the clock on the table near her bed. It was close to five. Even though she'd gotten less than twenty minutes of sleep on the hotel's excessively soft mattress, she needed to get up and take a shower. She wanted to get to work early and find Peter, run her idea by him—prove to herself that she was still her, still one hundred percent focused on Gray's recovery, despite the infinitesimal amount of Alexander's blood running quietly through her veins.

For one quick moment, she stared at the wall in front of her, at the hotel's nondescript version of abstract art. The Miró lookalike reminded her of internal organs—liver, spleen, lungs, with rivers of blood intersecting. Blood. It seemed to be part of her stream of consciousness now, not to mention a turn-on, an odd combination of fear and desire.

She let her vision blur then, let the shapes in the painting become just saturation of color. What had Alexander done after she'd left him? Had he given in, taken what he'd needed from the one who thought they were true mates? Her gut twisted at the image of his mouth anywhere near Bronwyn, let alone feeding from her vein. But what was his choice? Starve to death? And what was her choice? Risk her life, and in turn risk her brother's future recovery?

She could never do that.

She turned, saw her cell phone beside the clock, and reached for it. The numbers on the screen blinked up at her, tempting her. Her hands shook as she punched in the numbers. Her heart thudded in her chest as the phone rang. Once, twice, three times—

"Hello?" A woman's voice.

Oh God. She was so weak.

"Hello?" A familiar, soft, tired woman's voice. "Who's there?"

Sara put her hand over her mouth.

"Is anyone there?" A moment passed, then another. "Sarafena?" the woman said softly. "Sarafena, is that you?"

Sara closed her eyes. The ache that moved through her was debilitating. It was the ache of a child who wanted to be held again, comforted—*forgiven.* And she knew her mother would have done that for her in an instant if she'd only let her. But she wouldn't let her. Not yet.

"Hi, Mom."

"Oh." There was a sigh of relief on the other end of the phone. "Honey, are you okay?"

"Everything's going well. As you saw when you

were here last month, Gray's progress has slowed down, but I think I've found a way, a new, innovative way to tamp down his—"

"Sara, please," her mother interrupted gently. "I know all about Gray. I want to know about you. Are you all right? When are you coming home? Just for a few days . . . Maybe for Christmas?"

Tears pricked Sara's eyes. It had been years of that question—ever since Sara had come to get Gray and bring him to Walter Wynn. And Sara's answer had always stayed the same. *Not yet.* She wasn't coming home until she could bring her mother's son back to her with his mind intact.

"Sara, are you there?"

"Mom, I sorry. It's late. I've got to get ready for work. I'll see you here in a few months, okay?"

Sara stabbed the end button and sat up. Her throat was so tight and she felt nauseous. She shook her head. She wasn't going to cry again today. It was useless. A stupid, useless reaction that weak individuals resorted to when they didn't get what they wanted. She grabbed the hotel phone and dialed a new number.

"Yes." *Dillon.* She was in the room next door. She'd followed Sara out of the house in SoHo, refusing to leave her alone and unprotected until Alexander gave her the word.

"I have an early call," Sara informed her. "I'll be ready in twenty minutes."

Dillon snorted. "Bated breath, Doc. Bated breath."

* * *

He was new, reborn and retooled.

Alexander followed two of Ethan Dare's recruits across the Brooklyn Bridge, Bronwyn's pure blood coursing through his veins. He felt unflinchingly strong, totally focused, his speed and vision outstanding.

Scurrying past a stone pylon, the pair of Impures glanced back, but they didn't see him—just as they hadn't seen him waiting in the shadows outside Dare's town house. Heavy snow rained from the sky, making the view of lower Manhattan look like the insides of a snow globe. The snow, combined with Alexander's flash movements forward, to one side, then another on the wood plank walkway, kept the recruits and any human up and out at five thirty a.m. from seeing him.

Once off the bridge, the two Impures raced past City Hall Park toward the Financial District. Alexander shadowed them, a sinking feeling growing in his gut as he realized where they were headed. He'd hoped these boys would lead him to Dare, but it looked like they were on a mission to pinch a few more Purebloods.

When they turned onto Liberty, Alexander slowed, found shelter against a building front, and watched as the pair stood outside the gates of the Manhattan *credenti*, talking with their heads bent.

How will you manage it, Impures? Your blood isn't welcome there.

Alexander's muscles twitched. He wanted to move. Hell, he wanted to know what these two were planning and how Dare's recruits were getting inside the *credentis*. He withdrew his knife and nearly flew into the snowy street, but paused when he saw three new Impures approach from the other side of the street.

Alexander's skin tightened and his fangs descended. *Jackpot*.

Ethan Dare *and* Tom Trainer.

Dare walked calmly over to the gate, pulled back the sleeve of his coat, and dropped his head. Alexander watched as Dare brushed the inside of his arm against the bars. The familiar groan of metal disengaging from metal. *So this is how the Impures were getting into the* credentis . . . Alexander sneered. But how the hell was the blood of a half-breed vampire powerful enough to open the gates?

Whatever the answer, they weren't getting inside today.

Alexander was off. He flew straight at Dare, but before he reached the half-breed, an Impure jumped straight in front of him, smashing him in the face with an iron-gloved fist. Alexander reeled back, his nose spurting blood. *Fuckers.* Growling, he hauled off and kicked the male in the head, sending him flying across the sidewalk and into the wall, grinning as he heard the sound of cracking bone. The second Impure came at him fast and furious, diving low, thrusting his knife deep into Alexander's thigh. Blood poured from the wound, but Alexander barely registered the pain. He slammed the recruit in the belly, then slashed his throat. Breathing hard, nostrils flared with rage, Alexander whirled around and sent his elbow into the chest of the other Impure and his fist into the bastard's face.

"Do you really care for the Eternal Breed, or do you secretly wish for its demise?" Alexander heard Dare call out as the extralarge Impure at his side ran at Alexander, blades flashing, fangs flashing.

Spinning around, Alexander cracked the Impure in the head with his fist. The male howled and retaliated with a slice into Alexander's other leg. As blood pooled on the snowy sidewalk, Alexander wished he had Glocks in his fists right now so he could end this bullshit. But there could be no gunplay outside—one shot off and the police would be on the scene.

He couldn't get a bead on Tom and Ethan, as the cowards kept flashing out of his reach.

"You aren't superior to me, son of the Breeding Male," Ethan taunted with a bitter chuckle. "I know who you are, what you are. You may have pure blood, but half of you is animal."

Refusing to lose focus, Alexander flashed, landing directly behind the massive Impure, issuing a battle cry as he slid his blade into the male's back. Hitting rib cage and missing heart.

Flash. Gone. The large Impure—Ethan and Tom with him.

The gasps behind Alexander had him whirling around, crouching, ready to continue the battle through stinging, bleeding thighs and a busted nose. But there was no enemy there—not the kind Alexander was expecting anyway. Several members of the *credenti* stood near the gates, huddled against the cold in their simple nightclothes.

Jaw tight, Alexander nodded at the dead Impures near his feet. "Take them in and dispose of them, unless you want NYPD up your ass."

They looked scared, but did as he instructed, running out to grab bodies and pull them inside the gate. Feeling like shit and breathing heavy, Alexander waited until the gates closed to try and flash home.

He dipped into his mind.

Nothing.

Dammit. With his injuries, he couldn't focus well enough to flash that far. Too much blood loss. He limped down the street, feeling the tug of night ending, the alarm bell ringing in his blood to find shelter. The tunnels weren't too far, ten blocks or so, and he picked up the pace. Like Hansel leaving bread crumbs, Alexander dripped blood, and it was a good thing too. Two blocks into his journey, a BMW rounded the corner, then screamed to a stop in front of him.

The darkly tinted passenger-side window slid down silently. "Get in."

Alexander grinned at the faces of his brothers and jumped in the backseat. "Perfect timing, *duros*."

Nicholas sped off, while Lucian *went* off. "What the fuck, Alex? Do you have a death wish or something? It's nearly dawn!"

"I had them, both of them." He eyed Nicholas in the mirror. "Dare and Trainer."

Nicholas's dark brows lifted. "Bodies on their way to the Order already?"

"They pulled the disappearing act again, but I did manage to take out a few of his recruits."

Nicholas drove with the speed and precision of a race-car driver, utterly focused. "All you get is a few recruits and I get blood all over my backseat."

Lucian chuckled.

"Yeah, sorry about that," Alexander said dryly, shifting his focus to the street they were racing down. Again, he felt the end of night nearing. "Let me out here," he commanded.

"What?" Nicholas barked.

"Right here! Stop the car."

"No way."

"There's access to the tunnels here, through the subway."

Nicholas cursed, but slammed on the breaks. "Where are you going?"

"I'll stay belowground," Alexander said, exiting the car.

"No more hunting solo, *Duro*," Nicholas called after him. "We wait until dusk and go together."

Alexander clipped him a nod. "Agreed."

Lucian glared at him. "You look different, your blood too. Have you *fed*?" He said the last word as though it were an accusation all its own.

"Drained the cow dry." His face as controlled as his words, Alexander lifted a hand in farewell. "Thanks for the save."

The sun was just rising as he rushed down into the subway and toward the secret passage that led to the tunnels. Bronwyn Kettler was certainly no cow, but he'd sworn not to reveal her generous gift to anyone. If the *credenti* found out, they would not accept her back in the fold, for she had fed a *paven* who was not her true mate.

Once in the tunnels, Alexander rejected the path that led him home, taking instead the one that would lead him to Sara. As he ran, his thighs bled and ached to be healed, but his heart was in far more pain. He needed to see her and hear her voice, even if she refused him. He snaked through a tunnel that had clearly been unused for a long time, then entered the hospital basement.

He palmed his cell phone and dialed.

The *veana* answered on the first ring. "You better be in the shade."

"I'm directly below you."

Dillon released an irritated sigh. "You're here? In the hospital?"

"What floor is she on?"

Dillon cursed. "Four. But she'll be heading your way in a few hours."

"For what?"

"Tests on the brother."

"Good." He was no longer surprised at the palpable relief that spread through his system at hearing he would see her soon. "Can you meet me down here?"

"For what?"

"I need a blow job."

She was silent, then ground her words out like crushing glass. "I know I didn't hear you right."

Alexander laughed, his gaze running the length of the gashes in his thighs, the blood oozing from them. "Just get down here, *veana*." Without waiting for a reply, he stabbed the off button and hunkered down in the black corner to wait.

30

The man wasn't tall, but broad in the shoulders and undeniably handsome. His long, blond surfer hair, dimples, and pale blue eyes were a stark contrast to his manner, which was closed off and just plain shady.

Sara didn't trust him as far as she could throw him.

Standing toe to toe with him inside Pearl's room on the juvenile ward, Sara once again explained the reason she was kicking him out. "Unauthorized visits are not allowed, Mr. Barnes."

"Alistair. Please." He gave her a tight-lipped smile. "The child needs her parent, don't you think?"

"Yes, unfortunately that *legal* parent is not here."

"Doctor—"

"I've tried several times to reach her, as has the social worker." Sara's gaze shifted to Pearl, who sat on the edge of her bed, looking flushed and worried. "Pearl, do you know where your mother might be? How I can get ahold of her?"

Pearl didn't even open her mouth before Alistair

jumped in. "Unfortunately, her mother can't handle the stress of this situation. She's asked that I watch over Pearl, and"—he lowered his chin—"of your care of her."

What was it? Sara thought, studying him. There was something almost familiar in his tone and the expression in his eyes. For a second, she wondered if he'd been a patient.

Keeping his back to Pearl, he continued. "And may I say that you are taking fine care of our girl?"

"I'm doing my best," Sara assured him.

"I'm sure you are." He seemed to grow a few inches as he stared down at her.

Sara didn't so much as blink. "And I won't stop caring for her until she is . . . well, herself again."

His eyes narrowed. "Good to know."

They stared at each other for a moment, and Sara wondered if the man felt some type of connection to her as well. What the hell was it? As if hearing her thoughts, Alistair's eyes darkened from baby blue to sapphire, and his nostrils flared as though he scented something unpleasant.

"I should be going," he uttered.

Sara heard Pearl mumble irritably under her breath, but she nodded at the man. "I'll walk you out."

After Alistair said good-bye to Pearl, Sara followed him out of the room and down the hall. Her beeper went off and she glanced down to read the text. The tests she'd ordered for Gray were ready to go, while the bloods she'd been waiting for on Pearl couldn't be located. *What the hell?* The shift in her focus had been ten seconds max, but when she looked up again, Alistair Barnes had disappeared.

Alexander moved soundlessly down the hall, past the morgue, and into an alcove where he would be obscured yet could freely watch Sara through a small square of glass.

"You trying to blow my cover?" Dillon whispered beside him, deep sarcasm threading her tone. "Because you know how much I enjoy that."

"I needed to see her."

"Well, there she is. You saw her. Now fuck off back to the basement."

"You'd better watch yourself, Dillon," he warned softly.

"Yeah?"

"Yeah, you're starting to sound a little like a possessive lover."

She turned and punched him in the very leg she'd healed an hour ago. "Shut up."

He grinned in the darkness. "Don't think I don't see it."

"See what? You're talking in circles."

"You like her." Alexander watched as Sara spoke to her brother, who was lying on his back, eyes closed. "I see the way you look at her."

"Morpho has screwed with your wiring, you know that?" Dillon uttered.

Alexander shrugged. "Can't say I blame you. She's something to see."

"Are we done here?"

"Your secret shame is your own, Dillon. *Paven*, *veana*, whatever you choose to lust over this week makes no difference to me, never has. Sara, however, is mine."

Dillon cursed. "You want to take over this assignment?"

"You know I cannot."

"Then shut it before I walk away and declare my debt paid in full."

Alexander chuckled softly, though his attention remained in a room he could barely see and in it, the woman he ached to touch. "So that's the brother."

"His name is Gray."

"They look alike."

"They're siblings, genius."

"What's she doing with the movie projector?"

"She has a theory about bringing back an old fear to his mind, then using temporary amnesia to place a new, gentle memory in its place. I heard her talking about it with the boss man this morning."

It happened in an instant. One moment Alexander felt nothing, the next every inch of his skin crawled with life. Eyes widening, he stared through the window, directly at Sara. "She wants to get rid of memory?"

"That *is* why the brother's here," Dillon said sardonically, as though she assumed he knew this information and was just trying to annoy her with questions. "Has been for years. Erasing traumatic memory from the brain is her life's work. You know, the fire she accidentally started when she was—" Dillon stopped talking. She turned, shook her head. "No, Alexander."

Alexander didn't respond, his gaze still trained on the woman who refused to come home, the woman he refused to let walk out of his life.

Dillon shook her head. "You can't do it."

"Do what?"

"Oh, please."

"Chill out, Dillon."

"You're one selfish prick, you know that?"

He turned on her, growled his response, "It would be a gift to do this for her."

"A gift?" She snorted.

"Yes."

"No strings attached, right?" she said with obvious sarcasm.

"I have to go."

"Good."

"I have training."

"Maybe you should feed first, clear your head."

"Already done." He pushed away from the wall and without another word, headed for the tunnels.

Standing brazenly on the lawn outside of Dare's town house, Nicholas breathed in his two favorite scents: sex and drugs. His body screamed for both, pushed him to go inside and find both.

But that was an urge he kept hidden, an urge he was forced to quell.

He took out his phone, dialed.

Lucian answered before the first ring died. "Dare on the move again?"

"Long-term this time," Nicholas told him. "He's gone. They're all gone. Including Trainer, who I thought would've been easier to kill than a fly once upon a time."

"Shit. You checked the entire house? Every bedroom?"

Damn right he had, stayed a moment too long in each one, in fact. "Bet they've gone into hiding. After Alexander's minimassacre they know we mean business. Dare must truly fear us now."

"I would say so." Lucian was quiet for a moment, then, "You know we're running out of time—you're running out of time."

"We'll find him."

"I say we contact the 'eyes.'"

Nicholas shrank inside of himself, and the scent of sex and drugs from the town house interiors searched out his nostrils again. "We'll never be able to fully trust them."

"Doesn't matter at this point. We need the help, and they see everything." He could almost hear Lucian shrug. "But it's up to you. Those street rats were your past. If contacting them will bring back your need for *gravo* or—"

"No," Nicholas interrupted brusquely. "They'll have no effect on me now. I'll do it."

After ending the call, Nicholas pocketed his cell and turned from the town house, headed toward his car. The thought of *gravo* made his mouth water. The dried, poisoned blood was a fucking menace to vampire society. It had killed his mother, not to mention his years as a *balas*, but there wasn't a day that went by that he didn't think about it, or a night he didn't crave the complete silence of emotion and the utter deadening of pain it provided.

31

Sara stared, completely disinterested, at the beautiful plate of roasted mussels in a tomato and basil broth.

"Are you going to eat that?"

She glanced up, smiled into the curious, ravenous eyes of her boss, Dr. Pete Albert. "No."

"May I?"

"Of course." She inched the plate toward him. She loved the East Village, and Lavagna had been a wet dream on her culinary brain for more than a year. Now she couldn't conjure up an appetite no matter how hard she tried. She refused to use her emotional state as an excuse, so work-related frustration would have to do. Good thing she had plenty of that. She sat back in her chair, focused on her boss over the easy candlelight.

"Listen, Pete," she began as he poured her plate of mussels over his rigatoni with sweet fennel. "I need to know what I can get away with legally in the McClean case. I want to go to the house, talk to Mommy."

He shook his head as though he'd heard it all before.

"I think you should leave it alone. Let the police and social services handle it."

"You mean wait six months?" she said dryly.

He paused, his fork in the air. "I admire your commitment to your patients, you know that."

"Thank you."

His eyes warmed. "I admire many things about you."

"I appreciate that—"

"But," he jumped in, "breaking rules and breaking laws is one helluva career-ending move."

She shrugged. "I don't know any other way. Things don't get done; problems don't get solved—people remain broken unless you're willing to go out on a limb . . ."

"Are we still talking about Pearl?"

The cozy one-room restaurant seemed to go silent, as if all the guests were leaning toward Sara and Pete's table, listening to their conversation, waiting for Sara's response. Total imaginary bullshit, but it felt that way for a moment.

Pete continued eating. "Just because Gray hasn't responded to the treatment yet—"

"I can't even get to the treatment," she interrupted. "I'm still working on the hypnosis."

"—Doesn't mean he won't respond."

Above her, the tin ceiling felt as though it were closing in. She understood that perseverance was the only way to get results. Odds were good that at some point Gray would give in and go under, and then changing the image in his memory would be cake. It was just that her morale was slipping, and she couldn't seem to stop it.

"Let's get back to talking about Pearl, okay?" she said.

He reached across the table and touched her hand. "Sure."

"I don't think her mom has any clue what's going on with her daughter. That boyfriend of hers . . ." Sara wasn't sure what happened first, if Pete jerked his hand away or she did, but the next thing she knew, her boss looked white as a sheet and was grabbing his stomach with both hands and moaning.

She leaned forward, concerned. "Pete? What is it?"

His face contorted with pain. "I . . . I . . ." He shook his head. "Oh God!"

"Are you all right?"

"I have to go to the restroom." His chair scraped back and he got up, heading for the back of the restaurant. Sara stared after him, then dropped her gaze to the mussels. Oh jeez. And she'd invited him—

The sudden quiet in the room—real, not imaginary this time—clipped her thoughts short and she looked up, hoping not to see Pete laid out on the mahogany floor, convulsing. But the silence had nothing to do with her boss. Walking through the restaurant, looking like six feet three inches of branded, terrifying sex appeal was Alexander. The other patrons seemed to either shrink in his presence or, and this was mostly the female clientele, stare covetously while their dates slumped in their chairs unable to compete with the godforce walking past. Even the staff stopped what they were doing and had the good sense to look nervous.

He sat down in Pete's chair and glared at her. "What the hell are you doing here?"

"Having dinner with a colleague." His scent seized her nostrils, made her stomach growl for the first time in twenty-four hours.

He lowered his voice. "Trainer is still out there and bloodthirsty."

"And Dillon's right over there."

He snorted, as though the *veana* he'd recruited to protect her had zero skills to actually do the job.

Sara leaned forward and whispered, "You need to leave. My boss will be right back."

"Don't count on it."

Her eyes widened. "What did you do?"

He shrugged. "Stomach issues."

"You gave him a stomachache?" she said, furious at his cavalier attitude.

"I suggested it."

"Unbelievable! Why the hell would you do something like that?"

Barely controlled possessiveness rolled off of him. "I don't want him around you. I don't want any male around you."

"Tough shit," she said, keeping her voice barely above a whisper.

A growl rumbled in the back of Alexander's throat as his eyes lowered. "Your mouth is exquisitely delectable when you curse at me."

A searing wave of desire moved through Sara and in her mind she saw flashes of his hands on her skin, raking up the insides of her legs . . . Goddammit! Why did he have to come here? Why couldn't he just leave her alone, let her get over him, forget he existed? She glared at him, asked with barely restrained calm, "How's Bronwyn this evening?"

His gaze caught hers and held. There was great care in their depths. "I wouldn't know. Lucian is responsible for that particular guest."

So he hadn't fed from her? Is that what he was saying? Or he had and he was done, like fast food? She didn't want to ask, couldn't bear the answer if it was the wrong one.

He was watching her, his eyes heavy lidded and filled with ire. "The man in the bathroom wants to fuck you. Did you know that?"

Yes, she knew. "What do you want, Alexander?"

"I want you to come home."

"That's not my home." She shook her head, as much to herself as to him. She had no home, wouldn't until Gray recovered. What Alexander offered her was another place for failure and pain.

"I want you in my bed," he persisted.

"I don't belong in your bed." Where she was good enough to screw, but not feed from . . .

"Why are you out with this man?" Alexander demanded, his voice remaining low and controlled, though his face contorted with rage.

She knew people were staring at them. "It's none of your business," she told him.

"I won't have it."

"Do you hear yourself? You sound like a caveman." She glanced over his massive shoulder to where the bathrooms were. "You need to go."

His face changed and his eyes softened. "I need you," he said gently.

"What you need is something I can't give you."

"Not true." His eyes blazed with heat, with something close to anticipation. "I wish to make you an offer."

She shook her head, her heart utterly deflated, her body and mind growing weary of the fight. "What does that mean?"

"You return home, and I will help your brother."

She froze. "What did you say?"

"His memory of the fire, the pain, all of it, I will remove it from his mind."

Sara shook her head. "What are you talking about?"

"I wish you had told me earlier. I wish I had asked." He nodded, reached for her hand. "I'm sorry for that. But I can help you now. I can remove the memory and the pain from his mind."

She kept shaking her head. The madness he was spouting was almost intolerable, cruel to say the very least. All these years, all the work, and she had barely made a dent in Gray's memory. As if it were so easy . . .

"Sara—"

"I don't believe you." She pulled her hand away, ignoring the feeling of immediate and painful loss. "Why would you say something like that? Suggest something like that? When you know how it would hurt me."

"Sara, it is the truth."

"It's not possible."

"It is," he insisted. "It is part of my abilities as a morphed Pureblood. I am able to remove memory through the blood."

The explanation stopped her, made her stare at him. The thread of hope she'd carried with her these past ten years suddenly trembled inside her tired body.

"There are risks to his memory as a whole," he continued, seeing the change in her expression. "But they're very low. I have every confidence he would—"

She stopped him with a fierce glare. "No." She had to think, had to process what he was telling her with what she knew to be real. The threads of hope pulsed within her, wanting to kill the fear and confusion that accompanied it. "Please, Alexander, I need you to go."

"Sara, you are a practical woman. Please do not react to this suggestion emotionally or irrationally."

Her eyes filled with tears. It was too much. Didn't he get that? Didn't he get the hugeness of what he'd just offered her?

She spotted Pete coming back from the bathroom, looking pale, but alive.

"The man returns." Alexander said the words like a snake hissing.

Sara locked eyes with him, her tone pleading. "If you care anything for me, you'll go now."

He looked ready to argue, but didn't. Instead, he nodded. "Think on my offer, Sara."

Pete drew closer. Sara uttered, "Please. Go."

Alexander leaned down, whispered in her ear, "If he touches you," he said, lapping at the sensitive skin of her lobe, "I swear I will hunt him down and rip out his heart."

As every ounce of blood in her veins went hot and electric and traveled south of her navel, Sara forced her gaze away from Alexander and onto the pale shell of a boss who was walking dispiritedly toward her.

Two hours later, Sara lay on her bed at the hotel room, sheets stripped, lights off, waiting for the inevitable to occur. He would come, and when he did he would once again claim he could fix her brother.

Traumatic memory gone. All visions of the fire and the terror and the pain of his burns.

Gone.

She rolled onto her stomach. Of course, she'd been trying to do that for more than four years now with very little success, and yet the amazing, all-powerful, morphed vampire could make it happen in an instant.

It had to be bullshit. Right?

She flipped to her back again, stared up at the ceiling, at the shadows the adjacent buildings made. What if he could do it? Really take the memory from Gray's mind? The thing was, Alexander himself was an impossibility, a miracle . . .

She turned in to her pillow and closed her eyes for a moment. *What if?*

She must've dozed off on the thought because when she woke up the shadows on the ceiling had changed. Now, instead of floating rooflines, the outline of a man stretched out above her. She sat up, turned toward the floor-to-ceiling windows. Alexander stood on the balcony, twenty stories from the ground, his black wool coat turned up at the collar, the tails striking his thighs in the wind. Her heart leaped into her throat at the size of him, at the brutality of his face, at the raw desire in his eyes.

She scurried off the bed and went to the window. But instead of letting him in, she went out to meet him. The frigid wind whipped at her face and her hair the second she stepped onto the concrete.

"I'm sorry to wake you," he said, his eyes taking in every feature on her face. "But I had to see you."

She stood a good three feet from him and hugged her arms to her chest. "I know why you're here, and I've thought about your offer." She shook her head. "I just can't do it, Alexander."

He took a step toward her. "You're freezing. Let's go inside."

She shook her head, backed up, put her hand out to block him because if he touched her it was all over. "I want you to understand. I can't take the risk."

His dark brows came together. "Which risk are you speaking of? The one to Gray's mind?"

"Yes."

"Sara," he said gently. "I told you—"

"You told me there was a small chance of permanent damage to his memory."

"Infinitesimal. Far less than anything you're doing to him now." Alexander studied her. "Is it truly your brother you're worried about?"

"Of course," she said far more passionately than she intended.

His pupils dilated as he watched her, his nostrils flared as he took in her scent. *I DON'T BELIEVE YOU.*

She pointed at him. "Don't do that!"

He shrugged. "I fear you're lying to me, and to yourself."

"That's ridiculous. I just don't want to do things your way, come back to your house and live with you." Her whole body was shaking now. From cold, and from concern that perhaps Alexander saw her mind and heart better than she ever could. "Go home."

His eyes locked with hers. "I am home. Wherever you are . . ."

The words cut deep into the near-broken heart in her chest. They were lovely words, yet so cruel because they could never be true. Why wouldn't he stop tormenting her?

She turned around and went back into her room.

Alexander followed. "Where are you going?"

"To the bathroom."

"To escape this conversation?"

"Fuck you."

"You are acting like a *balas*, Sara," he said as she shut the door.

She crumpled into a ball on the other side of the wood, hoping he would just go away and leave her alone tonight. Just tonight. Tomorrow she would be herself again: strong, quick, able to take on moody patients, irresponsible parents, and, yes, irresistible vampires with self-serving agendas.

But he didn't. He stood outside the door. "Sara?"

She said nothing.

"What is it really?" he pressed, his tone gentle now as if he really wanted to know, wanted to help her know. "Are you afraid your life's work will have no value? Is it that you will have no identity, no purpose if he's cured?"

Her heart started to race and she scrambled over to the tub and turned on the shower.

"Is it that you can't face him?" he said louder. "Face what you did if he truly gets well?"

"Shut up!" she roared, a sick strain of panic racing

through her blood now. Fully clothed, she climbed into the shower and sat under the spray, desperate to drown out not just his not-so-bullshit analysis of her, but the questions they were bringing up in her mind. It was supposed to have been her. She was supposed to have fixed Gray, cured him, and brought him home to their mother. If she wasn't the one to do it, what did that make her but a huge time-wasting failure? If she wasn't the one who fixed him, how would she ever gain forgiveness for breaking him in the first place?

She heard the lock click open, the door creak back, and Alexander walk into the bathroom. The shower curtain ripped back, and he looked down at her, his body suddenly engulfed in steam.

"Jesus." He stripped bare, then climbed in, knelt down in front of her. "Let me help him. Let me help you."

Her eyes lifted to his. "You don't want to help me—you want me to come back. It's all that matters to you."

Alexander cupped her face as water sluiced down her back. "Yes, that is what I want, what I must have. God help me, the need to have you near—the need to see you safe is excruciating and undeniable. But does it matter? The motivation?"

Tears, like droplets of blood, fell from her eyes and her words came out choked and pained. "I'm scared."

"Of what?"

Her head dropped forward. "If I let you do this, I'm a failure. Don't you see? You've brought him back. That wasn't the deal . . . *I* broke him, *I* fix him."

"Look at me," he demanded. "Look at me, woman."

Again, her eyes lifted to his impassioned gaze.

"You are no failure. You are this." He touched her chest, her heart. "You beat with life and with love. You are brilliant, extraordinary, amazing, my captor and my friend. And make no mistake, you have kept Gray alive, as you kept me alive that morning on your doorstep." His voice dropped. "You need to stop punishing yourself."

Sara's lips trembled and she blinked, tears falling to her cheeks.

He shook his head. "I love you, Sara."

Her breath caught in her throat. "What did you say?"

He ran his hands over her face, gently placed her wet hair behind her ears and leaned in, kissed first her top lip, then her bottom. "What I have never said to anyone, have never felt for anyone but my brothers. I love you, and as impossible is it may be, you belong to me as I belong to you."

His mouth covered hers completely and for one brief moment Sara thought about resisting him, resisting her feelings, her need to touch and be touched by this *paven* who claimed to love her. But the moment died a quick death and Sara leaned in to the kiss, her arms wrapping around his neck, her tongue slipping between his parted lips, telling him yes, *yes*—she was his and they belonged together, connected, fused.

Alexander groaned, and his hand went around her waist, his fingers gripping her wet clothes as overhead the shower rained down on them both. He made love to her mouth, his tongue stroking hers, his teeth nipping at her lips hungrily. He loved her. Even under the hot water and the sweet assault of his mouth, she shivered with the memory. Not a day would go by that she didn't hear him say those words, not a night when she didn't remember his eyes, tender and true, as he confessed what she already knew; there was an unbreakable, remarkable bond between them that was only broken by a hunger for blood.

Alexander pulled his mouth from hers and stood up, his eyes heavy-lidded and lust-filled as he lifted her out of the tub and placed her on the white bathmat. With deft hands, he peeled the clothes from her body until she stood before him wet and naked, her expression filled with longing. She needed him inside her body, his weight on her, his eyes locked to hers as he moved in and out.

"You're cold?" he asked, concerned.

She smiled softly, sadly up at him. "No. But I am lonely, empty."

He gathered her up in his arms, gave her a kiss on the tip of her nose, then carried her out of the bathroom. The bedspread was pulled back and Alexander placed her down on the soft white sheets. For a moment, he stood there, looking down at her, his eyes fierce with longing, his cock standing up proud. Behind him, the glass door remained open and the November wind sent achingly soft snow into the room.

But Sara felt nothing but heat and need, and she reached for him. "Please, Alexander."

"Yes, love." He leaned down, his hands splayed on her ankles, up he raked to her knees, her inner thighs until he had her legs spread so wide her cunt wept for him. "You in me and me in you. For hours, forever." He entered her with one hard thrust and stayed there, the head of his cock kissing her womb.

Closing her eyes to the delicious feeling of being impaled, marked, Sara moaned, "Oh God, yes. Stay there, right there."

"Always," he whispered against her mouth, pressing deeper inside of her. "Look at me, Sara." His eyes blazed down into hers. "Your cunt is so hot, so wet, like a sweet fist, tempting me to move."

His words made her skin tremble, and she squeezed the muscles around his erection until he groaned. "The perfect fit," he uttered, tucking a hand under her ass and pressing her even closer, his cock thrusting impossibly deeper. Breathless, completely filled by him, Sara wrapped her legs around his waist and again squeezed the muscles that surrounded him.

Alexander grinned down at her, growled sensually, "Keep doing that and I'll come."

She smiled back. "Promise?"

He leaned down and nibbled at her lower lip. "Yes, and again I will be struck by my hunger for you." He started to move then, slowly at first as he kissed her softly, tenderly.

As he pumped inside of her, Sara let her hands explore him—his legs, his buttocks, so taut with muscle. Then up to his lean waist and rock-solid back, the skin straining to contain the sinew and bone—then over his shoulders, so terrifyingly massive, and his neck, his face. With gentle fingers, she traced the brands on his cheeks, then lifted her head and lapped at one with her tongue.

Oh God, the taste of him. Honey and passion fruit . . .

Alexander hissed and she felt his body go rigid, felt his cock grow even harder, stretching her. Grinning, she turned her head and traced the brand on his other cheek with her tongue.

How did he taste so sweet? She could get drunk off his skin, his . . . blood . . . She let her teeth graze over the rough brand—

"Fuck!" Alexander howled, pulling out of her, the sound of suction lost echoing in the room. "Your lips are dangerous, both pairs . . ." He grabbed her knees and pressed her legs all the way to her shoulders, spreading her so wide he had perfect access to every wet inch of her. He was inside of her in an instant, sinking back into the hot glove of her body and thrusting away. "Yes, dangerous, delicious . . ." Panting, keeping his eyes locked on hers, he slammed into her over and over. *MINE.*

Sara's breaths were coming in gasps, every inch of her screaming for him, tightening for him, wanting him to feed from her even if it cost her her life. She was a fool, drugged and desire-filled. She reached between them and palmed her breasts, tugging at her nipples until they beaded hard and dark.

Alexander's gaze slipped and he groaned at what he saw. "I'm sorry, Sara. Can't go slow. Too sweet, too hot, tight . . ."

"No," she uttered as she pumped her hips, keeping his frantic pace. "Fast. Hard. Please."

Alexander covered her mouth, thrust his tongue inside just as he thrust his cock deeper inside her body. Her breath caught in her throat, heat coiled within her, and her veins pulsed with the blood in her heart. She couldn't stop the building passion inside her and she didn't want to. Jutting her hips up, squeezing her cunt, she cried out, crashed, went over the edge. It was too beautiful, the sensations running through her, so frantic and sweet, and she refused to release it until he came inside her.

Her mouth moved from his and found the brand on his left cheek. She growled low and nipped at the rigid flesh with her teeth. Alexander cursed, bucked wildly. Sara suckled the brand into her mouth, played the damaged skin like a nipple with her tongue.

Fingers digging into the skin of her shoulders, Alexander slammed his cock so deep within her body Sara felt him in her belly. Hot seed spilled into her cunt, and Sara squeezed the muscles that surrounded him, wrapped her arms around his neck and hugged him close, reveling in the spasms and jerks of his climax.

He loved her.

She smiled, reveled in the feel of his weight atop

her. She nuzzled her head into the curve of his neck, her eyes open and unfocused. His shoulder spread out before her, looking massive and edible. She licked her lips, watching as his skin seemed to pulse. In her muddled brain she heard herself say that it was the same spot that had opened and closed so many times before—the spot she'd tasted, and beneath it, the blood that could change her . . .

Something snapped, her mind, her hunger . . . and she couldn't help herself. She lowered her head and bit down hard on his shoulder.

Alexander reared back, his cock coming free of her. "Sara!"

Oh God. She looked from his eyes to his shoulder. Shock and fear blasted through her. She tasted blood on her tongue. *What have I done?* She covered her mouth with her hand. "I couldn't help it."

"Shit. No." Eyes wide, Alexander sat back on his heels.

"I couldn't stop myself. I'm sorry."

He turned and checked his shoulder. "You broke the skin."

"Alexander . . ."

When he turned back to look at her, his eyes were black-red. "Do you taste me?"

Scared, she shook her head, lying to him without using the words. She knew what he thought would happen to her if she ingested his blood—even one drop. And maybe he was right, maybe it had happened already.

Alexander looked angry, shocked, and Sara stammered through another apology. "I'm sorry. I don't understand why I would do that. I don't understand anything right now. I'm so sorry." But even in her fear and confusion she realized she wasn't sorry. Not even a little. As she stared up at him, she wanted to continue what she'd started, taste what glistened on his shoulder now, bright and red and succulent as a peach.

Her heart plummeted to her stomach. What the hell was happening to her? The hunger, not for food, but for him . . . Oh God, what had she done? And what would happen to her next?

"Sara, you could become *Imiti*. Fuck! You must swear to me—" He froze, his attention drawn to something above her head, on the wall.

Sara sat up and turned to look. At first she thought she was dizzy, but then she realized that the plaster was moving, shifting like the pages of a book. Instinctively, Alexander moved in front of her as words formed on the wall.

"What's happening?" she asked. "What is this?"

Alexander stared at the message.

THE IMPURE LIVES IN THE NIGHT. THE SECOND ROMAN BROTHER DIES IN THE SUN. COME TO THE HOLLOW.

"I have finally been summoned."

32

The blood she had given had been a great loss to her, a compromise to her moral code, and yet it had granted her the answers she'd come to the Roman house to find.

Bronwyn took out the last piece of clothing in the drawer and placed it in her bag. Edel was already outside in the car, waiting to take her back to the *credenti*, back to her family, back to her work. She'd wasted enough time here, had been an unwanted guest for far too long. Her pride had taken a beating.

She snatched up her bag and headed for the door. The eldest Roman was supposed to have been hers, but she'd fed him, let him drink from her, and had come away with absolutely no impulse to quell her own hunger. She'd sat across from him as he swore to keep their feeding a secret, every molecule in her body screaming the truth—Alexander Roman was not her true mate.

She walked out into the hall and headed for the

stairs. She had done something wrong in her research, somehow misread the genetic markers. Alexander didn't belong to her, but she needed to find out who did. And there was no time to spare.

"Running away, princess?"

Dressed in black and standing in what had been a living area yesterday and what now looked like combat central with targets on the walls and burlap bags hanging from the ceiling, Lucian eyed her, two sizable knives in his clenched fists.

He looked ready for war.

"I'm going home," she said.

"But I barely had time to do my job," he drawled.

"What job is that?"

"Stand in for Alexander as you're potential mate." He grinned wickedly. "I was really looking forward to it."

She lifted her chin. "Somehow I think you'll get over your disappointment."

"And I think you're wise to give up on the whole true-mate bullshit."

"Oh, I'm not giving up," she said quickly, resolutely. "I'm still going to look. Just not here."

Lucian growled, turned around, and rammed both blades into the very center of one of the burlap sacks. "Just keep yourself locked up nice and tight, princess. There are dangerous males about."

Her gaze moved over him and she nodded. "Damn right there are."

His fierce eyes narrowed, but Bronwyn could've sworn she saw a spark of amusement in their depths.

Yes, going home was right. "Good-bye, Lucian." She turned and grabbed the door, yanked it open, then whispered, "Be careful," before she closed it gently behind her.

The ancient ten had returned to the Hollow. They sat at the glass table, hands folded, their eyes—the left ones branded with thin black circles—following Alexander as he walked over smooth, soft sand toward them.

"You have failed, son of the Breeding Male," said Cruen, his electric blue stare deadly. "Abductions have slowed, true, but Ethan Dare is still at large."

"The failure here is yours," Alexander returned with venom. "I came to you and told you that the half-breed has the powers and abilities of a Pureblood morphed male and you refused to believe it. Why do you think you could not track him! He is being protected."

There was a collective gasp among the members, a rustle of red robes as they turned to whisper panicked mumblings to their neighbors. "What is this?" and "Impossible!" and "How could it be?"

Cruen stood, called for calm among his peers, and when he had their attention, pulled his lips up tight in a grin that had nothing to do with humor. "I still refuse to believe it." He looked around at his peers. "Alexander Roman lies. He lies to explain away his failure."

Alexander swore in the ancient language, his knuckles white, fists ready to fly into the old *paven*'s bony face. "Dare can flash and so can his recruits. He used his blood to get into the *credenti*."

The *paven* chuckled. "Impures can never be anything more than what they are—a waste of blood."

Alexander sniffed. "You an Impure, then, Cruen?"

Something halfway between a growl and a scream shot from Cruen's throat and he opened his mouth wide and flexed his brick red fangs.

Alexander stalked over to the table and stood before the Pureblood. "Unless you're going to use those," he snarled, "put them back in your head and tell me why I am here."

Cruen started to stand, but the *veana* with the long snow-colored hair beside him slammed a hand over his arm. He hissed at her, but remained seated. His gaze lifted and Alexander saw the true force of evil within those pale blue orbs.

"This is the last time we will call on you, son of the Breeding Male," Cruen spat out. "You have twenty-four hours to bring Dare to us or Nicholas Roman will be morphed. Perhaps he will bring us what we seek."

Sara had the room for one hour.

Hopefully, it would be all she needed.

Venturing a glance at her brother, who was lying on the hospital bed she'd set up in the media room on the first floor of Walter Wynn, Sara noticed that his body looked rigidly still and his eyes were clamped shut.

She tried again, the slow, calmness in her voice concealing the profound anxiety running through her insides. "You are relaxed, Gray. So relaxed that the muscles in your feet, your ankles, your knees, your legs are so heavy you cannot lift them. So relaxed that your belly, chest, and shoulders are sinking into the bed. So relaxed your neck, face, and eyes are limp." Sara turned on the projector and the blank wall before Gray's bed erupted with light. There was no sound, only visions. Only images of fires, one after the other after the other.

She turned to look at him and said gently, "Open your eyes, Gray."

His face twitched as if he was trying to shake his head, but his muscles were too weak.

"Open your eyes now," she said again, a little stronger this time.

Like a lover going in for a kiss, or a fish stretching for food, Gray pressed out his lips. He was talking—in the only way he could and Sara knew what the movement meant.

No.

Normally, she'd give up at this point, let him be, let him rest. But not today. She didn't have the time or the patience for his petulance. She leaned down close to his ear and whispered tersely, "Open your eyes, dammit!"

He flinched, but slowly his eyes opened and he stared up at the screen. He didn't gasp, didn't turn away, scream, or get agitated in any way, as she'd thought he would—as she'd hoped he would so she could take the next leap into the treatment. What he did do was stare up at the images, eyes unblinking like some scene from *Clockwork Orange*, tears welling in his eyes, then snaking down his cheeks.

Fuck. Fuck Gray and fuck me.

Sara flicked off the projector, went to stand in front of him, her emotions high as they had been for days. "Look at me, you stubborn bastard."

He did, his eyes bright with the tears of a tormented soul. She recognized the look, she'd seen it in the mirror on more than one occasion.

"Is this it?" she asked him, shaking her head. "Are you ever going to let me help you? Or am I done? Do you want me to be done?"

He stared at her.

"Because I've had offers. Not pretty and probably painful as shit, but there's someone who can help you in a way I can't seem to."

Gray dropped his gaze and looked away.

As he always did.

Jaw tight, those goddamn tears pinching the back of her throat again, Sara pushed off the bed and went out into the hallway. "Bring him back up," she told the orderly. "I'm done."

Soul weary, Sara headed for the stairs, for her office and for the twenty remaining patients who actually wanted her help.

* * *

Drugs were being sold in Washington Square Park in broad daylight, bodies too, and the scent of both made Nicholas's prick stand up. He shoved his BlackBerry into the pocket of his coat, the message from Alexander thoroughly imprinted on his mind. Twenty-four hours until he was sunlight intolerant. Hmm. How much did he care? What living he did do usually happened after the sun died anyway. If it wasn't for Lucian and the very real possibility that when he morphed he would become the next Breeding Male, caged and tested by the Order, he might just forget this whole battle, tell the Order to kiss his Roman ass, tell the troll standing in front of him now to return to his bridge.

"So what do we get for assisting the Romans?" The short, hairy "eye" in front of him grinned, his fangs worn down from too much *gravo*.

"I can offer you money or blood," Nicholas said. "Which do you want?"

"I'd say we wanted you, Nicholas," the "eye" said with a cackle. "But you work the streets without a master now, don't you?"

His gaze unwavering, Nicholas stood utterly still.

"Those ribbed fangs of yours were a real draw, even as a young *paven*." The "eye" leaned closer, his breath resembling a decades-old trash can. "I'm curious—what do you do with the money you're paid for one of those fancy fucks? Don't have another *veana* to buy *gravo* for, do you?"

Nicholas had a knife to the "eye's" back before the *paven* could take his next breath. "I will ask you once more before I rip you open, neck to asshole—money or blood?"

A chirping sound erupted from the "eye's" throat and he forced out, "Three hundred grand for the location of the Impure."

"By tonight."

"Agreed."

"Good to see you, Whistler." Nicholas slapped the *paven* on the back, shoved his knife into the waistband of his jeans, and took off into the park.

33

Tom Trainer had changed. Strong body, keen eyesight, developing fangs, and the kind of hearing a bat would envy. So he was hardly surprised to overhear a hushed discussion between Dare, Alistair, and Mear three rooms over, in the new compound Ethan had procured for them. He was, however, surprised to hear his name mentioned, and when the male voices dropped another decibel, he jumped to his feet and went over to the door to listen.

"You did promise him, Commander." It was Mear.

"He's not ready yet," Ethan said tightly. "He will go after that doctor and not only forget his obligation to me, but cause a disturbance that might hinder my plan."

"But, Commander, I could—"

"Do you want a dead lover, Mear? Because if he goes and my wishes aren't carried out to the letter, I will slice him apart in front of you, understand?"

"Yes, Commander."

"He will have his day to drain the pain-in-the-ass doctor. Today I must take back what is mine. If what Alistair says about the doctor is true, if she indeed has vampire blood in her veins, the *balas* and its host are no longer safe there. Mear, you go with Alistair. Make sure there are no problems."

"Yes, sir."

Tom hid behind the door as the two recruits passed by him. They were going to Walter Wynn.

His blood, renewed, strong, lustful, and hateful, cried out for her.

Sara.

Ethan Dare was his commander, and he would follow him in all things. All things, but one.

Today, he followed Mear and Alistair—right out of the iron gates and into the street.

34

Sweat ran from Alexander's neck to his chest and arms, but he didn't slow. Hadn't in the past three hours. Hyped up and ready for battle, he'd run the tunnels, then sparred with three Impure guards, before following Lucian on the course he'd erected in the living room.

Night had fallen now and as the burlap bags swayed back and forth, Alexander weaved between them, slamming his blades into the center of each. Planted in the hallway, fresh from his own workout, Lucian cleaned weapons, while Nicholas performed a little cyber recon on Google maps as he waited for news from the "eyes."

"It's too bad Bronwyn's gone," Nicholas said, typing furiously. "Knowing who Dare's family connections are—who could be helping him . . ."

"You can blame Luca for that," Alexander muttered as he ripped a burlap sack from top to bottom, sending beans raining all over the floor. "She just couldn't handle being around such a charming personality all day."

Lucian glared at the destruction. "Hey, save it for the Impures, Alex. That's my work there."

Nicholas eyed Alexander and grinned. "Yes. Charming."

The screech of a car's brakes outside the house dissolved Alexander's dark chuckle, and had them all up and headed for the window. Alexander got there first, his gaze dropping to the curb below.

"What is it?" Lucian asked, coming up behind him.

"Dillon's car," he said, already turning around to go. "Halfway up on the curb. Something's up."

The brothers were out the front door, down the steps in mere seconds. They rushed over to the town car, ignoring the driver, to find Dillon slumped in the backseat. "What the hell happened to you?" Alexander demanded.

Dillon lifted her head then, let the top half of her body fall back against the seat. No bruises, no blood . . .

"Oh, shit," Alexander uttered as he saw the man sitting beside her in the back, dressed for a freaking summer day in jeans and a T-shirt. "You took Sara's brother from the hospital?"

"The human," Dillon whispered, her tone pained. "Trainer—he tried to attack Gray. I had to . . ."

Alexander's guts dropped into his boots. "Sara?"

Dillon squinted up at him. "She was with a patient. She's okay. She doesn't even know."

Alexander gestured to Nicholas and Lucian. "Take him in, call Leza, and tell her to get over here."

When Gray was out of the car and headed into the house, huddled against both brothers for support, Alexander leaned in and tried to remove Dillon from the backseat. He wasn't sure what kind of injuries she'd sustained, but knew they were internal.

"Trainer's body is still in the room," she said, letting Alexander pull her out and onto the sidewalk.

"Dead or out cold?" he asked, helping her up the steps.

She was pressing her hand against her right side. "I don't know. Didn't have time to check."

"Why the hell were you with the brother? Why weren't you watching her?"

"She asked me to go to him." They got to the door, inside the entryway. Dillon pushed him off of her. "I'm okay. You have to go back."

"She'd better be unharmed." Alexander turned to go, to flash, just as Dillon collapsed in the doorway, blood seeping from her side.

Sara entered her office, and with a heavy veil of exhaustion dropped into her chair. Long-ass day, and now she had the pleasure of going back to her hotel room, ordering a pizza, and watching some bad TV as she stared out at the balcony hoping the other half of her heart would show up and maybe make her cry again . . . maybe make her come again.

Her skin vibrated at the thought. Or she could take his deal. Her throat went dry. She was so damn thirsty. Had been for two days now. And not the kind of thirst that can be satiated with a few glasses of water. Her lust, her perverse need to possess Alexander had done something to her, changed her physical structure, and now his blood was all she thought about.

Over the years, she'd treated a few patients who were "human vampires," mostly adolescents who were desperate for love, their beliefs and rituals self-destructive and impossible to maintain in society. And yet Sara couldn't help wondering if one of them had perhaps met up with a friend of the Romans.

She sighed, grabbed a few files from the stack on her desk. Her gaze flew over the pages: Derek Kennedy wasn't tolerating meds, diarrhea . . . *fine, fine*. Pamela Newl was back for the fourth time—twelve-year-old daughter brought her in this time . . . Pearl McClean: second set of lab results—*never got the first*. With keen interest, Sara scanned the labs, thinking that Pete was probably right about letting the cops and social deal with the mom. Unfortunately, Sara rarely did what was "right" in these kinds of situations. Instead, she did what she had to do to get the answers she—

Sara sat forward in her chair, her pulse knocking harder in her veins, louder in her ears. She stared at the file, the labs. "Jesus Christ."

She grabbed the phone, dialed the extension for the nurse's station in the juvenile ward. The second it was picked up, she jumped. "This is Dr. Donohue. Is Pearl McClean in her room?"

"Dr. Donohue, Pearl was released an hour ago."

Blood drained from Sara's face. "What?"

"You signed her out yourself."

"No—" A hand stole around Sara's mouth, the other reached around her, grabbed the phone, and yanked it from the wall.

Instinct jumped in Sara's blood, and she drove her heel into the ankle of the attacker, grabbed at his hand, and clawed at his flesh. But whoever it was held her in an iron grip.

"You can forget about Pearl," the man whispered, his mouth near her neck. "She's with the commander now."

Sara's eyes widened and her nostrils flared trying to get air in her lungs. *Fuck no!*

Tom Trainer.

She bit down on his hand, then flinched at the sudden pain. Her teeth, they hurt, felt loose . . .

Tom jerked her back against him, keeping his hand over her mouth, but snaking his arm across her belly. "I've missed you, Dr. Donohue."

The fight in Sara hummed, wanting to get out, get wild. She slammed her elbow back into his gut, over and over, but he barely flinched.

"I thought about holding you again, touching you," he said, sadness threading his tone. "I thought about it every time he touched me. It was like we were all together. The three of us. Maybe that's how it's meant to be."

Recalling a technique she'd read about in a case study, Sara sucked in her breath, hunched her back slightly, and spun in his arms, stopping when she faced him. Without a thought, she kneed him hard in the groin. When he sucked in air, she did it again, a huge jolt straight to the balls. But he didn't back off, didn't do anything but breathe heavy and grip her so tightly against him that she could manage only tiny gasps of air.

He smiled down at her. "I look different, don't I? I feel different. I *am* different."

She couldn't give a shit. She struggled in his arms.

"A friend shared his blood with me," Tom said.

For one brief moment, Sara froze, looked up at him. "Shared blood . . ." Oh God. That's what she'd missed. The look in Tom's eyes—she'd seen it before. The cuts, the look of pleasure in Pearl's eyes—she had fed too.

"Jealous?" Tom leaned down and ran his tongue over the skin at the base of her neck. "I'd be happy to show you how it's done."

Sara struggled against him, but her breath was shallow in her lungs.

"My fangs aren't as sharp as some, but they'll get the job done." He chuckled. "Too bad your favorite patient won't be able to witness your transform—"

"What?" she managed to utter. "What patient?"

"The one who always comes before the rest of us."

Gray? God, no. Her eyes searched Tom's maniacal ones. "Where . . . ?"

"Why do you love him so much?" A snarl erupted from Tom's throat and he released her, gripped her shoulders and pushed her back, rammed her against the wall.

Gasping for breath, her back screaming in pain, Sara cried, "What did you do? Tell me right now, you sick fuck!"

Tom slipped his hand under her chin, his palm putting pressure on her windpipe. "I would have given you anything. Done anything for you. That vegetable couldn't even say your name."

Kicking out, she fought wildly, like a cat. But it was no use. She was losing air, losing oxygen.

Then suddenly, Tom was yanked off her. She slumped to the floor, grasping her throat, trying to pull air into her lungs, feeling as though she might vomit and pass out simultaneously.

"No, Alexander." Nicholas's voice, somewhere in her mind. "He's mine."

"He touched her."

Alexander. He's here. She pulled in air and cried, "Gray . . . ?"

"He's fine, Sara," Alexander said. "Dillon brought him to me."

"Trainer is mine," Nicholas growled, his mind single-tracked.

"No," Sara said, gasping for breath, pulling herself

up, stumbling over to where Alexander held Tom by the throat. "He's mine." She grabbed the knife from Alexander's waist. "I'm done with this bullshit."

Tom grinned as she approached. "You don't have the guts, bitch."

Without deliberation, Sara hauled back and ran the blade deep into Tom's stomach. The effort exhausted her and she dropped into a chair.

"Oh God, Sara." Alexander gathered her into his arms, held her against him like a child.

In the back of her mind, Sara heard the snap of a neck being broken and a crack of bones as Nicholas finished him off.

"Take her home," Nicholas said quickly. "I'll clean this up."

"Do not dispose of him. We need his memories."

"Where are you going to exit? Roof?"

"Window."

"I'm on it."

Tucked into Alexander's chest, Sara heard the cut of glass, felt the blast of frozen air, then the moment of weightlessness before they were flying.

35

Dillon lay on a bed in one of the Romans' spare rooms, getting sewn up by the vampire doc, while six feet away, the man she'd saved watched with a sneer on his full lips. Gray Donohue was also ass-to-the-bed, his face littered with a few bruises and one cut above his left eye that he'd gotten when Dillon had punched Trainer in the head and he'd fallen back, hitting Gray and knocking him into a food service cart. While his sister's eyes were always a very animated, passionate dark blue, this guy's gaze was metal gray and cold as the death he longed for.

Dillon knew his expression had nothing to do with Tom Trainer's attack. The damaged human male before her hated life, living, existing in a world he felt no connection to, didn't have a place in. Having lived inside herself for two hundred years, Dillon understood the penchant for apathy-laced rage. Not that she was ever going to share her "feelings" with anyone. She didn't do feelings, and wasn't looking for sympathy.

"This may sting a bit," the doctor said, applying some kind of solution to Dillon's wound.

"Shit!" Dillon jumped at the blistering sensation, hissed at her. "You think?"

Leza shrugged and attempted to look repentant. "The wound's incredibly deep. Nearly took out your liver." She smiled. "Let's give this an hour, shall we? Then I'll heal it the rest of the way."

"Sure," Dillon muttered, feeling as though someone had planted bowling balls made of acid inside her organs. "Thanks a million."

As Leza walked out of the room, Dillon caught Gray staring at her, his metallic gaze accusing. *You saved my life for what exactly?*

"What the fuck are you staring at, human?" she barked, her gaze dropping to his hands, the heinous burns that ruined his flesh. Fine. He had a scarred exterior, a shitty life. Yeah, well, internal scars were just as debilitating, just as much of a mind fuck. You didn't see her going around with a perpetually pissed-off puss 24-7.

The door burst open then and Sara rushed in. Her eyes were wild with fear, her expression so anxious Dillon almost wanted to call her over for a hug of support. Almost.

When Sara spotted her brother on the bed, she ran over to him and ran her hands over his skin, his face. "Are you okay? Look at me! God, are you okay?"

"He's fine," Dillon said when the guy refused to make eye contact with her. "Just a few bruises."

"What happened?" Sara asked without turning around.

"Your ex-patient wanted to take out the competition."

"Oh God."

Gray turned his head then and feigned sleep.

"Let him rest, Doc," Dillon urged, knowing Sara was barking up a tree that just wanted its branches cut off.

It took Sara a good five minutes before she moved, before she allowed her gaze to lift from her brother's face. But when she did, she came over to Dillon and shook her head, let out a heavy breath. Her grateful blue eyes took in every inch of Dillon's face. "Looks like I owe *you* a debt now."

The ripe bruise encircling Sara's neck wasn't lost on Dillon, but she kept her eyes off of it and her mood light and easy. "Finally. Someone owes me for once."

Sara reached for her hand, sincerity glowing in her eyes. "Anything you want, D."

Dillon lifted her brows. "Anything?" She'd meant to come off playful, but it was there—she knew it was there in her eyes as she looked up at the human woman she'd been protecting. Attraction. And Sara knew it too.

A smile split Sara's features and she leaned down and kissed Dillon squarely on the mouth. Just once, soft, a peck. When she stood up again, she had the nerve to look impish. "How's that?"

"Not exactly what I expected."

Sara went from impish to insulted in under a second. "What? I didn't bring the heat?"

Dillon laughed. She couldn't help it—the girl was too damn likable. "You and me, Doc—friends. Good friends."

"Fine," Sara muttered. "Have it your way, but don't say I didn't try."

Laughing, though it hurt like hell, Dillon envisioned the expression on Alexander's face when she told him all about the momentary, innocent girl-on-girl action she'd had with his woman.

Yes, she mused, watching Sara return to her brother's side. Busting Alex's chops—good times.

On the roof of Walter Wynn Hospital, Alexander and Nicholas hovered over Tom Trainer's dead body, good times as unattainable an idea as removing the Eternal Order from power. Time ticked loudly away, reminding Alexander that he had to retrieve Trainer's memories before it was too late, before his brain shut down completely and Ethan's hiding place remained a mystery.

Baring his fangs, he dropped his head and struck. He went deep, and directly into the temple. As a premorph he'd barely been able to break the skin without a brutal strike, now it was like a knife through butter.

A tunnel stretched out for miles in his mind, on both sides, still shots of memory played, one frame after the other. Alexander saw Tom as a child, playing on his lawn, Tom hiding in a closet, a rabbit in his lap, his hands encircling the poor creature's neck.

"Easy, Alex," Nicholas warned gently. "Don't get emotionally involved in what you see. Concentrate."

Circling around the memory, Alexander pressed forward, navigating around memories he did not need or want until he got to the recent past. When he saw Sara, he backed up, then slowed . . .

Yes. There we are.

Dare, sex, the town house, the battle with Alexander and his brothers, and the move to the new location. He centered in and sucked, Trainer's blood memories flowing into him. It was quick and when he pulled out, the release of suction echoed in the freezing air as his mind quickly processed what he'd taken in.

Nicholas eyed him. "Taste good?"

"If you like sewer with a side of infection," Alexander said, standing up, wiping his mouth with the sleeve of his coat.

"Did you get a location?"

Alexander shook his head. "Just visuals."

"Could you make it out? Was it the city?"

Alexander walked to the edge of the roof, frustration stabbing at his gut. He couldn't tell what the location was or where it was, yet it felt familiar to him somehow.

Nicholas jogged after him. "The 'eyes' have thirty minutes to collect. Maybe they'll drop another piece of the puzzle."

Maybe. Alexander stared out at his city, his mind working at hyperspeed. "Dare has a boss."

"What? Who?"

Alexander shrugged. "Don't know. Trainer didn't know either."

Nicholas lifted his brows. "Well, if that's true, it explains the extraordinary power of a mere Impure. But how would the power transfer? Through blood?"

"We will ask, *Duro*." He pulled Nicholas into his side, ready to flash. "Right before we kill him."

36

Sara stood naked in front of the mirror in Alexander's bedroom, her skin still damp from the shower. Tipping her chin up, she inspected the bruises on her neck, ran her hand over them, and swallowed. The throbbing pain had her gritting her teeth. *No more fear, Dr. Donohue.* Trainer's dead—the threat of him gone for good.

And yet she remained here, in this house, his house.

"Cruel, cruel girl."

"You're back," Sara said, the pleasure in her tone blatant.

Alexander came up behind her, dressed in black combat gear and looking like something the U.S. military would keep a secret from their enemies.

Grinning, he looked in the mirror at her. "How are you?"

"I'm not sure yet," she said honestly.

"Your brother . . . ?"

"Is sleeping. He still won't talk to me."

"You'll try again."

"And again." She smiled weakly. "What about you? How are you? What do you need?"

Wrapping his coat around her naked flesh, he breathed her in, then shook his head. "For now, I need your excessively brilliant brain. Some ideas, profiling."

She liked that. "Okay."

"After running from his previous residence, Ethan Dare continues to elude me. Trainer's memories gave me little. I see room after room of simplicity, but it's not an apartment or condo, and I can't tell if he's remained in the city or not."

Sara let this information sink into her brain for a moment, then said, "Well, I think that after leaving his home—or feeling as though he was forced out of his home—he'd find somewhere completely opposite, somewhere he feels no positive connection to. In fact, he may have run to somewhere he could do real damage and not care."

"Damage . . ." Alexander nodded, his eyes heavy and thoughtful. "I'll think on that, run it by my brothers."

"Hey, Alex?"

His gaze lifted to hers, his expression surprised at what she'd called him. "Yes?"

Sara turned in his arms, looked up into his beautifully fearsome face. "I want you to do it."

"Do what?"

"Take the memory from Gray."

"But you—"

"*I*," she interrupted passionately, "am a fake."

With a soft growl of reproach, Alexander cupped her face. "No, Sara."

"And a phony," she continued, nodding. "You were right—back at the hotel. I am worried about the risks to Gray's mind, but honestly I'm more worried about myself. Half of my life was paying for the accident I caused, the other half was spent trying to fix it. It's like, what am I without the pain, you know? The guilt? What am I without the constant cause?"

"You are the woman I love."

The *woman*. Not the *veana*. She'd never be his *veana*. Her heart stilled with momentary sadness, but she asked again, "Will you do it?"

He leaned down and brushed his lips over hers. "Yes."

A loud rap on the door startled them both.

"The 'eyes' have come through, Alex," Nicholas called through the wood. "We have a location."

Alexander nodded at Sara. "We will talk of this more later."

She didn't want him to go, but she released him. "Be careful."

"Of course."

"No, I mean *really* careful. As in, don't give Bronwyn anything that needs to be healed, okay?"

"Bronwyn has gone home."

It was as though the sun had risen in her chest and she nearly squealed with happiness. "She has?"

He nodded, grinning. "She knew, as I always did, that we were not true mates." He took her in his arms then and kissed her, hard and sweet, his tongue grazing her teeth. But when he broke away, his smile was gone, and his eyes registered concern.

"What is it?" she asked him.

"Nothing." He frowned, backed up. "You will wait for me."

She nodded. She wasn't going anywhere.

Turning, he strode to the door, but when his hand reached for the handle, he froze. "Room after room," he muttered. "A place he would hate, would want to destroy." Then he suddenly roared, "That's what I saw—the *credenti*!"

From the other side of the wood, Nicholas yelled, "Yes! How the hell did you know?"

37

Alexander flashed to the front gates of the Manhattan *credenti*, taking Lucian and Nicholas with him. Grazing his fangs against his wrist, he waited for the blood to flow. When it leaked red and strong from the puncture wounds, he ran it along the iron lock. As the gates disengaged and swung slowly back, Alexander readied himself, weapons drawn. His attempt to keep Sara out of his thoughts kept failing. Even as he ran, quietly and stealthily through the parklike setting inside the *credenti* grounds, he thought about his mouth on her, his tongue. He'd lapped at the tips of her teeth and had felt something . . . something disturbing, yet something that had made his body roar with lust.

A loose canine.

How was that possible? Had she told him the truth about ingesting his blood—

"Two recruits at ten feet," hissed Lucian as they headed away from the guards and past a small field of snow-dotted crops. "Shadows everywhere. Watch yourselves."

Alexander resumed his course around the field.

Snaking to the right, Nicholas gestured with the barrel of his gun. "The Barracks."

Alexander's gaze shot to the long stretch of housing in the distance. *Shit*. That's what he'd seen in Trainer's mind. Row upon row of rooms . . .

"He's holding members in there," Alexander said. "Let's go."

Alexander took off at top speed, the brothers following him across the field, over a small rise before stopping short just a few feet from the Barracks doors. A line of at least ten recruits blocked their way—ready and waiting, weapons drawn.

"Kill or be killed, *duros*," Alexander called as he ran straight at them, flying, firing, dodging knives and bullets, taking down two recruits before he was even on the ground again.

He leaped at a recruit, slamming them both to the icy grass, narrowly missing being skewered by the ten-inch blade in the Impure's fist. He rolled them both until he was on top, then smashed his elbow into the male's face, grabbed the knife, and plunged it into his heart. Flashes of gunfire echoed to Alexander's left and he jumped to his feet, taking a quick assessment of his brothers and the damage done. Nicholas was firing on a cluster of three recruits who circled him, while Lucian was pounding his fist into an Impure's side.

With four recruits dead, Alexander knew his brothers could handle the remaining six. He signaled to them, letting them know he was going in, going to find Dare, end this fucking nightmare once and for all. He stalked toward the Barracks, firing on one Impure who got in his path. But another bastard came from behind and ran his knife straight into the back of Alexander's leg, grinding it all the way down to his calf. Hissing, Alexander reached back with his gun and took the Impure out with one shot to the head. Undeterred, limping slightly, he slammed the doors of the Barracks open and stalked inside.

Training his guns on anything that moved, Alexander passed by *credenti* living quarters, small, barely furnished rooms filled with *veanas* and *pavens*, Impures and Purebloods, all huddled together looking terrified.

Alexander sniffed the air.

Where are you? Where are you?

In one room he passed, a young *veana* around ten years old caught his gaze and gestured to the room across the hall. Alexander nodded at the brave one, then changed course.

But before he reached the door, a massive Impure jumped out and clocked him in the face, then triple punched him in the gut. Grunting, Alexander fought to stay upright, fought his desire to shoot the shit out of the Impure and the room behind him. He scented Dare, but the half-breed wasn't alone. There were *vea-*

nas, innocents with him, some heavy with their swell. He had to take the perfect shot.

He heard the scramble of feet, movement behind the huge Impure, and when the *paven* dove at him, two knives in his fists, Alexander slammed his head into the *paven*'s gut, then quick as a blink, reached around the male's body with both Glocks and fired. Alexander heard a gasp, then a female's terrified cry as Dare went down.

"Holy shit," he heard Lucian snarl behind him.

Guns in his fist, Alexander rolled sideways, ready for more, but the huge Impure was up, rushing at Dare's still body. Before Alexander could react, the Impure threw himself over Dare in a bear hug and they vanished.

"*No*!" Alexander roared, raising his guns and firing into the floor where Dare's body had just been.

As the innocents scattered like rats, Nicholas grabbed Alexander's wrists. "Stop. Christ. He's gone."

"The recruits!" Alexander shouted, whirling around, ready for Dare or his Impures to flash, return.

"All dead, *Duro*," Lucian assured him. "It's done."

Breathing heavy, Alexander took in the sight before him, all the vampires in the Barracks, young and old staring at him with wide, frightened eyes. Was it done? Was it? He turned back to his brothers, who looked like they'd been playing soccer with their faces, and growled fiercely, "There's no body."

"They'll have to know he's dead," Lucian said, eyeg Nicholas for confirmation. Nicholas nodded. "Dare as stone cold. The Order will know."

Fuck, Alexander wanted to believe that. He stared at ie both of them, his younger brothers whom he loved. verything they'd known, everything they'd enjoyed r the past hundred years was gone. Peace had be- me war, and the days of self-governing had been iven over to the ones who ruled without thought. The rder, the *credenti*, the Eternal Breed as a whole had be- me part of their lives now, and Alexander feared that ven if he stopped the premorphing of his brothers, the nnection to this old life and new world would not be vered.

"We need to take inventory," he said, his tone com- ianding and controlled once again. "Sweep the entire rea and make sure no recruits remain. Then we must e to the *veanas* and their *balas*, find out where they be- ng and to whom. After that, we'll return home." He irned his focus on Nicholas and frowned. "To wait nd to watch."

38

"You're angry and confused. I get that," Sara said gently. "I know you don't want any more tests or pills or hypnosis. I'm done with all that, too."

Gray's eyes snapped up to meet hers. His attention at long last.

"Can you trust me this one last time?" she asked him. When he didn't look away, Sara took a breath and continued. "My friend Alexander, he's offered to help you."

"That's right, human" came a strong, clear masculine voice behind Sara. "You'd better buck up, because I'm coming for your blood."

Sara looked up to see Alexander walking into the room, limping slightly as his injury attempted to heal from last night's fight with Dare and his recruits. An hour ago, Dillon had given him her breath, but according to Leza the stab wound had torn cartilage and it needed a good twenty-four hours to mend properly.

"My brothers are coming to assist," Alexander told her, though his eyes were on Gray. "Why not make it a party, yes?"

"A coming-out party," drawled Lucian, strolling into the room, Nicholas behind him, both vampires looking like punching bags with eyes.

Sara noticed Gray's attention shift from the blacked-out windows to the blackened eyes of the brothers. "Do we really need everyone?"

"Yes." Alexander gestured to the pair. "Nicky, Lucian. Hold him down."

Sara jumped up. "No, Alexander, please. He hates being contained like that."

"Perhaps." Alexander's gaze was trained on Gray. "But not this time. Look."

The pulse in Sara's neck kicked, and she turned back to Gray. His eyes were on Alexander, his chin titled upward and his expression . . . She squinted. What was that in his metal gray eyes? Was that interest and a thread of . . . trust? Her heart lurched. God, how long had it been since he'd looked like that at her?

As he came to stand beside Gray, Alexander shook his head. "He knows he will fight, and he wants this done."

"How do you know that?" Sara asked, her emotions running a race inside of her. Fear and hope battling it out for first place.

"Please trust in me, Sara," Alexander said.

Nicholas and Lucian clustered around the bed, and

Nicholas put a hand on Gray's shoulder. "Easy now, Brother."

Taking a deep breath, Gray stretched his arms out for the brothers to hold him. Sara's mouth dropped open and she shook her head. He did know, he understood that whatever Alexander was offering might be the real deal. But how?

"You might want to turn away for a moment," Alexander warned her, his hands gripping Gray's skull.

"Not a chance," Sara said, catching Lucian glancing her way, his devilish eyes flashing with begrudging respect.

Alexander struck quick, and Sara flinched as her brother sucked in air, his body going instantly rigid. *Please work*, she begged silently, no longer giving a shit about her own sense of failure. She just wanted Gray to recover, to talk again, to have a chance at a real life.

Suddenly, his body jerked, and as the brothers pressed down on his arms and legs to keep him steady, Gray cried out and went into full-on convulsions.

Unlike Trainer's rank blood and diseased mind, Gray's blood was uncommonly sweet for a human, and his brain was open and ready. Alexander moved through the man's memories with experience, pushing his way back in history, jumping rapidly until he snagged on to an image that carried emotional weight. It took only seconds to find what he wanted and veer off the cerebral roadway to see the young, undamaged pair of children he sought: Gray and Sara. The image of little Sara made Alexander's chest tighten, and the temptation to remain and watch her climb a tree, her bare feet raking up the bark with the effortlessness of a monkey, was powerful. But he had sworn to take great care and speed within the head of her brother and so he pushed forward, flying through doors in time, one after the other until he came to a late-summer evening, a young Sara walking up the stairs in a pitch-black house, a candle in her hands.

"Go back to your room and stop following me, Gray," she whispered behind her.

But the boy must have continued because Alexander was following Sara up the stairs and down a hall. At a closed door, she turned and put her finger to her lips. "Stay here," she whispered. "I'll be right back."

Sara opened the door and disappeared behind it. Alexander felt Gray's impatience, his concern. Then the door opened and Sara came rushing out clutching a book to her chest, the candle forgotten. "Got it," she said excitedly. "It was under the bed."

Gray rushed after her, down the stairs and toward their bedrooms. They were inside only a moment when chaos erupted in the house. Everything happened at once. Alexander smelled smoke, heard a male scream. He saw fire at the top of the stairs, then turned to see Sara. Her face was pale and terrified as she realized what she'd done. She pushed past Gray and ran toward the staircase, screaming and crying. But a woman came running in from another room and grabbed her, held her back.

Alexander saw only the woman's profile, but something about her stopped him from focusing on Gray and the boy's need to get up the stairs to his father—something about the woman made his pulse speed up. He paused the memory and circled around, taking in one feature after the other until he saw the woman's face.

No. She was no woman.

Celestine.

Shock slammed into Alexander's lungs and he lost focus, falling back into the past, tumbling as his mind fought to understand what it had just seen. He was bombarded by images; Celestine pushing a *balas* from her body—holding a newborn *balas*.

"Focus, Alexander," he heard Nicholas urge sternly. "Take the memory of the fire."

But Alexander just hovered there, unable to stop staring at the Impure female he knew as well as he knew his own brothers. How could it be? Impossible. And yet there she was. After their escape from the *credenti*, Celestine had remained with them for nearly ten years, cared for them as they'd protected her. Then one day, she'd walked out to find blood and never returned. They'd all thought her dead, mourned her for decades, and here she was—alive, mother to two *balas*—

Oh God. *Sara.*

"Move along, *Duro*," Nicholas said, his tone grave now. "You stay too long in his mind."

"Please, Alexander." It was Sara; her anxious voice stole him from his startling revelation and he leaped forward in time again, searching for the last scene he'd witnessed.

He saw Celestine holding a hysterical Sara back. He saw Gray running for the stairs, up the stairs as his mother screamed at him. Alexander ran with the boy through the fire, as he kept low, when he found his father in the hall, his body consumed by flames. On a scream, Gray reached out to him with both hands . . .

Forcing himself out of the emotion and deep pain, Alexander circled the scene, focused, then drank, taking deep pulls of the fire memory into his mouth. It took only seconds and when he was certain he'd retrieved the entire memory, he withdrew from Gray's skull and opened his eyes. The Impure—for that's what he was—lay calm, asleep on the bed. Alexander pressed his thumb against the entry wound for a few moments; then he stepped back, his blood and Gray's blood racing through his veins.

"Let him sleep," he said softly to no one in particular, his mind reeling with the shocking images he'd just witnessed, not to mention the repercussions. "We will know soon enough."

"Alexander—" Sara began.

But Alexander was already up, walking away, out of the room. He couldn't stay there, look into Sara's eyes and pretend he was looking at the human female he'd believed her to be. Not yet. What he'd seen, what he now knew, was astounding, remarkable. Celestine had survived, and her *balas* . . . both the male and the female were in his home, under his care—and both had vampire blood in their veins.

Jesus. Sara could be . . .

Growling, he ran, flew down the stairs and toward the tunnels. He wanted to rejoice at the possibility before him. If he were merely a Pureblood, it wouldn't be possible. But he was a descendant of a Breeding Male. His true mate had to be a vampire, yes, but she could be either Pure or Impure. Sara could be his now—she could be his true mate.

He should have been hopeful and yet the only thing he felt was dread.

After Alexander's swift departure, his brothers were quick to leave as well. But Sara remained by Gray's side, taking his vitals every fifteen minutes, dozing in her chair, waking up to see if he was awake, and wondering what she was going to say to him when and if he did.

If the memory was gone, she reasoned, the trauma would be gone too. But he would still be left with fire-ravaged hands, and questions. Many questions. Then there was the flipside. What if he was exactly as he was before—or worse, what if he had no memory at all?

Feeling jumpy, she stood to take his vitals again, pulling out her stethoscope and placing the diaphragm against his shirt. Suddenly, a hand shot up, white-knuckled, and gripped her wrist.

"Sarafena."

Sara gasped, stared down into the open, gunmetal gray eyes of her little brother. His voice, deep and masculine now, so unfamiliar, yet so beautiful, washed over. "Gray. Oh God. I can't believe it." She touched his face, his forehead, his hair. "How do you feel? Are you okay?"

He nodded slowly, though confusion moved over his features as he tried to process his past, his present, and what had happened a few hours ago in this room. "Sara," he said, lifting his hands for her to see. "Explain this to me." He swallowed. "How?"

As the ache built in Sara's throat, she took his hands in hers and sat down beside him. "A little at a time," she said. "First step is rest, okay?"

He nodded again. "We'll talk later."

"Of course." She smiled gently. She'd give him small doses of memory until he could understand it without the trauma. Then they would see . . .

"And you'll thank him for me?" Gray said.

Him? Oh God, he meant Alexander? She leaned toward him. "You understood? Seriously? You knew he could help you?"

"Yes."

"How, Gray?" she entreated.

The beautiful young man before her smiled softly. "He spoke to me. In my head. About you, all you've done, how you've hurt." His eyes grew momentarily sad. "He said that it was time for you and me to go home."

Tears filled Sara's eyes and she shook her head, unable to speak. Alexander was truly more than a desire, more than the male she loved. He was a great friend.

"Hey, human," came a voice behind her.

Sara looked back, saw Dillon behind her, completely healed and grinning. "Hey, vampire."

"I'll stay with him." She flicked her chin toward the door. "You should go. See about the other one you love."

Yes. She needed him now, as he needed her.

With one last squeeze to her brother's hand, Sara got up and let Dillon take her seat. As she turned to go she swore she saw her brother's eyes flash with interest as the bodyguard dropped down into the chair beside his bed.

The cage had once been a place where his hunger could rage out of control, where he could be the animal he believed himself to be.

Now it simply kept him from the one he loved.

Fully clothed, Alexander sat back against the rock wall and fought his hunger for her as he fought the truth of what he'd seen inside Gray's head. He breathed in, frowned. "Your brother is well, Sara?"

The unlocked metal door swung back and Sara came inside, her heady scent and honest beauty a shocking contrast to the ugly frigidity within his cell. Her blueberry eyes sought out his in the near darkness and when she found him, she went to him and knelt before him. "He spoke to me."

"I'm glad."

"He sounds so . . . old. Like a man. It's hard to remember him as anything but a boy, you know?" She shrugged, her smile so bright it took his breath away. "He wanted me to thank you."

"It was all for you. No deals, nothing in return. I just want to see you happy."

She moved closer, until their legs touched. "He told me what you said to him, in his mind. Oh, Alex . . ."

The love Alexander had for her transcended his need to torture himself at that moment, and he allowed himself to say the words that hovered on his tongue. "Healing his mind . . . it wasn't your fault, Sara. You couldn't have fixed him—not the way you wanted to."

Sara stilled beside him, her brows coming together. "What do you mean?"

He shook his head. "His memories were too thickly ingrained. Blood drain was the only way."

"What?"

He hesitated, feeling as though he were unleashing a world of new problems onto her. But what was the alternative? She would know soon enough.

"Alexander?" Her eyes implored him to tell her the truth.

He reached up, brushed his knuckles over her cheek. "I saw your mother."

"What?"

"In Gray's mind. As I was trying to find the fire, I saw her."

"Okay. Well, that makes sense. You saw her because she was in his memory—"

"Sara, I recognized her."

The stillness in the air held them both hostage for a moment; then Sara started shaking her head.

"She was a teacher in my *credenti*," Alexander continued, knowing no other way through this but the truth. "The one I told you about the night in the lighthouse, remember? She was an Impure, a half-breed. The Order had called on her, as they do all Impures—it was her turn for sterilization. She wanted a new life as much as we did. I helped her escape."

Sara stared at him, looked as though she'd been punched in the stomach. "That's not possible."

"I felt the same way when I first saw her," Alexander said gently, but he was afraid nothing would soften the blows he'd already given and the ones that remained. "She cared for us: Lucian, Nicholas, and I. She was like a mother in ways our own could never be. But she disappeared one day—we thought she'd died. We searched, but—"

"My mother is a vampire!" Sara blurted out, her words echoing off the rock walls.

Alexander watched her pale face, the panic, the mental attempts to make sense of what he was telling her. Finally, he nodded. "Yes."

Her mouth ajar, Sara's eyes fell to the floor. "My brother . . ."

"Yes."

She was silent for at least a minute, and Alexander just waited, waited for it all to sink in, then come up again. What would her response be? Would she despise what she was—would she despise him for telling her the truth? When she finally spoke, it was a soft, mumbled clutter of thoughts. "This explains everything . . . what's been happening to me . . . how I've been feeling after . . . how desperately I wanted your blood . . . and how I haven't stopped wanting it, wanting you."

He hated having to be the one who laid this burden at her feet. "I'm so sorry, Sara."

She looked up at him, shaking her head, her nostrils flaring. "Damn right. You should be sorry. You jackass!"

"I know. I wish to God I had never—"

She grabbed the collars of his shirt, roared, "You said you loved me."

"I do." *What the hell?*

She yanked him forward, and although she had considerably less strength than him, he allowed her to do it. "You realized I was a vampire and you ran from me?"

"You're not angry about this?"

"Not at finding out what I am. Shit, I'm relieved. I knew something was going on with me, that something had changed. I thought I might be losing it. Then

I thought it was about your blood, that I had ingested it." She jerked him away, released him. "I'm angry with you."

"What?" He stared at her, stunned.

"It was safe to tell me you loved me when you thought I was just a human, when you couldn't have me—when you couldn't risk trusting me."

His face blanched.

"Because, that's what this is really about, isn't it?" she tossed out, her ire fueling her passion. "Trusting me with your heart, trusting me with your hunger?"

Alexander felt his fangs elongate. Oh, damn, her scent. The angrier she became the deeper her scent flowed. "Don't do this."

"Don't do what?" she yelled at him. "Call you on your shit?"

Alexander couldn't stop himself, he grabbed her shoulders and forced her onto her back. Poised over her, he flashed his fangs, his mind racing, his blood craving, his cock straining in his pants. "Stop. Now."

Looking up at him, Sara felt the coil of heat that always slammed through her when Alexander had her on her back. She knew him now, knew that he would never release the animal inside himself, truly give it over to her if she didn't push him to the very limits. Yes, she was angry—furious at her mother for never telling her the truth, furious at herself for not making at least one illogical guess about this outcome after that first taste of Alexander's blood. She stared up into his charged, ravenous face, eyes that were deadly and hungry, but were filled with a pain she understood, the pain a child, a soul, a heart feels when it believes itself unworthy of love, and she forgave him.

"It wasn't a mistake," she said softly, as her *paven* breathed fire above her, his face tight with emotion, body shaking with need. "How we met, how close we've become, the wound on your shoulder—how it opened whenever I was near. Your blood knew the truth—it called out to me—it belonged with me, with my blood, coursing together."

"The wound closed up again—"

"When we weren't together. Kind of like your heart—open to me, closed to the rest of the world. We have a bond that's proven itself to be unshakable. It's how it was meant to be." She raised her head and kissed the key-shaped brands on each of his cheeks, smiled when his body jerked in response. "I love you, Alexander Roman. I was always supposed to love you—and you me."

His groan was laced with both pain and pleasure. But that was okay. It was as it was supposed to be.

Her eyes filled with tears. "I will never keep myself from you. I will never discard your love like trash." Her voice caught with emotion. "And I will never starve you."

Alexander's eyes glittered with feeling. "I can't . . ."

"You can. You have to." She tipped up her chin and kissed him, soft and loving and hungry, her tongue slipping into his mouth, playing with teeth, the tips of his fangs. "Drink from me. Mark me. Make me yours."

Against her mouth, a moan of raw, desperate pleasure escaped Alexander's throat. "Not in here."

"It has to be in here." She reached between them and started removing her clothes. "Help me."

For one moment, Alexander looked ready to refuse; then he pushed back and with hands that shook, he stripped her naked.

Sara lay back on the cold rock floor and beckoned for him. "I'll stay in here until you're starving," she said passionately, "until you understand you can trust me, that I give to you unconditionally, out of the purest love. I'll stay here until this cage becomes a place of peace, of pleasure—not torment." Her eyebrow lifted. "I will stay in here until you can't resist me."

"I could never resist you." His eyes burned cherry black fire.

"Good. I'm counting on it."

"Wait! No . . . Sara!"

He reached out to stop her, but it was too late. Sara had her wrist to her mouth, her teeth bared. She bit down into her own flesh, then sucked in air as two pinprick holes delivered not only pain, but the specks of blood she needed to tempt him. A growl erupted from Alexander as he watched, his eyes trained on the blood, his fangs descending even farther.

Reveling in the glorious sting, Sara dragged her fingertip over the skin of her wrist, then lifted her finger to his mouth, swiped the bloodstained pad across his bottom lip.

Alexander's nostrils flared, his eyes rolled back in his head, and he cried out into the cold air of his prison. "You are my true mate." His head dropped and his eyes locked to her. "I need no mark to know this." He licked his lower lip.

"Please, Alexander," she whispered, emotion and passion surging within her. She knew what she wanted, and for the first time in her life, she felt completely deserving.

His eyes were brilliant, excited, hungry as he stood and quickly removed his clothes. When he stretched out over her, she opened for him. *Forever.* He was hers forever. The concept was unbelievable, impossible—but she knew better than to fall prey to that word. Nothing was impossible. Their love had proved that.

With one deep thrust, Alexander was inside her, deep, protected, where he belonged. Sara wrapped her legs around his waist and held on tight. When his head dropped, nuzzling at her breast, she knew what was coming and she couldn't wait. She arched against him.

I LOVE YOU.

The words entered her mind just as his fangs struck her heart.

Sara gasped, reared up, felt as though she'd been hit by a bullet, but in seconds the pain ebbed and pleasure like she'd never imagined possible flooded through her trembling body.

It felt as though his mouth were on her clit, suckling, pulling her into the most intense climax of her life. And she couldn't hold on; she came, hard and uncontrolled, and as she bucked her hips, Alexander drank, fed, took deep pulls straight from her heart into his.

Sara felt the change come over her, like honey flowing from her toes all the way up into her mind. She was herself, but so much more. She was his. She was eternal.

Alexander pulled away from her chest, his eyes filled with a love, with a pleasure that couldn't be contained. He kissed her then and she tasted her own blood on his tongue, sweet as nectar, sweet as the promise of a long, lasting future with the one she loved. He kissed her again and again—her cheek, her neck, her collarbone.

"You are mine," he growled into her ear, making her shiver. "Forever. My eternal love." He bit down gently on her lobe, laved at the curve, then flicked the tender spot behind with his tongue. Suddenly, he stilled; then his tongue lapped. Once, twice, a third time.

His hands came up to her face and he pressed her ear forward. "Dear God."

Sara pulled back. "What's wrong? What is it?"

His face was a mixture of shock and amazement, love and understanding. He took her hand and placed it behind her ear. "Do you feel it?"

Her fingers grazed something. Something small, rough.

"The key," he uttered, then broke out in laughter, his cock still deep inside of her. "My brand, my mark. It was hidden. All this time." His eyes locked with hers and he began to move. "Oh God, my Sara."

"I love you, Alexander," she said, her arms going around his neck, pulling him close.

"And I love you. My truest mate." He thrust into her, going as far as her body would allow, and when Sara could no longer control her own need, her own hunger, she bit into the skin of his shoulder, the spot that belonged to her, that had called to her so many times, and when she tasted the eternal sweetness her new life's blood, she drank deep.

The Beginning

Minnesota

Christmas had come to his old friend's neighborhood. Lights glowed from rooftops and around white picket fences, and snow was piled in three-foot drifts atop the dead grass, easing the way for the five vampires who walked up the drive.

Alexander turned to Sara, keeper of his heart, blood of his blood, and grinned. "Are you ready, my love?"

"Yes." The tense smile she flashed him showed her beauty, and the tips of a nearly mature set of retracted fangs that had come with the pleasure of feeding from her true mate.

Coming to stand beside his sister, Gray offered her a squeeze on the shoulder. "It's all she ever wanted, Sara. You back home. There's nothing to feel nervous about."

Alexander reached for the brass knocker, but never made it. Didn't have to. The door was pulled wide and there stood the female he'd escaped the *credenti* with so long ago. Celestine. She looked the same, her dark hair pulled into a knot at the top of her head, her heart-shaped face pale but shrewd. Her pale blue eyes went to her children first and she bit her lip. "Sarafena. Grayson. You're home. My life can be lived once again."

Alexander looked down at his mate, smiled as he saw her eyes fill with tears and her hand reach out for the older female's pale one. It would take time, as all things of value did, but he would help them both find happiness and forgiveness within their own hearts, as each, in their own ways, had helped him find a new life.

"Well, now . . ." Celestine caught sight of the three men behind her children. "My old friends."

"In the flesh," Alexander said, taking the female's other hand.

Celestine smiled, the tips of her canines showing. "Come in, all of you. There is much to say, much to explain."

Alexander followed Sara and Gray into the house, Lucian and Nicholas trailing behind.

"Lose our number, eh, Celie?" the young albino quipped, stalking into the foyer.

Celestine snorted. "Still an asshole, I see, Luca."

Everyone laughed, but the merry sound was short-lived. Before them on the foyer wall, the pale green paint had begun to move, sway, pulse.

"Oh God, no," Sara muttered under her breath.

Alexander growled and blocked both females with his body. But nothing could stop what was happening, nothing could erase the two words that leaped out at him.

DARE LIVES.

"Alex."

Alexander turned at the sound of Nicholas's call. Still outside on the stoop, the middle brother was doubled over, panting, his hands shaking with a sensation that Alexander knew all too well. Soon the *paven* would be hit by a rod of pain so fierce and debilitating that the very breath would be ripped from his lungs.

Dare lived.

And Nicholas Roman had just been sent through morpho.

ermont *credenti*

As the blue light of day succumbed to the pale laven-der of evening, a bitter cold moved over the land, hook the snow from the trees, and curled around he *veana* and the *balas* who sat on the front steps of he small *credenti* elementary school. The snow on the round, which had been melting just a few hours ear-ier, now glistened under the rising moon as water uickly turned back to ice. It was nearing six p.m., nd in accordance with the laws of the Order, it was ime to end the labor of the day and begin the calm of ight. Behind them, the school was dark and empty. Most residents of the *credenti* had left their work or chooling and had entered their homes for their fam-ly meal and reflection. Kate Everborne, however, had o family to go home to. What she did have was a be-ief that reflection was for unthinking drones and the nwelcome responsibility of a seven-year-old *balas*, who once again had to be watched until his mother showed up.

"She's not coming."

Kate glanced down at the boy. With his large black eyes and shock of white hair, he didn't blend in well. She knew how that was. "She's coming. She's just late."

"She's always late," he grumbled.

"Give her a break, kid. She's doing the best she can."

"She should work inside the *credenti*. Like you. Do what *veanas* are supposed to do."

The smile on Kate's face was false and forced. The last thing in the world she wanted to be doing was living inside the *credenti*, any *credenti*. And her work at the elementary school, passing out lentils and fruit during midmeal— Well, that was utter bullshit, a cover-up, a way to control her.

But she didn't have a choice. Not yet.

"She dishonors my father's memory by leaving the *credenti*," the boy continued.

"You're a good kid, Ladd, but right now you're acting like a brat."

He crossed his arms over his chest. "I don't care."

"Yeah, I can tell."

"I don't care about me and I don't care about her." He puffed out his lips. "Maybe I wish she'd never come."

"Maybe she wishes that, too," Kate said dryly.

Ladd's eyes grew wide and *balas*-wet as he stared

up at her, took in what she'd just said, and molded it into the worst-possible abandonment scenario.

Ah, shit. Kate released a weary breath. She could be a real asshole sometimes. "Listen, kid, I didn't mean it like that. I was talking about the feeling of freedom some vampires feel when they step outside—"

"I'm here. I'm here." Mirabelle Letts came running across the tree-littered play yard toward them, her feet sinking calf deep in the heavy snow. She was a pretty *veana*, small, curvy, with soft brown doe eyes that did their best to exude happiness. Slightly breathless, she called out, "Sorry, Kate."

"No problem," Kate returned, coming to her feet. She was just relieved the *veana* had shown up. She really sucked with kids, wasn't sure what to say to them, how to comfort them. Sticking her in a school hadn't been the Order's smartest move, but hell, she hadn't been about to complain—not with two months left on her work release.

"Mommy! I see you!" Ladd jumped to his feet and waved his arms like he was landing planes, all anger gone now.

Kate chuckled at the quick recovery. At Ladd's age, it seemed that no matter what a parent did, said, or forgot, they were always a welcome sight.

Give it a few years, kid.

No more than ten feet away, Mirabelle waved back at her child as she waded through the snow. "Training went over and there was a gardening demonstration—"

Something shot out of the shadows of the trees, cutting off Mirabelle's words. A *paven*, tall and dark. In under a second, he was on Mirabelle. Kate opened her mouth to scream when she saw a silver flash. A knife! Oh, shit. No! Terror locked the scream in her chest, and she fought the dual pulls of running to help the *veana* and protecting the young *balas* at her side.

Before she could make her choice, the *paven* slashed both of Mirabelle's thighs, then plunged the knife deep into her chest.

A piercing scream whipped through the night and jerked Kate from her horror. *Ladd.* He tried to run to his mother, but Kate caught him in her arms and held him back. Blood rushed river-quick from the wounds on Mirabelle's legs, and as the attacker yanked the blade from her chest, she dropped to the ground.

The dark-haired male suddenly glanced up, locked eyes with Kate, and grinned. *Fuck.* It was there in his eyes, in his smile—hunger to spill blood. He was going to take out her and the kid. The town was a quarter mile away, on the other side of the forest and playfield. Could she get there with the boy? If not, she was going to have to fight off this *paven* herself or—

God, did she have it within her anymore? The power, the gift that had both saved and sent her to prison ten years ago? Or had the Order removed it for good?

The butcher *paven* started toward her and Ladd. Knowing she couldn't outrun him, not with the boy, Kate delved inside her head, attempted to find and harness the power she'd been gifted as a *balas*.

But it was gone.

"Help!" she screamed, praying there was one soul disobeying the Order tonight, walking through the forest or meeting someone behind the school. "We need help over here!"

But she heard nothing. No one.

She shoved Ladd behind her back, opened her arms to the evil coming at her, and flashed her fangs. *Come and get it then, asshole.* His smile widened, the moonlight catching the tips of his fangs. Then suddenly he stopped, lifted his chin, and sniffed the air. With a growl of annoyance, he turned around and ran back across the field and into the trees.

What the hell?

Kate sucked in the bitterly cold air scented with blood and screamed again. "Help!" Hoping to God that Mirabelle was still alive, Kate raced to her side, Ladd behind her. The *veana*'s eyes were open, but her quick, shallow breaths signaled how close to death she was. Kate dropped down in the snow and pressed her hands to the gaping wound in the female's chest. Forcing up the healing energy all Pureblood *veana*'s possessed, she blew on the wounds in Mirabelle's thighs—back and forth, back and forth, each breath a show in pure determination and desperation. But the cuts were so deep, the femoral artery calculatedly severed. Red death seeped between her fingers, over the *veana*'s chest, spilling out onto the pure white powdered floor.

"Goddammit!" Kate screamed. "We need help here!"

What a lost cause. They weren't coming. No one was coming. All those selfless, community-first, pious bastards were huddled around a table in their homes *reflecting* while one of their own needed them.

Ladd laid his head on his mother's belly and howled in misery.

Mirabelle's eyes were glassy as she hovered somewhere between this world and the next. Her gaze flickered toward her son, then back up to Kate. "Take him," she uttered through short gasps of breath.

"Shhh," Kate said. "Don't talk."

"Take him. Please. He can't be tested."

Lifting her head again, Kate yelled one last time into the frigid air, "We need help!"

"No!" Mirabelle rasped. "Please. Don't want them . . . Please, take the boy."

She was delusional, had to be. Kate shook her head. "He'll be okay. Don't worry."

Mirabelle whispered something.

"I can't hear you . . ." Kate lowered her head, her ear to the female's mouth.

"He will be . . . caged if they find out."

"Find out what?" Kate uttered, keeping her ear close to the female's lips.

And in the last seconds before her death, Mirabelle revealed not only her secrets, but her desperate plea to save her son's life, all to the one vampire on earth who could do nothing for her.